PRAISE FOR THE FIERY TALES

"Evocative, erotic. . . [A] sensual treat!"
— **Sylvia Day,**
#1 *New York Times* bestselling author

"Hot enough to warm the coldest winter night."
— **Publishers Weekly**

"Sophisticated and deeply romantic."
—**Elizabeth Hoyt,**
New York Times bestselling author

"Sure to delight!"
— **Jennifer Ashley,**
New York Times bestselling author

"The most luscious, sexy take on classic fairy tales I've ever read!"
—**Cheryl Holt,**
New York Times bestselling author

"Sets the classic fairy tale(s) ablaze!"
—**Anna Campbell,**
bestselling, award-winning author

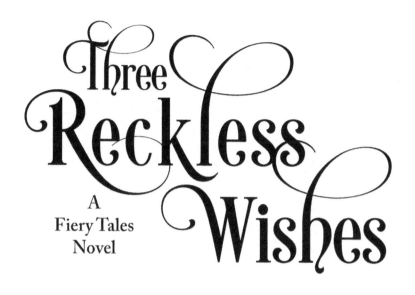

Three Reckless Wishes

A Fiery Tales Novel

LILA DIPASQUA

DiPasqua

Copyright © 2018 by Lila DiPasqua

Cover: Carrie Divine/Seductive Designs

Photography: © Period Images

Interior Design by Woven Red Author Services, www.WovenRed.ca

Edited by Linda Ingmanson

PRINTING HISTORY

First Edition: Lila DiPasqua—Oct. 2018

ISBN: 978-1-7752352-1-7 (trade pbk)

ISBN: 978-1-7752352-0-0 (e-book)

To my beloved readers who patiently waited for this book.
I'd be nothing without you. I utterly adore you.

And to all single parents everywhere who do their best everyday
to make ends meet—much like our heroine, Isabelle Laurent.
You are unsung heroes.

Lastly to Mom.
"Fai la nanna, pupa bella . . ."

CHAPTER ONE

Paris, 1661

. . .There are times I have dreamed of it. I am naked in his embrace. His hand moves down my body, warm fingers grazing lightly across my skin. The sensation is so sublime, I cannot contain my sound of bliss. I arch to him, hungry for more.

He alone ignites this fire inside me, one I cannot extinguish any more than I can stop these vivid dreams—so shamelessly unbridled. Nor can I quash the feelings he stirs within my heart.

Oh, how I long for his heart, his smile. His arms around me. I want to know the feel of his skin, the taste of his kiss.

I want to indulge in all the carnal delights he favors.

I want to surrender to his every wicked desire.

Down to my very marrow, I feel there is a connection between us. One destined in the stars. If he would simply notice me, touch me, he would feel it too. . .

Marc d'Emery, Marquis de Vigneau, slammed the journal shut. "*Merde.* I can't read anymore, Luc. I'm at a full cock-stand, and we're just minutes from my sister's *hôtel.*" He tossed the journal across the moving carriage to the empty spot next to Luc de Moutier, Marquis de Fontenay. "I'll admit it. That's stirring stuff—and I can understand the appeal of her writing—but the last woman you should be thinking about is a dead one."

Luc tightened his jaw as he stared out the window. A blur of gray town houses and indistinguishable people threaded past as dusk descended. He agreed. He should have ceased his fascination with the journal and, more importantly, with the author of the evocative writing long ago.

In the three years since Sabine, his brother's new wife, had given Luc two journals, he'd read them so many times, he had the blasted things memorized. He couldn't seem to put them away and forget about them. Forget about *her.*

Isabelle Laurent.

Sabine's deceased twin.

He was the subject of Isabelle's writings. The object of her desire and affection. It completely staggered him that these passionate posts had been written by a female completely untried and unschooled in the carnal arts. And just as astonishing was the affinity she'd harbored for him.

One he'd known absolutely nothing about.

He hadn't even known Isabelle existed until Sabine entered his brother Jules's life and Luc learned all about his sister-in-law's only sibling. The late famous playwright Paul Laurent had been Sabine and Isabelle's father. *Jésus-Christ,* Luc had attended Paul Laurent's theater more times than he could count and wasn't aware the man had daughters at all—despite having spoken to him countless times.

And not once—not one bloody time—while Isabelle had watched him from the side of the stage with such adoration and tender desire, recording every little tidbit she observed about him, had he noticed her.

Not a single sighting. Not even a glimpse.

All the while, she'd duly noted what he wore. Which of her father's plays he appeared to like. Which parts made him laugh.

Deriving such astute deductions about his personal tastes.

Deriving such astute deductions about far more—things the rest of the world didn't see about him. Things he thought he'd hidden from everyone's eyes.

Except Isabelle's.

The more he'd learned about her from her journals, the more he wanted to know her and was amazed how similar her own personal tastes were to his.

On many subjects.

For a woman he'd never met, he knew her better than any female he'd ever had in his life. For a woman who'd never once spoken to him, she knew him better than anyone else ever had.

How absurd is that?

She came to life on the pages of her journals. Lived and breathed so vividly in his mind. And he couldn't help but wonder, more times than he should have, about the sound of her voice or her laugh. The feel of *her* skin.

Her taste.

Isabelle Laurent and her enthralling journals, documenting the last years of Isabelle's life, had him completely beguiled.

And utterly burning.

Just having the thing near him tightened his groin and warmed his blood. He didn't have to look down at the brown leather-bound volume on the seat next to him to know it was there. He was all too aware of it. And *her*. She was in his thoughts constantly. It was completely illogical, but he actually *mourned* the loss of her. The loss of ever getting to know her.

Worst of all, his fascination with Isabelle Laurent hadn't diminished over time. It only strengthened.

It was beyond insanity that he wanted—no, was obsessed with—a *dead* woman.

And he had no bloody idea how to alter this lamentable state.

How the hell did he get her out of his system?

He had a vague description of her: dark hair and eyes—a sharp contrast to her twin sister's fair coloring. In his mind's eye he'd formed a mental image of Isabelle Laurent—and that very same dark-haired, dark-eyed beauty was making appearances in every one of his erotic dreams.

Passages from her journals playing out in the most mind-melting detail.

Each time he'd awaken, his cock stiff as a spike, the pressure in his sac immense. Ravenous for her.

For a woman who'd been dead for eight years and who was haunting him in the most maddening ways.

If only he'd known she'd left home, after her family had lost their theater and wealth, to work at one of his family's châteaus as a servant—in the hope to be near him. If only she hadn't perished in the servants' outbuildings on his lands at the hands of a madman who was now thankfully dead and gone.

Leon de Vittry had left so much devastation in his wake. A sickening number of innocent women he'd murdered had been discovered at the bottom of his privy, the natural smells having masked the stench of death. He might have spared Isabelle that particular indignity when he murdered her, but her fiery death at the hands of that monster had been no less horrific.

It had taken five long years to learn that Vittry had murdered Isabelle. And to prove Vittry had had a hand in the conspiracy against Luc's family that ultimately led not only to the false treason charges laid against his father, Charles de Moutier, but to his execution as a traitor to the Crown, as well.

How ironic was it that treason was about the only sin his piece of *merde* father hadn't committed?

The one accusation he hadn't deserved.

After stripping him of his title, he'd been hanged—a further humiliation bestowed on him as members of the aristocracy were not executed by public hangings on a gibbet. While Luc was awaiting his own fate in prison, the guards had tried to taunt him with details of how Charles had writhed on the end of a rope. What those guards didn't know at the time was that they'd given him the single greatest moment of his life. He hadn't felt grief, as Jules had. Luc hadn't shed a single tear over Charles's death.

Instead, he'd been flooded with…*relief.* Satisfaction.

And a morbid sense of jubilation.

Just knowing that the devil—as he'd often called him in the quiet of his mind since boyhood—had suffered just *once* quieted some of the rage that had festered inside him for so long. Charles de Moutier had caused more than his fair share of human suffering to many.

He deserved the punishment he got.

There wasn't a doubt in Luc's mind that Charles, at this very moment, was standing right next to Vittry—burning in hell.

After all he'd been through with Charles, and his family's disgrace, his life had *finally* been set right. He and Jules had regained favor with the King. Reclaimed their family's vast fortune that had been confiscated. And cleared their sullied name as enemies of the Crown. During their exile from Paris, when polite society had turned its back on them, when he and Jules had been stripped of everything, including their dignity, nobility, and, for a time, their freedom—while under arrest for suspicion of treason—Luc had not only longed to reform the Moutiers' ruined reputation, but to take it to new heights of power and prestige.

To that end, he needed a wife with exalted bloodlines and vast wealth. A union that would enhance his family's esteem and already laden coffers.

The problem was, he just couldn't stop comparing each suitable choice to Isabelle—when it shouldn't matter that the women didn't have the same wit, intellect, and natural sensuality as the deceased dark-haired beauty dominating his mind day and night.

"Are you utterly certain you never saw Isabelle at Laurent's theater?" The question had fallen out of Luc's mouth uncensored. *Damn it. Just let this go.* His words sounded pathetic even to his own ears. They were laced with desperation. A desperation to learn more—*anything more*—about the elusive and far too captivating Isabelle Laurent.

He liked women. The women who'd graced his life had been his greatest source of joy. He loved discovering all the interesting little quirks and habits that made each one unique. And then there were those delicious sweet spots on their bodies, the ones that made them moan and scream for him.

He adored discovering those even more.

He didn't deceive women. Nor make promises he wouldn't keep. He always made it clear that his interest was solely in a carnal connection—unbridled mutual pleasure.

Without emotional entanglement.

He'd spent his entire life maintaining a certain level of detachment—from everyone. He was most at ease when he was in complete control of his world. Soft feelings made him turn away. He'd learned a long time ago to keep a tight rein on his emotions at all times.

Or else…

Yet, the tender feelings Isabelle's writings had inspired were beyond unsettling. And he was too damned seasoned to be unraveled by the mere words of an ingénue.

Smiling good-naturedly, Marc shook his head, the shade of his dark, curly hair likely to have been very similar to Isabelle's own locks. "Luc, I'm beginning to worry about you. This obsession you have with this dead woman isn't at all healthy. Why don't you focus on, say…a live one? They're much easier to bed."

Luc sighed, frustrated. "I know it's been years since the theater closed and the playwright passed away, but surely someone caught a glimpse of her. A dark-haired young woman who perhaps resembled Laurent a little?" He had no idea if she'd resembled her father at all. Paul Laurent's prestigious theater had been highly popular among the upper class before the civil unrest, the *Fronde*, when all of Paris went mad. And Luc's world collapsed around him.

Marc shrugged. "And what if they did? What difference does it make?"

He wished he knew the answer to that. He had no idea why learning more about this deceased young woman should matter at all.

Marc leaned in and rested his elbows on his thighs, his smile returning. "You know what you need?

To stop thinking about Isabelle Laurent... "What?"

"To commence negotiations with the Duc d'Allain for a marriage contract between you and his daughter Sophie—"

Luc groaned. "Good Lord. No, not her. Unless she has changed since my exile, the woman speaks incessantly. There's only so much inane conversation about her shoes a man can tolerate."

Marc chuckled. "Aside from her somewhat wanting conversational skills, she is a beauty. Claiming your conjugal rights won't be much of a hardship." He grinned.

"Unless she's still talking about her footwear while I'm fucking her."

That garnered a bark of laughter from his friend. "All right. Forget the Duc d'Allain's daughter," Marc said, still softly chuckling. "What you need, my friend, is to enjoy yourself tonight. This masque is a perfect place for you to reenter society. You can mingle about with anonymity, reacquaint yourself with old friends, and perhaps make some new ones."

He didn't have any old friends.

The few Luc had once trusted had turned their backs, distancing themselves from him as soon as Charles had been arrested for treason. Though the King's pardon had come three years ago, Luc had stayed away from Paris, spending every moment seeing to the extensive restorations his properties desperately needed after years of abandonment and neglect while in the Crown's possession.

He'd refused to reenter society until everything was perfect.

He had to prove to himself that despite his banishment from Paris and his imprisonment before that, he had not broken. He'd not only restored his châteaus, he'd brought them beyond their former glory.

Better still, he'd destroyed and removed anything that reminded him of Charles de Moutier from his childhood homes.

"What new friends are there to make?" he asked. No doubt there would be some who'd still be leery of socializing with a man whose family had been labeled traitors to King and country.

His former short temper with the male aristocracy, and quick-to-duel tendencies, had never made him popular among the men in his class.

His popularity had come from the finer sex, with whom he'd always felt the most at ease.

"Well, Juliette Carre comes to mind. She is one woman you *need* to meet."

Luc crossed his arms casually. "Oh? Why do I *need* to meet Juliette Carre?"

"Because she doesn't talk incessantly about footwear. In fact, she has everyone in Paris completely charmed. And she's a courtesan," Marc added.

Luc lifted a brow. Marc was well aware he'd sworn off his old ways. His days as an unrepentant libertine, bedding beauties around the realm, were over. He wanted nothing to distract him from his plans. Or the new image he wanted to forge.

Merde. He was already distracted enough by Isabelle Laurent and her bewitching journals.

"Now wait." Marc held up his hand. "I know your 'plan' and what you're thinking. Allow me to explain the benefit here. Though there are plenty of courtesans around, this one is different. In truth, rather exceptional—a vision, with a polished wit to match. Luc, you've got to see her. When she enters the room, she is utterly enthralling. Every man of consequence is vying for her. And she is very selective. Any man who beds her has the immediate respect and regard of every male in the realm. A definite boon for you should she favor you. I heard that the Duc de Savard gave her a significant sum—without ever bedding her—just to be considered as her next choice. And two weeks ago, the Marquis de Renier and the Comte de Northy practically came to a duel over the comte's refusal to relinquish his seat beside her to the marquis, despite being outranked socially. After everything that's happened, if you really want to make a grand impression, bed Juliette Carre." Marc's usual smile returned. "She's one woman who won't bore you. She'll be here tonight. If there's anyone who can make you forget all about Isabelle Laurent, the beautiful and captivating Juliette most certainly can."

Dieu. He'd be willing to pay a king's ransom to snap the spell Isabelle's journals had cast on him. How he wished simply bedding a courtesan would do that. Luc glanced down at the brown leather-bound volume resting beside him on the velvet seat. Looking so deceptively innocuous.

It had the most powerful pull on him.

It was so potent, no one, not even the newest, most coveted courtesan in Paris, no matter how charming or beautiful, would be able to obliterate it.

*****

Isabelle crossed the grand entrance of the Comtesse de Grandville's *hôtel* with the elegant, unhurried strides she'd perfected. Her dear friend Nicole was by her side as the stout majordomo led the way.

Be calm…

Anyone observing Isabelle—or rather Juliette Carre—would never know that the confident smile she wore belied the disquiet churning in her belly. The din from the masque—its chatter and music—emanated from behind the tall white-and-gold double doors at the far end of the vast vestibule.

Resonating around her.

Growing louder and louder the closer they got to the comtesse's grand salon.

Isabelle was grateful to have Nicole with her. Her mere presence gave her the boost of confidence she needed to get through yet another event as Juliette. This persona she'd adopted was still so new to her. Only a few months old.

And there was no room for error.

This was her only means to survive. And after all she'd been through, she was most assuredly a survivor.

Discreetly, Isabelle smoothed the skirts of her costly gown, then checked her dark blue demi-mask with white plumes, making certain it was securely in place. *Your appearance is fine.* She stilled her fidgety fingers immediately.

Be calm.

She'd had the same knots in her stomach the last time she'd selected a new lover.

Thanks to Nicole's tutelage, there were several prospects to choose from. Isabelle had been lavished with expensive gifts and extravagant sums from a number of powerful men. After much thought and discussion with Nicole, Isabelle had made her choice—the Duc de Vannod. He'd petitioned her with a generous sum of money and a magnificent silver-and-diamond pin. He was attractive. Widowed.

And tonight, she was going to inform him that he was the one she'd selected.

She took in a quiet breath and firmly tamped down her nervousness.

Pleasing Vannod both in and out of the boudoir—and ultimately leaving him wanting more, weeks from now when she'd end the affair—was imperative if male interest in her was to continue to grow. And grow it must. Though, there was just one problem.

She was a complete fraud.

Behind the façade of Juliette Carre was merely a woman who'd been raised around her father's acting troupe and knew how to put on a convincing performance. A woman who'd utilized the education her father had provided his daughters—an education far superior to what most highborn women received. At each salon *Juliette Carre* attended, she'd charmed and heightened her appeal, as she was able to discuss novels and the arts and debate topics of interest with deftness. Able to read, write, and speak Italian, thanks to the Italian actors she'd been raised around. Juliette Carre was always poised, witty, graceful—attributes men with prominence found attractive.

It didn't hurt that Juliette Carre was from a long line of courtesans, her mother having once been a popular Venetian courtesan. That was the story she weaved, the tall tale she'd told everyone who asked about Juliette's past.

As to Juliette's sexual experience, it wasn't nearly as vast as everyone thought.

Not even close.

The number of men she'd ever had sexually was the grand sum of…two.

One was the sweet and gentle Marquis de Cambry, whom she'd selected—thanks to Nicole's help once again—upon Juliette's debut in Paris. And the other wasn't much of a man at all. Roch had been nothing but a scoundrel of the highest order, preying on her vulnerability, taking full advantage of her dire circumstances and her naïveté.

But she was no longer naïve.

She was practical, realistic. And determined.

"Everything is going to be perfect tonight, my darling. You'll see," Nicole reassured, affectionately looping her arm with hers.

Clearly, her dear friend sensed her agitation.

As she glanced at the beautiful fifty-six-year-old woman beside her, Isabelle's smile turned genuine and warm. Full of affection. Years ago, when her father's theater had been the center of society, she'd been completely awestruck each time the stunning woman with the sumptuous gowns, lush blonde curls, and glittery jewelry attended her father's comedies. Nicole captivated everyone, both men and women, then and now. Though her hair color had changed slightly, Nicole was just as striking, fascinating, and engaging as ever. And just as sought after by men, who still vied for her attention and craved the company of the renowned former courtesan and respected writer. Nicole's intellect and extraordinary talent for penning poetry had garnered the admiration of the intellectual and social elite. As such, she was invited to all the finest salons in Paris, where lords and ladies, and the literati came together, regardless of social rank, to discuss and debate literature and language, art, politics, and philosophy.

Nicole was an inspiration to her.

In fact, to all woman with few choices.

Thirty-seven years ago, Nicole de Grammont had arrived in Paris with little money, her parents, low-ranking nobles, recently deceased. Yet, despite her diminished circumstances and the limited future she faced, Nicole quickly rose in popularity, gained the acceptance of the aristocracy, becoming the most adored courtesan the city had ever seen. She was so revered that a number of men came forward following the birth of each of her two children to claim the babes as theirs and amply providing for them. Genuinely kind and savvy, Nicole had amassed a fortune over time. And with the aid of her besotted benefactors, she even managed to secure respectable marriages for both her son and daughter.

If Nicole could elevate her children in society and give them a life free from poverty, Isabelle could do the same for her son Gabriel.

And she would.

Nothing would stop her.

"I know it will. Thanks to *you*." How could she ever repay Nicole's generosity and kindness? How could she ever thank her enough for all she'd done, beginning the night Isabelle had arrived on her doorstep, not knowing where else to turn, with no funds. And a hungry young child. It was Nicole who'd placed a roof over Isabelle's head and that of her eight-year-old little boy. It was Nicole who'd, albeit reluctantly, schooled Isabelle in her role as a courtesan and gained her admittance to the most prestigious salons in the city. It was Nicole who'd sponsored her writing, allowing Isabelle the creative outlet—a place to escape into the novels she wrote and published anonymously—a series that had become astoundingly popular about the lives and loves of two princess sisters who met and eventually married two princes.

Only in her books and with her son did she let down her guard.

Only in the pages of her novels did she experience the love she'd once dreamed about with the only man she'd ever dreamed of.

The most beautiful man she'd ever beheld. Then and since.

Only on the pages of her novels was she reunited with her beloved Sabine.

The stunning news she'd learned months ago from Nicole still had her reeling. How incredible was it that her beautiful twin sister had actually married the man *she'd* always dreamed of? Jules de Moutier. God, how she missed her every single day. The news of Sabine's marriage to Jules had elated her. And left her with a sense of longing, on so many levels. She and Sabine had been inseparable. They'd shared secrets. And dreams. Despite their differences in personality, no two sisters had ever been closer. Isabelle had been far more impetuous and adventurous than her levelheaded twin, coaxing her twin into mischief multiple times, sneaking about their father's theater without his knowledge, spying on the patrons.

Spying on the gorgeous Moutier brothers.

Yet Sabine would hardly recognize her now.

There was very little left of the Isabelle her sister once knew.

And she had no one to blame but herself.

Isabelle swallowed hard against the knot that had formed in her throat. This was no time to allow emotions to overtake her. She'd made it her practice to limit her thoughts of her sister. It was far too heart wrenching to think of her. For nine pain-soaked years, she'd been without her other half. Hadn't hugged her. Laughed with her. Isabelle hadn't even been there to see her wed. To see her joy. Did Sabine have a child of her own now? For years, Isabelle had been isolated, unable to let anyone know she was still alive. Not after Leon de Vittry had attempted to kill her. He was mad and vicious. He would have surely finished what he'd started, not to mention murder everyone she loved, if he'd learned she'd survived the fire.

But Vittry was dead now. So was Roch. And Sabine was impossible to reach while she lived on an unknown island in the West Indies with her husband.

Nicole affectionately squeezed her arm. "Vannod is an excellent choice. You've done so well since you've arrived in Paris." Her smile was always infectious.

"Thank you, Nicole. I'm so very pleased you think so."

Isabelle might have done everything wrong.

But Juliette was doing everything right.

The sheer number of men she had vying for her was the indisputable proof. So was the small wealth she'd already accumulated. From now on, she, and she alone, would manage her finances, have dominion over her funds and control of her future. She was well on her way to rebuilding some semblance of a life for her and her son. She'd managed to keep everyone safe. Her family. Her child. Herself. Even when mere months ago, she and Gabriel had been suddenly tossed out onto the streets from their home—Roch's home. Her options were bleak and narrow. Suitable employment at a château was scarce, and even more so with a child in tow. Lord knows she'd tried. No one had wanted her.

They'd all turned her away.

Moreover, the pittance they would pay would never safeguard Gabriel from the poverty she'd known after her family had lost everything during the *Fronde*. It was her life's mission for her son to be spared what she'd been through.

Nicole dipped her head and said in her ear, "I think you'll find your arrangement with Vannod to be mutually pleasing." Another touching attempt to ease her nerves.

Though she doubted her words, nonetheless, she responded politely. "I'm sure you're right."

Nicole made it no secret that she enjoyed sex and believed every woman should. Isabelle didn't have quite the same enthusiasm for it.

The virginal curiosity she'd once had about the intimate act between men and women was long gone. Her sexual experiences in no way resembled the passionate encounters she'd witnessed between couples in the dark corners of her father's theater and the alley outside. Yet, she'd learned how to put on a passionate performance nonetheless when needed.

And she did it by closing her eyes and conjuring up thoughts of the most beautiful man she'd ever seen—Luc de Moutier.

Though her romantic girlhood notions of him were dead, Luc still served a purpose in her life. Each time she surrendered to an encounter, she imagined that it was Luc's hands and mouth on her body.

It made it easier.

And she would allow Luc into every intimate act she'd have with Vannod as well. Whatever it took, however long it took to give Gabriel the life he deserved.

They reached the doors to the grand salon.

Isabelle squared her shoulders and brightened her smile. She was ready.

"Now remember, my darling, do not announce your choice until the end of the masque," Nicole said. "Let them continue to dance and prance about you until the end of the evening. The harder they have to work, the more they will want you."

The doors swung open. A crush of people was suddenly before her. The salon was full to capacity, the men and women in the center dancing the final steps to the *menuet*.

A fresh wave of nervousness crested over her. Those nine words that would sometimes assail her rose up in her chest, straight from the heart. *"This wasn't what my life was supposed to be…"* She swallowed them down before they could escape her lips and quashed the urge to flee back home.

Enough. You can do this. You shall do this, she assured herself. *The duc will be well pleased and brag to all his friends.* She'd be fine. Gabriel would be fine.

And tonight, everything was going to go as planned.

CHAPTER TWO

…I almost touched him!

My Fair Prince was at the theater again tonight. (I have decided to name Luc as such after Sabine told me she has dubbed her beloved the Dark Prince.) I convinced Sabine to sneak into the audience with me. I stood so close to where my Fair Prince sat. But, alas, I lost my courage to reach out and touch the fabric of his doublet as I'd planned. I know one day I will touch him. And he will touch me.

And it will be beyond my wildest imaginings…

There she was again.

Luc caught another glimpse of the woman with the luscious dark locks. He was at the Comtesse de Grandville's masque, immersed in the crowd that lined the perimeter of the grand salon—several rows deep. She was at the center of the room with the others who danced the *allemande*, moving in perfect unison to the violins and harpsichords.

He'd been bored. Frustrated. In his absence, he'd forgotten just how tedious most of his peers were. He'd never been as well liked or as well regarded as his brother Jules. The few men who'd recognized him tonight had already distanced themselves. Clearly, it wasn't going to be easy to convince everyone that his lengthy, humbling exile and his service in the King's navy had changed him.

For the better.

Had curbed his temperament.

The seething rage that had once pounded in his veins, always goading him to find a male counterpart to unleash it on, no longer plagued him.

He'd been debating over the last several minutes whether he should leave early from the masque and start afresh at the next social gathering.

That was until he saw the dark-haired beauty in the deep blue gown.

And her bedazzling smile.

Until he noticed the most adorable little dimple at the corner of her mouth that adorned that smile.

Dieu. A mere flash of her fine profile, demi-mask and all, and he was captivated by her. Who was she? Which aristocratic family did she belong to? If any.

Luc pressed forward through the throng, several strong perfumes assailing his nose along the way, until at last he reached the edge of the dance floor.

At last, an unhindered view.

Normally in social settings, he kept his back to the wall, a longtime habit that made him feel more relaxed, but he was drawn to the beauty with the dark blue demi-mask and white plumes. She placed her palm against her dance partner's raised hand and turned in a circle in time with the music and dancers around her.

Besotting yet another male in the room.

Her mask unfortunately hid half her face, but not that captivating smile. It graced the sweetest mouth he'd ever seen. She had the most perfect lips. Just the right fullness to drive a man wild.

A man could spend hours in oral worship of that lush mouth.

Riveted, Luc watched each elegant turn and movement she made. With his thoughts so disordered by Isabelle, he knew full well that it was her coloring that had initially drawn his gaze to her. Particularly her dark hair and the fineness of her features. Though there were others with dark hair in the room, this woman resembled just what he'd imagined Isabelle to look like. He couldn't help but notice her mouthwatering curves accentuated so delectably by her gown. And the top curves of those gorgeous breasts presently visible above her décolletage. She was flushed from the dance, her skin a pretty pink. Looking so silky soft.

His blood warmed. There was something about seeing a woman flush with pleasure that undid him.

Every time.

He fucked hard. Loved to make a woman come hard. He sought out women who matched his intensity in the boudoir. The rush it gave him to rock a woman's body with powerful orgasms was the sweetest, headiest aphrodisiac. He left them sated, languid, their skin flushed pink from the pleasure he took from their bodies. And the pleasure he gave in return.

Merde. Luc could feel his cock hardening by the moment. *Easy, now...*

The last thing he needed was a stiff prick. He wasn't here to bed anyone. He was on a mission—to begin reclaiming his place in society. And find a bride. Yet, as she danced past again, her beautiful dark cascading curls flouncing over her shoulders with the movement of her body, Luc's urge to ingratiate himself with the pompous asses in the room completely dissolved.

She was by far the most interesting person here. And he was going to learn exactly who she was.

His mysterious beauty circled her partner once more.

Then caught his gaze.

Abruptly, she stopped, surprising him. Her raised hand, pressed against her partner's palm, dropped slightly, and he could have sworn that her eyes widened within her mask. Yet she composed herself quickly, brightening her smile for her dance partner, and continued on with the *allemande*.

What the hell was that about? Did she *know* him?

He was now more intrigued than ever.

A hand suddenly clasped his shoulder. He snapped his head around and managed to quash the urge to knock the hand away in the nick of time—a purely visceral impulse to being touched, especially anywhere near his back.

Especially by a man.

Christ. It was Marc, and he was sporting his usual genial grin from behind the gray mask he wore. "How goes it, my friend?"

Marc's hand on his shoulder was a heavy, uncomfortable weight. And despite the layers of clothing Luc had on, it was singeing his skin. That familiar, unwanted anger began bubbling in his blood. Luc turned his body to face the only male friend he had in the room, a purposeful move that caused Marc's hand to slide away naturally.

The relief was instant, rushing through Luc, washing away the tension in his muscles, the anger receding the moment the touch was gone.

Marc seemed oblivious to just how far Luc had come. In the past, Luc wouldn't have bothered to master the fury. It would have suffocated him until he'd intentionally provoked a duel or some sort of physical altercation with the man responsible for the unwanted touch.

"I've not exactly received a warm welcome," Luc responded, returning his gaze to the dance floor, scanning for the beauty in blue now suddenly missing. She was a finer way to occupy his thoughts. The dance had ended, and a new one had begun. "In fact, I may develop a chill from the icy reception I received from some," he added.

Marc chuckled. "Be patient, Luc. It will take some time."

"I know."

He spotted her just then. On the other side of the dance floor, a number of men surrounded her, engrossed in her every word. Clearly, they were as captivated as he was.

"Who is that woman over there?" he asked, jerking his chin in her direction. "The one with the dark hair, blue gown, and white plumes on her mask?"

Marc stepped up to the edge of the dance floor and scanned the crowd. "Ah, yes. I see her." He paused for a moment, his lips pursed slightly as he studied the woman. Then his smile returned. Actually, it was a great big grin. "I believe *that* is none other than Juliette Carre."

"The courtesan you spoke of?"

"The very one. And it seems she's caught your eye—even when you claimed you wouldn't be interested. I told you she would appeal to you."

He couldn't deny that. Thus far, she appealed to him very much.

"I'm going to talk to her."

Marc chuckled. "You'll have to first get through her crowd of admirers. Vannod is there, practically panting for her. Everyone knows he wants her."

Vannod and the others didn't concern him in the least. He was intent on learning everything there was to know about Juliette Carre. From her.

And why on earth she'd reacted to him so oddly.

*****

"Please excuse me, gentlemen." Isabelle smiled. With a curtsy to the four men before her, she turned and made her way through the crowd. Her mind reeled over the man she'd spotted during the *allemande*.

It can't be… Can it? It isn't… Luc?

Nicole would know for certain who the man with the dark blond hair and the black-and-silver mask was. He was tall. Muscled. And he'd sent her insides into a frenzy with one look.

So similar to the physical reactions she'd had years ago when she'd first set eyes on the fairer Moutier brother.

It took several long agonizing minutes of being jostled about in the crush before Isabelle spotted her friend engaged in conversation with a tall silver-haired gentleman in a black mask.

"My apologies for the intrusion…" she said the moment she reached Nicole, hating to interrupt a conversation her friend was clearly enjoying, judging by her genuine laughter at the man's whispered remarks. She had Nicole's attention immediately. Isabelle kept her smile bright as a sad realization occurred to her: while Nicole's smiles were almost always real, Isabelle's were almost always not. But then again, she was Juliette. And Juliette was nothing more than an essential charade.

There wasn't anything authentic about her.

Isabelle's genuine smiles were only for Gabriel and Nicole and one rather overlarge dog named Montague.

"Might I have a brief moment of your time…in private?"

"Of course, darling," Nicole said. There was a flash of concern in Nicole's eyes before she schooled her features with practiced skill. Excusing herself from the company of the disappointed gentleman beside her, Nicole looped her arm with Isabelle's, then together they made their way to a quieter corner in the room.

"What is the matter?" she asked sotto voce the moment they stopped.

"Do you see the tall gentleman across the room?" She described his clothing and mask with enough detail to aid Nicole in spotting him in the mass.

"Oh yes, I see him."

"I believe that is Luc de Moutier," she whispered in Nicole's ear.

Could he have returned from the West Indies or wherever he'd been all this time?

Nicole shook her head. "Impossible, darling. He's taller and his shoulders are far broader than the Luc de Moutier I remember. And his hair looks darker too."

It was true. He did seem taller, his body more powerful. And the hair coloring wasn't quite right from her vantage point. But no one had seen Luc de Moutier in years. Especially her. He might not be quite the same as the seventeen-year-old boy she'd last seen eleven years ago at the theater and had so adored.

Her insides were in chaos. Her emotions were awhirl.

What if it was him? Could he help reunite her with Sabine?

"Besides," Nicole added, "if Luc de Moutier were ever to return to Paris, there would be quite a stir. That isn't the sort of news one would miss. If he was at the masque tonight, I'd have learned of it."

That was an inarguable fact.

Everyone confided in Nicole de Grammont. She'd be among the first to learn of his attendance at the masque. If the elusive Luc de Moutier were truly here, someone would have certainly recognized him standing in the crowd—regardless of the demi-mask. The gossip-mongers in the room would have spread the news of his presence as fast as fire.

Instantly, she quashed the disappointment that threatened to crush her and placed thoughts of her sister back in that place in her heart in which she kept her sealed.

"He does keep looking at you," Nicole said of the gentleman in question, giving him a friendly nod. "And he is quite handsome. It wouldn't be too difficult for a woman to enjoy his attention—*fully.*"

She knew exactly what Nicole meant by fully—in every carnal way. Sex was merely an unavoidable part of the role Juliette played. Something she did because she had to. Yet, at the moment, as she took in the sculpted aristo, she didn't feel the normal aversion to Nicole's remark.

Nicole gave her a smile. "If you prefer this man to Vannod, make the duc wait. It won't harm Vannod to learn more patience. It'll spike his interest and determination further. Men *always* want what other men have."

The gorgeous male across the salon captured Isabelle's gaze once more. He stared back at her openly. Then a slow, wickedly sensuous smile formed on his lips. Her stomach fluttered, taking her by surprise—again. This was the first man, aside from Luc, who'd inspired any sort of real interest. Or physical reaction.

She was definitely drawn to him.

And for the first time since racing out of the burning servants' quarters at Luc's father's château years ago with Gabriel in her arms—a mere infant at the time—followed by empty years in a sham of a marriage, she actually felt a flicker of desire low in her belly.

It was startling.

It felt good.

And it had everything to do with the attractive man across the room who'd reminded her of a time when life was so very different. When she was so very different.

When her future wasn't so fractured.

Nicole was right. Vannod could wait. She enjoyed dancing. And she was intent on joining in the next dance—especially as she noted that her enigmatic lord had just stepped onto the dance floor. His focus on her and that sensuous smile hadn't wavered for an instant. She glanced about, confirming his interest was truly directed at her.

And it was, unquestionably.

Her curiosity was piqued. Her heartbeat was quick with excitement she hadn't felt for too many years to mention.

She was going to learn more about this tall, alluring aristo.

From him.

CHAPTER THREE

Luc stepped in front of one of the male dancers, cutting into the man's spot, ignoring the protest. Bowing to his female partner, Luc then took her hand and waited for the music to begin. He didn't particularly care for dancing, but he was making an exception this night. Anything that would get him before the intriguing raven-haired female.

And her beautiful flushed form.

He'd seen her excuse herself from her admirers. He'd seen her speak to a woman he was all but certain was the well-known Nicole de Grammont. They were clearly talking about him—given the way they'd both continued to glance at him as they spoke. *Dieu,* he liked the way she looked at him. Very much. As though there was no one else in the room.

He couldn't help but reciprocate the very same way.

This pull to her was beyond enticing. It beckoned him from across the grand salon.

Out of all the women here, she was the only one he wanted to learn more about. Her initial reaction to him had to have been in error. She must have mistaken him for someone else. If this was the courtesan Juliette Carre, then they didn't know each other. He'd never met her before.

But he was hell-bent on changing that.

The longer they stared at each other, the more strongly he felt a delicious heat rushing through his veins. It had already grown to a level that was impossible to ignore.

Without exchanging a single word.

The attraction was raw. Instant. He couldn't remove the smile from his face. As he watched her enter the dance floor and take her place in the *menuet*, giving her partner a curtsy—her attention deliciously drawn back to him again and again—his every rakish instinct told him that a carnal encounter between the two of them would be nothing short of intense. And it had nothing to do with the fact that she was a skilled courtesan.

And everything to do with the palpable allure between them.

The music began. His heart pounded to its own beat. He moved to the next female, anxiously waiting until the dance rotation brought him face-to-face with *her*. He was one dance partner away. Another few steps. Another turn to the left. Then one more to the right.

And finally, he clasped the hand of the one woman he wanted to dance with.

Surprisingly, her hand was cooler than he would have imagined, given her flushed skin. Was she…*nervous*? Before he could dwell on that, she smiled at him.

Jésus-Christ. It practically knocked him back.

Her smile was even lovelier up close. As for that little dimple near the corner of her mouth, it was just too damned adorable.

This woman had a smile that was utterly contagious. "I couldn't help notice that you've been watching me, mademoiselle."

"I could say the same of you, my lord." He liked the sound of her voice. There was a delightful playfulness to her tone.

And she smelled so good. The light scent of jasmine seduced his senses. He was having a difficult time concentrating on the steps of the dance. "Have mercy on us mere mortals. You are so fine to behold, I couldn't help myself."

She laughed. "Mere mortals? Are you suggesting I am a *goddess*?"

They turned with the music, then clasped hands again. He purposely grazed his thumb down her palm, then wisped across her wrist, enjoying the small gasp she gave at the light sensation. His groin tightened. She was highly responsive to him.

How delectable was that?

"Yes, that is what I strongly suspect," he said. "Though, I think further investigation is in order." He was running out of time. He'd be on to the next partner in moments. And he wanted to be alone with her. So badly. "Meet me in the library at the end of the dance, beautiful Juliette. I promise, you will enjoy every moment."

*****

Isabelle's skin still tingled where he'd caressed her as she moved to her next partner in the *menuet*—an older, potbellied gentleman.

"I promise, you will enjoy every moment…"

Those seven little words from Lord Seductive's lips had lanced straight into her core, making her sex clench. Her every nerve ending hummed with awareness.

Who in heaven's name is he?

He'd managed to rattle her when she didn't believe she could be rattled by any man anymore.

It was a challenge just to stay in step, her mind turning much faster than the turns in the dance. How in the world had a few charming words, a light caress, and a sexual proposition incited any responses from her body? Much less such potent ones? Regardless of who he reminded her of, he shouldn't have had this kind of impact. Not with so little effort. It wasn't as though she hadn't been propositioned before. Lord knows she'd been on the receiving end of a forward caress many a time. She'd heard every sultry word and flowery phrase a man would utter to a woman he was trying to bed. Yet no one had spiked her pulse or left her feeling heated from the inside out.

Except the man who wanted to meet her in the library.

She was even more drawn to him than before. And more curious about him than ever. As she turned in time with the music, she couldn't help casting a glance in the direction of the enticing aristo.

Her stomach lurched. He was gone.

A slim man with an orange mask and a ridiculously long purple plume had taken his spot in the *menuet*.

She quickly scanned the other dancers one by one, in case she'd missed him somehow. She hadn't. He was nowhere on the dance floor. Dear God, had he left for the library already? Was he there at this very moment waiting for her?

The mere thought made her insides flutter.

Again.

Something told her Lord Seductive wasn't full of idle words. He could—and would—make good on his promise of pleasure. A thrill rippled up her spine. Whoever he was, her intense attraction to him was unbalancing. And gave her pause.

She had to preserve the façade of being seasoned and sophisticated about sex at all cost.

He couldn't know that she found him in any way daunting.

Nicole had taught her to place her lovers in one of two groupings: those who paid for her favors. And those she favored whom she enjoyed for free. It made men work harder to earn the preferable grouping. And to remain there. Yet she hadn't had enough lovers to forgo a fee.

She could simply return to Vannod. But if she didn't meet the seductive lord in the library, she might never learn who he was. Not to mention the liaison could bolster her socially too. *Liar. Those are not the only reasons you want to meet him,* a voice inside her countered. For the first time in a very long time, she'd found a man who was desirable. *Exciting.* She hadn't felt either for any male in too many years. He offered a rapture she'd never known. Nor had she realized just how starved her senses were—until he touched her.

He'd addressed her as Juliette. Clearly, he had taken the time to learn her name. As she moved from dance partner to dance partner, her desire to go to the library mounted.

So, he intimidates you. So what? That's no reason to back away.

He was a challenge. She'd dealt with many challenges in her life. Besides, Juliette Carre was a courtesan. And courtesans had clandestine encounters with gentlemen. It was expected.

She could have at least one she was actually interested in.

As the final strains of music faded away, she made up her mind. She'd meet the handsome aristo in the library. She'd keep to her role—and perform it convincingly. As she had thus far.

Moreover, she'd learn just who was behind the mask.

*****

Luc arrested his steps in the library and softly cursed.

Dieu. He was pacing again.

He hadn't been this restless since his time in prison, when he filled the long, empty hours with endless pacing and torturous thoughts of his possible execution.

Waiting for Juliette to arrive was almost as excruciating.

With a far more decadent outcome *if* the lady arrived.

Placing his hands on his hips, he blew out a sharp breath, exasperated with himself. His proposition to her had been ridiculously abrupt.

She may not come…

He hoped to God that wasn't the case. That the simmering desire between them would be enough to draw her to the library. To him. Damn it, he was normally more adept at charming a woman he was attracted to.

And she has a crowd of men out there wanting the very same thing you want from her. Perhaps propositioning her at this very moment—far better than the way you did.

A pang of jealousy slammed him in the gut, taking him by surprise. Where the hell did that come from? He wasn't the possessive type.

Not ever.

Luc strode over to the window and braced his palms against its frame, staring absently out at the courtyard as rain began to streak down the pane of glass. This whole situation had him uncharacteristically unbalanced. The last thing he expected to happen tonight was to meet a woman for whom he was practically panting. And who so closely resembled the mental image he'd had of Isabelle Laurent.

For the longest time, he'd been convinced that if he could have had just one encounter with the real Isabelle, it would have been enough to snap the spell she'd cast on him. But that was impossible. No matter how much he wished it. He'd begun to despair that the ghost of Isabelle Laurent would forever torment him.

And now, incredibly, beautiful Juliette had come along.

Could being with her be just like being with Isabelle? He'd never pretended to be with one woman while bedding another. Nor had he ever paid for sex—not when it had always been offered for free. Yet, he'd be willing to pay this one gorgeous courtesan a king's ransom if she could just give him back his mental peace.

Then he could purge Isabelle Laurent from his system. His thoughts. His dreams.

There was no question. He had to break this hold she had on him so he could move forward with his life without this maddening fascination he had for a deceased woman.

The sound of rustling skirts snagged his attention. He spun around. The sight of Juliette standing at the threshold of the library made his heart skip a beat. She had a slight smile on her delectable mouth. And those luscious breasts of hers were rising and falling more quickly than normal with each soft accelerated breath she took. A telltale sign of arousal. His cock thickened in an instant, his prick suddenly feeling as heavy as lead.

She is here.

And fuck…she wants you.

She looked so good standing in the doorway. Part of him wanted to stalk across the room and tear off her demi-mask just so he could take in the beauty of her entire face. But he was afraid to do anything that would alter this moment. It was all too perfect, from the desire crackling between them to the sheer perfection of the woman before him. How fucking fortunate was he? Of all the men vying for her, she'd selected *him*. And she was a courtesan. A woman whose very occupation it was to fulfill men's fantasies. As he drank in the sight of her—every sweet inch of her edible little form—he knew she'd already done her job.

She was every bit the extraordinary beauty he imagined Isabelle would have been.

Before him was his fantasy come to life.

Christ. Not just his. She was every man's fantasy come true. He fully understood the clamoring Marc said she caused, why every man of means threw riches at her—just for a moment like this.

Yet again, he found himself unable to hold back a smile. He'd made this beautiful woman a promise—and he couldn't wait to fulfill it. He was going to see to it that she did indeed enjoy every moment. He was going to show her the extent of his gratitude and the depth of his desire for her.

One stunning climax at a time.

*****

Isabelle watched as he approached, all that tall, strong, masculine beauty coming her way.

Anticipation gripped her.

The way he moved was riveting. With the confidence of a man who knew just how to take a woman to ecstasy and back. Her sex was already slick. The bud between her legs had begun to pulse. This man incited her breathing, ignited her blood. She'd stopped believing she'd ever find anyone who could set her on fire this way. Her long-dormant body was fully awake and starved for what he offered. It was completely ludicrous, but she was actually battling the urge to launch herself at him.

Clearly, she was even lonelier than she realized if a stranger in a mask could discompose her this way.

Lonely or not, you are going to experience true passion.

For once, she wasn't going to have to close her eyes and force herself to pretend she was with Luc de Moutier just to get through the experience. This man made it easy. Everything about him made her *want* this encounter.

Her seductive lord stopped before her, his body all but touching hers. Her heart was thundering so loudly, she feared he'd hear it.

She wanted him so badly… *For goodness sake, compose yourself.*

Leaning in, he reached behind her—his arm brushing her waist—and closed the door. She felt the sensation right through her clothing.

The lock clicked into place.

He straightened and smiled down at her. "I'm so very pleased you're here."

Dear God. His voice was low and oh so sultry. She gazed at his enticing mouth and for a moment couldn't help ponder how he'd taste—the thought taking her by surprise.

She had certain rules, ones she never broke during her carnal encounters. One of which was no kissing.

The only act of intimacy that wasn't for sale.

The only act that hadn't been tainted by Juliette and her occupation. Or by the things that had happened to her before she became Juliette. Roch had disliked the act of kissing, and thankfully, she'd never been forced to endure it with him.

If truth be told, neither Isabelle—nor Juliette—had ever experienced a real kiss.

During sex, she knew how to detach and put on an engaging performance. But a kiss was different. Designed to be romantic. And, perhaps, ridiculous though it was, she wanted to experience it with a man—someone significant—who truly deserved that level of intimacy from her. Whether he'd ever know it or not.

"Juliette?"

His voice snapped her out of her thoughts, and she realized she hadn't responded to his welcome.

"I'm glad you're pleased, my lord," she said. "But there is something that would please me."

His beautiful smile returned. "Do tell, and allow me to fulfill your wishes."

She flinched at the word *wishes*. From her experience, only dreadful things came of making wishes. Long ago, she'd made three. Every one of them came true.

And had leveled her life.

"It would please me to know whom I have the pleasure of speaking to." Somehow, she managed to utter the sentence without sounding as breathless as she felt.

His disarming smile never wavered. He surprised her by taking her hand in his. It was strong and warm, and she liked the feel of it enveloping hers—far more than she would have ever expected.

He led her to the center of the room, then stopped abruptly. In one swift movement, he gripped her hips, picked her up, and set her bottom down on the large ebony-and-gold side table against the wall.

Her eyes widened.

Lord Seductive braced his hands against the side table on either side of her knees and gazed into her eyes. She had to quash the urge to squirm.

Dipping his head, he brushed his mouth over her bare shoulder ever so lightly. She lost her breath. The sensations rippled down to the tips of her breasts. She tightly gripped the edge of the table with both hands. He trailed his lips up her neck—a slow, silky stroke—all the way to the sensitive spot beneath her ear. Pressing a hot, knee-weakening kiss there.

She barely caught the mewl that shot up her throat.

"No," he whispered in her ear before pulling back, his face mere inches from hers. Her quickened breaths mingling with his.

She blinked. "No?" Try as she might, she couldn't make out the color of his eyes given the shadow his mask cast and the limited light from the hearth on the other side of the room.

"Identities stay hidden until midnight. Those are the rules at any masque. Masks are not removed until then." His smile graced his sensuous mouth once more.

"My lord, you know who I am. You could tell me your name without revealing your face."

He placed his hands on her knees over her gown. Her heart skipped a beat. She immediately knew what he was about to do. "This desire between us and this moment are perfect. Let's not change a thing." He spread her legs apart.

Her sex responded with a warm gush. Isabelle dug her nails into the edge of the table, acutely aware of the void between her legs and the ache to be filled.

The likes of which she'd never experienced before.

He stepped between her legs. "All you need to know about me at the moment is that I'm the man who's going to make you come—several times—before we leave this room." He gripped her hips and yanked her close. His solid shaft coming in sudden contact with the sensitized bud between her legs. A soft cry shot up her throat. Her hands flew to his shoulders and held on, her breaths ragged. He was applying perfect pressure where she needed it most.

He rolled his hips, the friction exquisite. She closed her eyes, unable to contain her moan. Her clit was throbbing hard against him now.

His hot mouth was back against her neck. She tilted her head, giving him complete access. After so many empty encounters, she reveled in this.

In this moment of real passion.

The kind she could lose herself in.

Anxieties that plagued her every waking moment—for her son and herself—melted away. Lost to the glorious sensations coursing through her body. It didn't matter who this man was anymore. Or that the attraction to him had been triggered by an old girlhood infatuation. All that mattered to her right now was the pleasure saturating her senses. She'd stumbled upon a small miracle; she'd found someone who had a magic touch, a man able to do what no other ever had. To pull her out of reality.

Into sexual oblivion.

Temporary as this was, she couldn't be more grateful.

"What say you, Juliette? Shall we begin?" he murmured in her ear and gently bit her lobe. She whimpered.

Good Lord, hadn't they commenced already? *You've let this get away from you before addressing essential preliminaries. Focus!* This wasn't just an amorous encounter between lovers.

She squeezed his strong shoulders and forced herself to push him away.

His head shot up, and for a moment, she thought he'd flinched at her touch before dismissing it as absurd.

Grasping her wrists, he pulled her hands from his shoulders, placed a kiss on one wrist, then held them. "What is the matter, *chère?*"

Gone was his beguiling smile. Confusion, or perhaps it was concern, was etched on his brow.

"Since you know who I am...then you must know there's a..." The usual words caught in her throat this time. She forced them out. "There is a *fee* for this." How she hated this part. Blatantly selling herself. Never more so than with this particular man.

A slight smile tugged at the corner of his appealing mouth. "Name your price, beautiful Juliette. Whatever it is, you are worth it."

God, how she wanted him. More than anything. Desperate for some friction—any relief from the torment between her legs—she squirmed against his delicious hard bulge wedged against her. The jolt of sensations snatched the breath from her lungs.

Without thought, a price tumbled from her mouth on a pant. She realized immediately that what she'd asked for was almost twice what Vannod had offered.

What any man had offered.

She wanted to kick herself.

You've just asked for an exorbitant amount. Despite his words, he was going to walk away for certain now! Her body railed against the mere thought.

"Agreed," he said, without hesitation. She couldn't have been more astounded. "Is that it? Or is there more you wish to discuss?" His voice was tinged with urgency. Hearing it only heightened her hunger.

"A couple more things. Are you married?" Foolishly, she'd let this go further than normal before knowing the answer to that all too important question. She didn't engage in sex with a married man—no matter how it limited her pool of income. Or how much she desired the man before her. She'd end this now if he had a wife. Isabelle held her breath, praying he'd say no.

"I am not married. Never have been."

Joy welled inside her. "Lastly..."

"Yes?" She could tell even by that one word that he was becoming impatient.

"No kissing." It was amazing just how much regret she felt voicing that sentence to *this* man.

He went silent for a moment, and she could tell she'd surprised him. Then his lips quirked in what looked suspiciously like amusement. He placed her hands down on the edge of the table where she'd gripped it before. "Keep your hands here," he said. Before she could respond to his odd request, he cupped her breast.

She went stock-still.

"Now then, you are going to have to be much more specific, Juliette. Where am I not permitted to kiss you?" He stroked his thumb over her nipple. "Here?" He repeated his caress again.

And again.

She squeezed her eyes shut. The sensations were rippling into her core. The ache between her legs becoming unbearable.

"No… I mean, yes," she said. "Right there is…*fine*." His strokes were melting her mind.

He slipped his other hand beneath her gown, his fingers grazing along her inner thigh, getting closer and closer to her needy clit. Every fiber of her being willed him forward.

"What about *here*?" He scored a finger along the slit of her *caleçons*. She practically jumped right off the table at the merest touch of her ultrasensitive bud.

"Well, sweet Juliette*?*" She could hear the smile in his voice. He was enjoying this. She was dying. "You're going to have to give me an answer, *ma belle*."

She licked her lips. He knew full well where she didn't want to be kissed. She'd play this his way, if she didn't first expire on the spot from lust. "*Yes…there…* There is fine, too… I meant on the—" He cupped her sex. Her thoughts scattered.

"On the *lips*?" he supplied, sliding his hand inside the slit of her drawers. He began massaging her slick folds with delicious deftness. With a whimper, she slumped back against the wall, arching for more.

"Y…Yes…*lips…* "

*****

Luc couldn't take his eyes off the sensuous woman before him. He continued to stroke her, giving her enough stimulation to keep her keen. But not enough to let her come. Her eyes were closed, her lips slightly parted, and her cheeks were pink. The way she was coming undone for him was so fucking inflaming.

If he'd been fascinated by her before, he was even more so now. He'd spent years as an unrepentant rake before his family's disgrace. More than one courtesan had favored him with a *gratis* tumble or two, just to boast they'd been with a member of the then preeminent

Moutier family. Particularly the youngest son of Charles de Moutier, Marquis de Blainville. Luc's once wild, unbridled reputation both in and out of the boudoir had always garnered him his share of women.

And he'd never met a courtesan who refused married men. Or a kiss.

Anywhere.

It would be a lie if he told her he wasn't disappointed. Especially when she had such a seductive mouth. He really wanted to find out why, what her motivation was behind her intriguing rules. But it was going to have to wait. At the moment, he was enjoying what he was doing far too much. She was so luscious. Her sex so hot, wet, and silky soft, already primed for the taking. And given how hard and heavy his cock felt, he knew he was in for a powerful orgasm with this woman.

As spine melting a climax as he was about to give her—if—*he hoped*—she'd be willing to abide by *his* one rule during sex.

She arched hard, trying to grind her engorged little clit against his palm. Famished for some friction. He easily evaded her efforts without ceasing his caresses to the rest of her slick sex.

With his free hand, he captured her pebbled nipple through her gown and gave it a playful pinch. She bit her bottom lip and gave him a mew she couldn't contain. *Jésus-Christ,* everything she did made him want to fuck her.

If she wouldn't let him taste her mouth, he was going to taste the rest of her. Every last sweet inch—starting with those delectable little nipples that were straining so hard for him inside her chemise.

He dipped his head and in her ear said, "I'm going to open your gown, and then these pretty nipples are mine."

She shivered with excitement. It reverberated through him all the way down to the tip of his prick, making him seep some spunk.

Mentally, he swore. He was picking up the bloody pace. *Get the preliminaries over and done with.* "But before we go any further, I have a rule too." Needing her undivided attention, he reluctantly released her nipple and withdrew his hand from her inviting cunt.

Her eyes flew open, soft pants continuing to slip ever so sensually past her lips. She met his gaze, clearly distressed at his cessation of their sexual play. Yet there was also curiosity in her eyes. And that pleased him more than she could ever know.

You have her attention now. Out with it. He untied his cravat, slipped it from his neck, and held it out before her. "You'll be bound while I take you."

He caught the surprise in her dark eyes. She glanced at the cravat in his hand, then back at him. *"Bound?"*

"Yes."

"Why?"

For many reasons... "For pleasure. Yours and mine. It heightens the encounter." Not exactly the whole truth, but all he was prepared to say. While there was nothing sweeter than a woman's complete surrender—bound with a silk scarf or cravat—he liked that kind of control. He needed it. And he valued every woman who'd placed their trust in him during sex and ceded it to him. In truth, he valued each and every pleasurable moment he'd ever had in his life. It helped combat the dark ones. Not to mention that having her hands rendered incapable of touching his back, even by accident, allowed him to relax and simply relish the experience. And kept the memories at bay.

She stared at him, incredulous.

"Think of it as merely a sex game. One where we both win. One I'll make certain you enjoy," he added. For a fleeting moment, he was mildly surprised that as a courtesan, if she hadn't participated in such sexual practices, she hadn't at least heard of it. Gatherings of debauchery among the aristocracy occurred frequently. And there were no shortage of courtesans present at them. Yet, oddly, she seemed to be hearing of the concept for the first time. He'd discovered it years ago while attending his first such party at the Vicomte d'Inville's château—the entertainment purely carnal, with every type of decadent diversion to suit all sexual tastes.

From the mild to the depraved.

Whippings were not Luc's taste, not on either end of the whip. In no way could he ever associate sexual pleasure with a lashing. He'd endured the lash more times than he'd ever allowed himself to remember. He'd practically raced from the room as a wave of white-hot anger surged inside him at the first sight of it back then. But the carnal play he'd observed that involved erotic bondage...well, that was entirely different.

That had become the most liberating, sublime diversion he'd ever known.

He wasn't the only one who indulged in such sexual play. But he was probably the only man who never took a woman unless she was bound.

Luc saw her pull her gaze from the cravat in his hand and move it to the door of the library. *Fuck.* She was contemplating a departure from the room. Perhaps a hasty one at that.

He immediately stepped back, giving her more room, not wanting to scare her into believing she was trapped. Or that he'd force this on her.

His body instantly balked at the loss of contact from her soft form.

Luc dragged in a breath and let it out slowly, trying to master his desire, his blood pounding in his veins. It didn't help that his sac was so tight and full, he wanted to howl in frustration.

Yet, no matter how badly he wanted her, if she was going to submit to him this way, it had to be of her own free will. He'd only ever had two women refuse. He'd walked away, respecting their wishes. Both times.

"Juliette, you are free to leave, if you wish." *Don't go...* "But if you stay, I swear, you won't regret your trust in me. This is about mutual pleasure. I'll make you come harder than you've ever come before."

*****

Isabelle's head was spinning. Her body feverish. She warred between wanting to yield to his startling—highly provocative—request.

And wanting to leave the library. Posthaste.

Try as she might, she couldn't seem to quash the desire to know what it would be like to submit to him in the way he suggested and experience the heightened pleasure he promised. To lose herself in this man who so reminded her of Luc. Her body was screaming, *SAY YES!*

But you don't know him. Don't know his identity. And she wasn't reckless anymore. She had a child now who had no one but his mother in this world to care and provide for him. She'd stopped trusting men with influence after Vittry and Roch were through with her. When one had tried to murder her and the other had so grossly deceived and manipulated her, she'd learned it prudent to distrust the male aristocracy.

There were three things she'd never risk again: Her life, her freedom, and her free will.

It was one thing to meet Lord Seductive in the library—especially after making certain to inform Nicole where she'd be. But to allow herself to be bound, rendered that vulnerable, simply because a stranger told her he was trustworthy, was far too careless, regardless of the amount of money being offered. Words were empty.

Especially from the mouths of powerful men.

She hadn't even brought Yves and Serge with her tonight, Nicole's largest servants who normally accompanied her to her carnal encounters. Yet even having them nearby wouldn't have been enough for her to surrender to such a request from this stranger.

No matter how hard the bud between her legs pulsed, no matter how eager she was for more decadent delights from him or how intrigued by his wicked game, she managed to drag the words she needed to say up her throat. And out of her mouth.

"I can't…"

She slipped off the table and onto her feet before he could react, then stepped away from him, putting distance between them.

And hating it.

He didn't make a move to hinder her retreat in any way. Instead, he placed his hands on his hips, and his smiled turned rueful. With a nod, he said, "I understand."

For some reason, that sank her spirits. She was wishing for…what? A protest and compromise of some sort?

A withdrawal of his condition to bind her altogether?

She'd have to be completely blind to miss that impressive part of his male anatomy that was still solid and erect and straining inside his breeches. Was he just going to let her walk away when he wanted her as strongly as she wanted him? This couldn't be just a sex game to him. Could it? There had to be more to his sexual practice then he was saying.

And she couldn't help wonder what.

Isabelle held his gaze, unsure what more to say. Willing him to somehow change his mind. The fact that he hadn't attempted to coerce her, as some men of his standing might have—as Roch certainly would have when he was this aroused—made her want to stay with him even more.

But not tied up and defenseless.

Silence saturated the air. His expression was unreadable, and she wished she knew what he was thinking. The quiet grew to the point of awkwardness.

You can't continue to stand here and stare at him. Bid him adieu and leave, Isabelle.

Instead, entirely different words escaped past her lips. "I-I would stay...if you were to withdraw your condition." She immediately cringed. That sounded pathetically desperate.

His smile didn't change. "It's how I want you. It's how I fuck," he said.

Her knees practically buckled at his blunt language. From this man's lips alone, it had the most stunning effect on her libido.

"It is wicked," he continued, with a lopsided smile on that tempting mouth. "It is also entirely intense and delicious. And you should try it—with me." His words, the timbre of his voice, and his heated gaze fixed her to the spot.

A triple blow to her defenses.

Dear God. If you don't leave right now, you run the risk of succumbing to his allure. And end up trussed up like a goose.

"I'm sorry," she murmured, then unstuck her feet from the floor and turned to go, her body rioting against her actions.

When she reached the door, she heard him call out, "Juliette."

Her insides danced with joy. She turned around, managing to keep her smile from showing. Everything inside her hoped he'd changed his mind and removed his condition.

"Yes?"

"Are you going back to Vannod?" he asked.

Not exactly what she thought she'd hear. "Perhaps." In truth, the answer was yes. She'd given up a small fortune by turning down Lord Seductive's sexual proposition. She wouldn't turn down Vannod's sum too.

He approached and stopped before her, his chiseled form now towering above her. No man on this side of the stars should be this gorgeous. She wanted to lean in and wrap her arms around him. Just to feel that strong, solid chest against her and his muscular arms about her—a longing she hadn't had for a male in years.

"He can't give you the pleasure I can," he said.

Oh, she didn't doubt that for a moment.

She'd never felt the intense pull to Vannod as she did to this aristo. *Though, I doubt Vannod harbors a penchant for tying women up during physical encounters.* From the extensive information Nicole had given her about the duc, he was just like her last lover.

Safe. Conventional.

Tolerable.

And for those times when it was more of a chore than others, she need only conjure up Luc de Moutier in her mind.

"My lord, it would be wrong of me to discuss one man's sexual prowess with another."

He placed his hands on his hips again and tilted his head, quietly studying her. She shifted her weight from one foot to the other, unsure what to do at the moment.

Then he swore under his breath. "I don't make exceptions. I don't withdraw my condition of sexual bondage."

Really? "Never?"

"Not ever. That is…until tonight. With you." Tossing the cravat he'd had in his hand carelessly to the floor, he clasped her shoulders and pressed her back against the door. There was nothing threatening in the way in which he did it. There was just enough sensual command in the action to spark a fresh flare of arousal in her belly.

He released her, then he flattened his palms against the door at either side of her head. His mouth was so close to her own. She held her breath, unsure what he would do.

"Easy. There is no need to tense up. I'll abide by your wishes. There will be no kissing—*on the lips*—though not ever tasting that beautiful mouth is going to be one of the greatest regrets of my life. It takes trust to allow someone to bind you. I'm going to earn your trust, *chère*. If you are willing, I'm going to give you a sampling of what I can offer—with no binding."

Every fiber of her being reveled in his words. "A…A sampling? As in a small taste?" *Oh yes, please!*

Lord Seductive then gave her a purely male knee-weakening grin. "I don't do anything in small measures. So, tell me, *ma belle*, does your next orgasm belong to me?"

Chapter Four

Merde. What the hell did you just agree to?

Luc couldn't believe the unprecedented promise he'd made just to have this woman. His need for this one female had eclipsed all reason.

And had him completely discarding a sexual practice he'd normally never forgo.

But he was on fire for her, desire scorching through his body. And the pressure in his stiff prick was driving him out of his mind.

Leaning on one hand, he ran the fingers of his other over the gentle swells of her breasts, gingerly following the contour of her scooped neckline. He heard her catch her breath, and she arched into his touch, purely involuntary reactions she couldn't help.

Dieu, he liked that. As much as he liked her quickened breaths. And by God, she was affecting his own.

He had enough experience to know that a small part of her was curious about being bound for pleasure—even with her reservations. He was intent on gaining her trust and her permission. In fact, he intended to have this highly responsive woman eager and begging to be bound for him. In time. The notion that he'd be the man to initiate this sensuous woman into this particular carnal practice sent a hot pulse down his cock.

As for now, he was going to relish every moment of his erotic dream come to life with the closest version of Isabelle he'd ever seen. In all likelihood, being with the real Isabelle might have been much the same way. No matter how much she'd professed to desire him in her journals, it might have taken some gentle persuasion to have her accede to having her wrists and ankles bound for sex.

"What's your answer, Juliette? Is your next orgasm mine?"

She licked her lips, the small act torturing him. How he wanted to lick, bite, and kiss those lips. More than anything. *Easy… One step at a time…* She was uncommonly antsy for someone of her trade. Truly, she was uncommon on so many peculiar levels for such a sought-after, highly paid paramour.

She gave him a quick shaky nod. It was so adorably earnest and awkward, he was forced to suppress his smile. Another peculiar behavior.

And for some reason, he liked that too.

She cleared her throat, then attempted to reaffirm her response. "Yes," she said, trying to sound collected. Yet it slipped past her lips so sensually breathless.

Jésus, she was refreshingly different. Not at all what he expected her to be when he'd pursued her. And she wasn't as blasé about sex as he might have believed. Nothing about this felt like a paid encounter at all, despite the staggering sum he was paying to have her.

"Well then, since we've discussed all terms and conditions and I have your permission to proceed…" He pressed both palms to the door again and moved in a little closer. Her sweet derrière gave an impatient little squirm. Another spurt of pre-come wept from the crest of his cock. "Open your bodice for me." He couldn't help notice her nipples were pebbled and straining for his attention.

And Lord knows he was famished for their taste on his tongue.

Her hand yanked loose the ribbon between her breasts in an instant. Next, the fastenings with hungry haste. Tugging at her clothing and stays, her fingers fumbled for a moment, until finally reaching her chemise.

She paused and looked up at him, her breaths shorter and sharper and matching his own.

"Go on," he urged, wanting to tear the clothes off her lovely form with a ferocity he'd never felt before.

She pulled her chemise down, slipping the fabric beneath her breasts, and gazed up at him, expectant. Waiting for his next move.

Before him were the most mouthwatering tits he had ever seen. A feral need rolled through him and practically shifted the ground beneath his feet.

"Arms above your head." The words slipped out sharper than he intended. For the first time ever, he was having a difficult time moderating himself.

By the flicker in her eyes, it was clear his request struck her as odd. After a moment's hesitation, she slid her arms up between his hands still pressing against the door, stretching her arms up above her head.

Those perfect little peaks of her breasts lifted up to him a fraction farther. His cock jerked hungrily.

Grasping her wrists in his hands, he pinned them against the door with intensity. She gave a little start.

Luc lowered his head, his mouth hovering over one taut nipple. "It's all right, Juliette. Just relax. I'll let go any time you say. *Instantly.* But for now, I'm going to suck these nipples the way they're aching to be sucked."

Luc flicked the tender little teat with his tongue. She jumped with a soft cry.

He smiled. "Ultrasensitive nipples. Perfect..." As perfect as the rest of her.

*****

Isabelle squirmed against the door again, unable to keep her hips still. Her nipples weren't normally this sensitive. There wasn't anything about her body that was acting normally.

There wasn't anything about this encounter that was remotely normal for her.

She was pinned against a door by a masked stranger—and she *should* demand he release her wrists, but she didn't want to.

He had her wild for him beyond all comprehension.

Pulling her wrists together in one hand, he cupped her breast with his other, his fingers capturing her taut nipple. And he gave it a pinch, holding it until it began to lightly throb, applying perfect pressure, sending spine-melting sensations pulsing from her breast. And echoing in her sex. She arched hard toward him, her senses swamped, sultry sounds emanating from her throat that sounded nothing like her own. He continued his sweet torture on the sensitive tip, plying it with tender twists and tugs. Just when she thought she couldn't take any more, he sucked her other nipple into the heat of his mouth.

Her head fell back against the door, her lips parted in a silent cry. The finesse of his fingers coupled with the silky pull of his mouth had her writhing and mewling and straining against her restrained wrists, lost to a level of lust she hadn't known she could reach.

"Please…" she panted. She was practically incoherent.

Suddenly, his mouth and fingers were gone. She snapped her eyes open, instantly distressed by his cessation. She found him smiling.

"Please *what*, Juliette? Please let me come? Do you want to come for me?"

How is that not obvious? "Yes!" He was teasing her. He knew exactly what she craved. She was seriously contemplating freeing her wrists so she could punch him. "Hurry!" She never made demands during sex. A courtesan always deferred to her lover's pace. But she was ready to jump out of her skin. She wasn't in the proper frame of mind to contemplate the error of her utterance.

By his grin, he didn't look as though he was interested in complying. "Not until I hear you tell me from those lovely lips what you desire."

Truly? Did he jest? He was as overwrought as she! Why was he wasting time with chatter? Isabelle dragged in a ragged breath, determined to move matters along. Good Lord, she'd recite the Greek alphabet if it meant he'd get on with it. "I want to…" Isabelle paused, realizing this was the first man who had ever asked her to voice her desires— in or out of the boudoir. How she wished she knew who this unique man was. "I want your hands on me. Your… Your mouth too. I want to come for you. Very much. *Right now.*"

His smile softened. He leaned in and, in her ear, said, "I like your answer. And I want to give you what you want. Very much. *Right now.*" She could barely focus on his words. Not when his free hand was at last back under her skirts. And moving toward the apex of her thighs.

More moisture pooled between her legs.

"Open your legs wider," he murmured in her ear, widening her stance with the nudge of his foot. His hand slipped past the slit of her drawers, and he plunged his fingers inside her. A whimper quivered up her throat, her hips thrusting forward—pure reflex—driving his fingers in deeper. She closed her eyes. She didn't know how many fingers he had buried in her. She didn't care. Not when she was consumed with an exquisite stretching sensation inside her sex. And the sense of fullness she craved. Of their own volition, her inner muscles clenched, giving him an unintentional squeeze.

A groaned rumbled from his chest. Softly, he swore. "That's right. Bear down just like that. Squeeze my fingers again." Her body responded to his command with another contraction of her vaginal walls, without her willing it. Or being able to stop it.

"That's it. You're going to milk my cock just like that once I've made you come, aren't you? You have the softest..." He withdrew his fingers with a slow, decadent drag. "The wettest..." He sank them back in deeply, "...snuggest little cunt. Perfect to drive a man wild." He stroked her sex again and again. The friction was glorious.

She needed more. Had to have more.

Or lose her mind.

"Most men pay little mind during sex to that sweet spot inside a woman's sheath," he said, his fingers still pumping in and out of her with masterful skill. Maddeningly holding her on the edge of her precipice. "But not I." She had no idea what spot inside her he was talking about. All she knew for certain was the fierce need for a release. "If you have not experienced it before, Juliette, it can be intense when rubbed just the right way. It takes a few moments to get used to the erotic sensation. Are you ready for it?"

She was beyond the point of no return. "Yes... Do it!" From his words, what resonated with her were precisely two—*intense* and *rubbed*. That was exactly what she needed. To have him rub her intensely. Faster. *NOW.*

Curling his buried fingers, he gave her short quick strokes over the "sweet spot." A sharp sensation shot through her core and vibrated up her spine. She cried out, jumping up onto the balls of her feet, the intensity taking her by surprise despite his warning. Milking a fresh gush of juices from her sex.

He tightened his hold on her wrists and struck up a steady rhythm. She tried to squirm away. The sensations were more powerful than she'd ever experienced.

"Easy, now... Don't fight it," he soothed in her ear, coaxing her along. "Ride through the sensations. Let it keep building..."

She was writhing and moaning, never so unbridled. She felt herself climbing higher and higher to a plateau she'd never been before with sensations that were so acute and engulfing.

"I love how you're soaking my hand. Your every reaction is so damned sensuous. I'm going to make you come right now. Then you're going to take my cock and let me fuck you until you come again."

More words!

She was on the brink. He was holding her on the edge, her orgasm blooming, then receding. Teetering back and forth. She nodded, no objection to his plan. Speaking was no longer within the scope of her ability.

He suddenly increased the pressure of his strokes, his fingers stroking harder and faster than before. She cried out as ecstasy exploded through her senses. Shuddering pleasure flooding her body. Her feminine walls contracting around his fingers in wild, uncontrollable clenches.

He yanked away his hand, tore her drawers from her body, and opened his breeches with the same impatient intensity, then lifted her. Without a moment's hesitation, he drove into her quivering core, pinning her to the door. Snatching the air from her lungs.

Her bare bottom in his hands, her spread knees at his hips, he buried his face in her shoulder and began hammering into her, tilting her hips just right, making constant contact with the bud between her legs with his every solid thrust. Her hands now free, she gripped his shoulders and simply held on. God, he was so big. And so deep. Plunging his whole length into her with one stunning thrust after another.

Then she felt it. The ripples of another hot wave of rapture mountaining by the moment. He rode her with blinding abandon as a second orgasm slammed into her. She surged hard against him, threw her arms around him, and screamed into his shoulder. He grunted but didn't relent on the pace or force of his thrusts, his shaft ramming her through the renewed contractions of her slick walls. She could hear his ragged breaths. She could feel his muscles were taut. Driving into her on and on until the delicious spasms inside her sex ebbed.

With a sharp groan, he suddenly reared back, jerking his cock from her core. Burying his face in her hair, he roared out his pleasure long and hard, his warm semen hitting her hip and thigh.

Isabelle tightened her arms around him. Feelings of euphoria hummed in her veins. She allowed herself to bask in the afterglow of one of the most powerful experiences she'd ever had.

She hadn't felt this good for a very long time.

That constant knot of worry that plagued her stomach was still notably missing. Her entire body was awash with a sense of peace she'd forgotten existed.

Gently, he lowered her feet to the floor. Her arms fell away from around his neck, and she slumped heavily against the door, not trusting the strength of her legs at the moment. Holding up her gown, he stepped back and met her gaze.

"Are you all right?" he asked with the touching concern of an attentive lover—as this man was.

"Yes." She was far better than all right.

By the smile that returned to his handsome face, she knew her answer pleased him. He stooped, picked up her torn drawers, then wiped her hip and thigh clean before cleaning himself and adjusting his clothing. Her gown fell back down into place.

His care in the aftermath only added to his appeal.

This aristo was forever surprising her.

She exerted the effort required to readjust her own clothing and closed her bodice.

He walked over to the hearth. "I'm sorry about this," he said, indicating the balled-up drawers in his hand, and then tossed it directly into the flickering fire. "I'll buy you new *caleçons*."

She felt so light, she could float off the floor. And she was smiling. A rare genuine big brilliant smile. "No matter." The loss of a single pair of drawers was a small price to pay for the soul-satisfying encounter she'd just had with him.

Pushing off the wall, she forced her legs to move forward and stopped before him. "Where did you learn that?" she couldn't help but ask. From her experience, his sexual skills were not common.

His beautiful smile grew ever so slightly. "Learn *what?*"

She laughed. "You're teasing, of course. Or perhaps you're shamelessly looking for a compliment on your carnal skills?"

"Perhaps."

She laughed again, unable to muster any real dismay at his cheekiness. "It would seem you can add humility to your repertoire," she teased.

It was his turn to laugh. "It would suffice to hear from your beautiful lips—lips that tragically I don't get to kiss—that you were well pleased."

"My lord, were I any more pleased, my heart might have stopped."

He leaned in and placed a soft kiss just below her ear, his mask against hers. "Mine too." Her stomach fluttered. He pulled back and gazed into her eyes. She could see his eyes better now that they were near the light of the fire—they were light in color. But still not well enough to detect their true hue. "Believe it or not," he added, "I was once a roué."

She shook her head with a grin. "Forgive me for pointing out the obvious, but you've just participated in a clandestine encounter with a courtesan. One might not believe your claim at self-reform."

He chuckled quietly. "Despite how it appears." He stroked the back of his fingers down her cheek. A long silky caress that reverberated down to her toes. "I have changed. I used to be very different. With a quick temper."

She raised her brows. "Should I be afraid?" That comment unsettled her.

"No. *Never.* My altercations have been with men of my peers. I'd never harm a woman. And the last woman on this side of the stars I'd ever harm is one who is as intoxicating as you."

Once again, he'd complimented her. If only he didn't look so sincere and wasn't so impossibly charming when he said it. And foolishly, like some sort of inexperienced adolescent in the bloom of her first love, her insides danced. *Dear Lord, you ought to be far more urbane about all this by now.* Especially compliments uttered by a self-admitted libertine.

"This night was a disaster. That is, until I met you. You, Juliette Carre, have made this evening exceptional. You have no idea how out of the ordinary this night has been for me."

Out of the ordinary for *him*? If only he knew how out of the ordinary this night had been for *her*.

"This hasn't been a typical evening for me either, my lord. I don't engage in amorous encounters masked. And I usually know the name and identity of my lover." Enough was enough. It had to be midnight. At least close to it. She was going to learn who her disarming aristo—master of the carnal arts—was right now.

She could hardly wait any longer.

"I think the time to be rid of these masks is long overdue." Yanking off her demi-mask, she then tossed it carelessly to the floor. She still couldn't stop smiling at him. "Your turn."

The smile he'd been sporting suddenly faded as he stared back at her. For a moment, hers faded too, and she didn't know what to make of his sudden sobering. At last, he spoke. "*Jésus,* I knew you were beautiful, but I never imagined you were this breathtaking."

Her smile brightened anew. "I'm pleased you approve, Lord Seductive."

His brows shot up above his mask. "Did you call me *Lord Seductive?*"

"Since I don't know your name, I don't know what else to call you—and it's fitting."

He laughed again. And she adored the sound of it. "Juliette, you are the one who has seduced me. And you've had me at a full cockstand from the moment I set eyes on you. Not to mention that my arousal for you has sorely tested the stitching on my breeches."

She crossed her arms and tried to affect a stern expression, but amusement over his banter was making her lips twitch.

"My Lord Seductive, you should be more concerned about the stitching of that demi-mask, for in moments, I am going to tear it off you—if you do not remove it yourself."

That only inspired a very large grin from him. He snaked an arm around her, pulled her to him, her breasts coming in quick contact with his muscled chest. Dipping his head, he brought his mouth to her ear. "Tearing things off me? Hmm… I've never had a woman do that. But since your *caleçons* are presently burning in the fireplace, in this instance, that sounds only fair. It also sounds far too appealing to pass up," he murmured, then lightly bit her earlobe. Making her shiver.

Straightening, and still with his handsome grin, he released her and placed his hands on his hips. "Go on. Remove my mask."

She couldn't believe he'd quickened her pulse with a mere love bite.

Oh, she was definitely removing this aristo's mask straightaway. Reaching up, she pulled it off in one quick movement.

Isabelle froze.

So did her blood.

She stared up at him, suddenly feeling as though someone had delivered a blow to her belly. She knew just who was standing before her. Had memorized the very distinct shade of those incredibly captivating light green eyes long ago. She didn't need to hear the next words from his mouth.

In fact, she barely heard him over the sudden ringing in her ears when he said, "My name is Luc de Moutier, Marquis de Fontenay."

A single word thundered inside her head over and over again. *No. No. No. No. NO-O-O!* But a strangled squeak was all that shot up her throat and out her mouth. She needed space. Air. Time to think. Spinning around, she made to flee. But she stepped on the hem of her gown. And landed on the floor with a hard thud, her palms and knees slamming against the wood.

She winced. His demi-mask, still in her hand, snapping in two with her fall.

"*Dieu,* Juliette, are you all right?"

She knew he was about to help her up off the floor of the library. Isabelle shot to her feet and bolted out the first door she saw before he could touch her.

Cold water splashed against her heated face and chest. She gasped, realizing she was standing in the courtyard.

In a downpour!

Oh God! Could this evening be any more disastrous? Her clothes and hair were already drenched. Her palms and knees hurt.

And she'd made a complete fool of herself—from her unceremonious fall to the floor, to her dash from the room. Straight into a rainstorm.

Oh yes, and let's not forget the best part of all, Isabelle: You just had unbridled sex with your sister's brother-in-law!

And charged him a fee!

Of course he reminded you of Luc de Moutier. He IS Luc de Moutier. You idiot!

She was desperate to get away from him. Her mind awhirl. Her heart in her throat.

Luc de Moutier... The Luc de Moutier!

Scanning about, she saw no way to leave except back through the same door she'd just exited. Or the doors on the other side of the courtyard that led to the ballroom—and every guest in attendance at the masque.

She was trapped. Soaking wet.

Utterly mortified on so many levels.

"Umm... Juliette?" His voice came from the doorway. She couldn't bring herself to look at him, wishing she would magically vanish into thin air. "Are you aware you are standing in the rain, *chère?*"

Mentally, she cringed. Some of her curls that had been so precisely arranged had already flopped onto her forehead.

"Yes, of course I am," she said, managing to sound blasé about the humiliating situation. Just then, a soggy plume drooped down from the top of her head and stuck to her nose. With as much elegance as she could muster, she peeled it away. Her earlier decision to add the extra plumes in her coiffure to match her demi-mask had proven to be a bad idea.

"And the reason for that is…?" he prompted.

"I adore the rain." *Brilliant answer. Couldn't you think of anything more half-witted to say?* She must look like a drowned rat, standing in an empty courtyard, her back against the stone wall of the Comtesse de Grand-ville's home as rain poured down on her. Her sodden curls and plumes a soggy mess.

How was she going to get out of this predicament?

And without everyone in attendance this night seeing her in this condition?

She'd be a laughingstock. Nicole would be a laughingstock by association. The gossipmongers' tongues would wag *forever* about it.

"I'll admit I've had various reactions from women upon seeing my face, *chère*, but this is…well, rather a first." She couldn't tell if there was amusement in his tone. "Is this because of who I am?"

YES! She swallowed hard. A lump had formed in her throat. And, much to her horror, she felt tears sting her eyes.

Don't cry!

Quickly, she blinked them back. This wasn't just any man she'd sold herself to. This man had always been significant to her—from the first moment she'd laid eyes on him at her father's theater when she was fifteen and he seventeen. He was the man of all her girlhood dreams. With all her many losses, thoughts of him had always been a light in the darkness. Of all the dreams she'd had of him, of meeting him for the first time, to what it would be like to be his and share physical intimacies with him—*this* was not what she'd imagined.

Not a *paid* encounter.

Never as a courtesan.

And most certainly never, ever as a mother forced to sell her body so that she and her son could survive.

"Juliette, come in out of the rain. You'll catch your death."

Relying on her acting skills, she smiled one of her far-too-common, inauthentic smiles and gazed out at the courtyard, still avoiding eye contact. "Nonsense. It's refreshing. And good for you."

Good Lord. *Refreshing and good for you?*

What were the chances that the ground would give way and swallow her up?

"I believe I'll stay out here awhile. Please feel free to rejoin the masque." *Go away!*

"You're not fooling me for a moment, you know," he said. "I understand exactly why you're behaving this way." His statement was uttered with such conviction, it made her snap her head in his direction. One of her plumes smacked her in the cheek and stuck to it.

"Oh?" She peeled it off her face. It was impossible for him to know the reason behind her reaction, no matter how poorly she was commanding the situation.

"By the way you're behaving, it's obvious you've heard of me. You've been made privy to the ugly gossip about what happened to my family, and you are leery to be in my company now that you know I'm a Moutier. But I can assure you, I am no traitor to the Crown. Never have been. And His Majesty is in agreement with that now. He has fully pardoned the House of Moutier and reverted title, funds, and lands. I spent years in the King's navy in loyal service to the Crown before I was dishonorably dismissed and falsely arrested. And after my release from prison, God knows I could have turned against the King. But instead, I continued to serve His Majesty in the only capacity I could—as a privateer for the realm. I may not have many friends here tonight. In fact, I believe the sum total is our hostess, her brother, and hopefully *you*—but there will be no royal repercussion in associating with me. I can guarantee it. And as to the rest of society—they will align themselves with the King's renewed perspective of my family soon enough."

A swell of compassion tightened in her chest. His words resonated with her. Luc had been through significant hardship too. Yet he couldn't be more mistaken in his assessment of her flight from him.

Before she could attempt to formulate a response, she heard the library door open and close. Then a female voice called out her name.

"Juliette?" Isabelle's stomach dropped. She knew Nicole's voice when she heard it. "Are you in here?"

Briefly, she closed her eyes. Her humiliation this night knew no limits. Having her refined friend see her in this sorry state only added to her mortification.

She responded reluctantly. "Yes."

Rapid footsteps drew closer to the doorway Luc filled with his muscled form.

"Good evening, my lord," she heard Nicole say from within the library.

Well, at least Nicole had managed to draw Luc's attention to the woman addressing him.

And away from the fool standing in the rain.

He was frowning now, clearly dismayed by the sudden intrusion. Nonetheless, he returned with a polite "Good evening."

Nicole's head then peeked out from the doorway's wooden frame. "Ah, there you are, darling." Ludicrously, she was speaking to her as though Isabelle were in the garden on a sunny summer's day. Completely ignoring the shambles her appearance was in.

How in the world had Nicole entered the library with the door locked? Flashes of her intense encounter with Luc flitted through her mind and the answer became clear. They must have somehow unlocked it during their vigorous passion play.

Over her shoulder, Nicole said, "Please forgive me, my lord, but I must speak to my dear friend." Turning to Isabelle, she continued. "Darling, I have our cloaks." Isabelle's gaze dropped to the material draped over Nicole's arm. Her spirits suddenly soared, as a way out with no one seeing the state she was in had just appeared. Thanks to Nicole. "Would you be so kind as to escort me back home? I have the most unbearable headache."

She wanted to throw her arms around Nicole and kiss her. She was willing to wager that Nicole had no such ailment plaguing her. Somehow, she'd realized Isabelle was in a terrible bind—and was saving her from her imbecilic predicament. Yet again, Nicole had her gratitude.

"Yes, of course," she readily agreed. Nicole and Luc stepped back to allow her to reenter the library. She could feel the heat of his gaze as she stopped just past the threshold and reached to take her cloak from Nicole's extended hand.

"Allow me, ladies." Luc took both cloaks and aided Nicole first. "Madame, I'm sorry you're not feeling well. I pray your headache dissipates soon."

Nicole gave him a nod and a murmur of thanks.

Then he came up behind Isabelle. She tensed. Heat emanated from his strong, sculpted form right through her soggy gown. She braced for his potent touch. He slipped the cloak onto her shoulders. His warm fingers brushed against her cool wet skin. A hot pulse vibrated through her.

"Thank you for a most wonderful evening, Juliette," he said softly near her ear. His sensuous male voice was as wickedly sultry as before.

Leave! Leave! Leave! Before anything else goes awry. She managed the words "thank you" and "good evening," threw on her hood, and walked briskly to the door of the library, despite her gown, weighted with water, feeling as heavy as lead.

She was out the door with Nicole in an instant and making a hastened trip across the vestibule. Ignoring the pull back to the library and his magical touch.

*****

Luc stared at the closed door of the library.

Glancing down near his feet, he saw his broken mask lying beside a small puddle of rainwater that had dripped off Juliette's dress.

The door suddenly burst open, giving him a start. To his surprise, Juliette was standing there, her hand on the latch.

"There is no fee!" she blurted, then disappeared as quickly as she'd appeared.

Leaving him staring at the closed door once more.

Luc placed his hands on his hips and shook his head, a smile tugging at the corners of his mouth. Of all his sexual encounters, this was inarguably—*unique.* He should feel slighted by the way she'd bolted from the room, but her antics were so unexpected and unconventional, he couldn't muster up feelings of insult. She'd left him even more intrigued and drawn to her than before. Once again, he hadn't anticipated her to be like this. Nor could he have anticipated having such an intense sexual encounter with her without *any* binding involved. *Merde,* his knees were still weak from the sheer force of his orgasm.

And *Dieu.* The look of her with her wet gown plastered to her body, those delicious nipples of hers protruding ever so delectably against the soaked fabric, wasn't an image he was going to be able to get out of his mind anytime soon.

And yet, of all the unusual things that had transpired between them tonight, nothing—*absolutely nothing*—staggered him more than the fact that she'd put her arms around him.

And he hadn't even noticed until the aftermath.

He'd been so completely engulfed by pleasure—the most glorious draining rush purging from his prick at his release—that he hadn't felt any of the usual suffocating urgency to retreat from the embrace.

Another unbelievable first...

Somehow, Juliette had even managed to vanquish the ghost of Isabelle Laurent for a time. He'd forgotten all about her. Juliette had had his undivided attention and so completely undone, he doubted he'd have noticed if the room burst into flames.

Maybe, just maybe, Isabelle Laurent was gone for good.

There were many things he intended to focus on in order to rebuild his life that had nothing to do with the beautiful courtesan who had just left the room. But he liked her. Very much. He liked many things about her, things that went beyond the physical, including her adorable quirkiness.

And, fuck, he *really* wanted to kiss her. He really wanted to introduce her to the sexual practice he favored. Moreover, he wanted to learn where this incredible woman came from.

And all the many secrets he sensed were behind those lovely dark eyes.

CHAPTER FIVE

Isabelle watched the note in the hearth burn. Slowly, it blackened and curled within the lambent flames. Images of a much larger fire flashed through her mind. Tall lapping flames climbing the walls around her. Scorching across the ceiling. The suffocating air, thick and smoky.

Burning her throat.

Isabelle turned away, battling the images back. She'd relived that inferno too many times in her worst dreams.

This was the second such note she'd received in the last week.

Nothing more than some hateful words sent to her anonymously.

Clearly, the author of the loathsome letters didn't care for her. Nicole had warned her to expect such letters from time to time. The more popular a courtesan became, the more enemies she'd have. Yet that held true for everyone who scaled society in any way. Not just women of her trade. Though she knew she should be nonchalant about such correspondence, she couldn't help feel the sting from its biting words.

Rapid footsteps suddenly thundering down the corridor outside her private apartments in Nicole's *hôtel* grabbed Isabelle's attention. She turned to the large double doors of her antechamber. The instant she heard a resounding bark, she knew exactly who was barreling toward her rooms.

The doors flung open. And slammed against the wall.

Her son raced toward her, waving a parchment, flanked by his oversized, inseparable companion in the form of a white, three-year-old Great Pyrenees dog named Montague.

"*Maman!*" Gabriel skidded to a stop before her and flung his arms around her waist. "Good day!"

She laughed and returned his embrace with equal enthusiasm. "Good day, my darling." He was the greatest joy in her life.

Montague was never one to be ignored, if you could ever ignore a dog practically the size of a small donkey. He pushed his big body in between them, nudging them apart so he could be the center of attention. With a barked salutation to her, he resumed his canine smile. His tail wagging vigorously.

"Good day to you too, Montague." She scratched his favorite spot, just above the base of his tail, and he curled his body to give her busy fingers approving kisses.

"*Maman*, I finished my lessons, and Monsieur Bernard allowed me time to sketch, just like a real artist!" Gabriel waved his parchment again, his excitement atwinkle in his dark eyes. God, how she loved that sweet face. From his dark hair down to his small feet, he was the most precious thing in her world. "Look at it, *Maman*! Look!" He was still waving it back and forth, making that very task quite impossible.

She laughed again and gently grasped his wrist, stilling it. "One moment, darling. Let me see your work."

"Do you like it? That's you." He pointed to the figure with the large gown. "And this is Montague."

Isabelle gazed at the sketch Gabriel had done and couldn't help but return his contagious smile. "I love it. It's wonderful!" She pulled him to her and pressed a kiss to the crown of his head.

He made a face.

"Too old for a kiss from your mother, are you?" she gently teased him. At eight, he was trying very hard to be older than his years. Yet, he still allowed her to cuddle him at night before going to sleep—as she regaled him and Montague with stories of faraway kingdoms, honorable knights, brave princes, and magical horses—the very same stories she and Sabine had invented together in their childhood—as Gabriel and Montague drifted into slumber on Gabriel's bed.

She'd promised Gabriel *two* stories tonight to make up for the one missed last eve due to the masque.

If only she'd made some advancement on the story she was writing—the next volume of her popular *Princesses' Adventures*. She had to turn it in for publication soon if she was to build on the excitement and momentum with the series.

The income her anonymous stories generated was something she couldn't simply forgo.

But she hadn't slept much last night. And her concentration today was nonexistent. Her mind was a constant whirl all morning, fluctuating between heated memories of the encounter she'd had with the last man on earth she should have given herself to, and the thought that she might have actually found a link back to her sister.

There was a knock at the open door of her antechamber.

Nicole stood at the threshold, already smiling at Gabriel, looking as elegant as always, dressed in her deep green gown.

"Grand-mère!" he exclaimed and raced toward her, Montague on his heels, both boy and dog stopping abruptly in unison. Montague wagged his powerful white tail unceasingly. Her little boy gave Nicole a proper bow, making Isabelle so proud, before the woman who had not only opened her home but her heart to them. Even insisting that Gabriel call her *grandmother.*

It gave Isabelle such delight to see the happiness her young son and Montague brought Nicole. They both drew smiles and laughter from her constantly.

"I made a sketch, *Grand-mère!* It's of *Maman* and Montague. I shall draw you in next."

"That's marvelous. I cannot wait to see it, Gabriel. Why don't you take Montague back to your room and finish your sketch, then show it to me?"

As soon as Gabriel and Montague raced off happily, Nicole didn't waste a moment. She closed the doors, then took Isabelle's hand and pulled her down onto the settee near the hearth. "I simply must apologize to you again, my dear. I assured you that Luc de Moutier was not in attendance last night. Yet that wasn't at all the case. I want you to know I rushed to you the moment I learned from the Duc d'Allain that Luc had chosen the Comtesse de Grandville's masque to reenter society. I feel terrible about misleading you."

Isabelle shook her head. "No, Nicole. Please, don't fret. You owe me no apology at all. I should have known it was him. It was my stupidity."

"What happened last night? Why were you in the rain?"

Isabelle cringed at the mention of her antics. She'd made a colossal fool of herself in front of Luc. And after all Nicole had taught her, there wasn't anything sophisticated about her behavior last night.

Thankfully, Nicole had not assailed her with questions during the short but very wet carriage ride back to her *hôtel*. In the light of day, in reflecting on her evening with Luc, it was even more mortifying.

And exquisite.

"It was a carnal encounter, though not exactly a typical one." *That is an understatement.* Erotic memories of last night flooded her thoughts. Her blood warmed instantly. "I had sex with the very man I once harbored the greatest *tendre* any young girl's heart could possibly possess—and who now happens to be my sister's brother-in-law. Oh, but that's not the extent of it. Before I knew who he was, I requested a sum in exchange for the encounter. A substantial one."

Nicole's brow furrowed. "Really? How much did you request?"

She told her the amount and watched the seasoned courtesan's eyes widen. "And he *agreed* to that much? For a single tumble?"

"It was far more than a mere tumble. It was...rather, he is..." The feel of his hands and mouth on her body, the shattering finesse of his fingers inside her were forever branded into her mind. Imprinted on her form. And then there were those stunning sensations of every plunge and drag of his hard length. The man believed in the deepest penetration possible. No short sharp thrusts with this man. He gave long, luscious strokes with his sex—tantalizing every nerve ending in her sheath down to the farthest depths of her core. She'd never been filled so completely.

She had never reached such a heightened level of pleasure. For the first time ever, she hadn't had to put on a performance at all.

"That good?" Nicole asked.

"No." Isabelle shook her head. "Luc de Moutier is far better than good. He is *exceptional.*"

Nicole smiled. "Why, that's excellent! All the rumors about him are true, then. Though I have heard he isn't the sort of lover for a novice at bed sport. He has very distinct sexual tastes. You've had a limited number of lovers. Did you not mind it when he bound you?"

She tried not to blush at the blunt question. "He didn't. Though he did ask to. But I refused him." Yet he'd still restrained her wrists for a portion of the time. Again, she couldn't shake the feeling there was more to this practice of his than merely a penchant.

Nicole looked at her as though she'd suddenly grown a horn in the middle of her forehead. Shock was etched on her face. "Let me understand this... He agreed to a hefty sum to have you *once,* and though he firmly practices bondage during *all* his sexual encounters—so much so that he's walked away from any woman who refuses to participate in it—he made an exception for you?"

"Well...yes... I suppose..." To an extent, though she wasn't about to relay every intimate detail.

Nicole let out a short laugh. "My dear, whatever you have done, you have beguiled this man and he is not one to be beguiled easily. I'm positively delighted for you. And I'm very pleased you've experienced your first gifted lover."

"Nicole, he is a part of my sister's new family—and by extension, part of mine."

"*And?* What is the problem?"

"The problem is this wasn't just a passionate interlude between a man and a woman—though that alone is bad enough given his connection to Sabine. What happened between us amounted to nothing more than a mere transaction. I sold him something he wished to purchase."

"Nonsense. I heard you tell him before we left there was no fee—though I cannot believe you forfeited that sum of money. You canceled it, nonetheless. If funds aren't exchanged, then it isn't a transaction."

"That was something I blurted out to further make a fool of myself. Because, clearly, after he revealed who he was, my running straight into a rainstorm, then standing there in it wasn't imbecilic enough for me last eve."

Nicole smiled and placed a hand over Isabelle's hand. "Isabelle, I wouldn't waste another thought on that. You have made yourself interesting. And that's never a bad thing when dealing with men."

Isabelle squeezed Nicole's hand. "Nicole, I don't wish to be interesting to him. Nor would I have ever offered to sell myself to this man—of all men—had I known his identity. I just want to reach my sister." The instant the words were out of her mouth, her stomach and heart clenched with opposing emotions. Longing and trepidation assailed her equally. Understandably, Sabine would want—*insist*—on knowing every detail that had transpired in Isabelle's life over the last nine years since they'd seen each other.

So many excruciating details to divulge—including her present vocation—that Isabelle had hoped her sister would be spared.

She'd written Sabine countless letters over the years, even though she couldn't send any of them and risk everyone's safety. And upon returning to Paris and learning they were at last safe from Leon de Vittry, Isabelle had written dozens more, when there was no address to send them to. Letters that were ultimately crumpled up and burned. Sabine had taken their three cousins and what remained of their father's acting troupe—in essence, all that Isabelle considered family—and now resided somewhere in the West Indies, whose waters were infested with pirates.

Moreover, not a single letter adequately expressed how vastly she missed her. Or how deeply she regretted her youthful, rash decision to leave her home and family behind to go work for Charles de Moutier—her head full of ridiculous girlish romantic dreams about Luc.

Little did she know that leaving home would set into motion a series of devastating events for her.

Gabriel was the only good thing to come out of her mountain of mistakes.

He wasn't a mistake. He was perfect.

"He's the only one who knows where Sabine is and has any potential access to her. Since no one had seen Luc de Moutier for the longest time, I'd despaired of ever seeing my sister again," she continued. "Now that he has reappeared, he could perhaps help me reach her."

If she knew she could trust him.

She had a thousand questions for Luc about her sister. How she was? Did she have children? Was she happy? Did she think of her anymore? Or did she limit her thoughts of her, just as Isabelle did, so she wouldn't miss her so much? So her heart wouldn't ache so unbearably.

"I don't understand," Nicole said "How is it that he didn't recognize you? Didn't you say that after your father lost his theater and your family was forced to move from Paris to the country with your cousins, you eventually left the farm to work as a servant for Luc's father at one of his châteaus?"

"Yes, before Gabriel was born. That is true. For a time, I did work at Château Serein, one of the Moutier grand estates." She could still see Sabine's stricken face when she'd told her she was leaving, having convinced their father to let her go. A foolish, fateful day when anger and fear got the better of her—anger over their life-altering losses of lands, funds, and future, and fear of the accumulating bleakness. She regretted the pain she'd caused every day that her family thought she was dead. And loathed herself for it. Worst still, she was utterly heartbroken that her father had passed away in her absence never knowing that his daughter was still alive. "It was there at the Moutier château that the fire occurred, the fire Leon started in his attempt to murder and silence me for his misdeeds."

That was the day Isabelle Laurent died—to all who knew her.

That was also the day she became Gabriel's mother.

"Luc didn't recognize me because he never visited his father or that château while I was there." She'd hoped each day that Luc would arrive, and actually notice her, when she'd been so invisible to him at the theater, no matter how long she'd adoringly stared at him. So young and foolish, she saw it as the only way to meet and marry the handsome lord of her dreams.

Given how horrible his father was, she wasn't surprised he'd never darkened the doorstep of Château Serein. The servants often gossiped about the fact that Charles de Moutier's youngest son didn't much care for his father. And the feeling was more than mutual.

"Since he doesn't know you, will you introduce yourself as Isabelle Laurent?" Nicole asked.

"I cannot blurt out that information. I don't know that I can trust him to help me reach Sabine." She was nothing if not overly cautious now. "What if he behaves as Roch did and uses it against me? I would be at his mercy. I have Gabriel's future to think about. I risk his wellbeing. Not just mine. And last night, I complicated matters. If I tell him the truth now, he'll know that I am…"

"A woman doing what she must and in control of her own future," Nicole supplied. "A woman who is among the few our society allows to embrace her sexuality as freely as any man. I see no shame in what we do. But I understand how you feel. And I agree that you should proceed with caution. I also understand this wasn't the future you envisioned as a girl. But there are worse ways for a woman to survive than to be given funds, jewelry, and pleasure."

"Yes, I know. Please forgive me. I meant no disrespect," she apologized. "My lack of sleep and last night's events are—"

Nicole instantly hugged her. "Hush now. No apologies are needed from you either. You and I are different women. While I have always enjoyed having a variety of special men in my life, I believe you'd prefer to have only one special man in yours."

Perhaps once. A long time ago, that was true. Not anymore. She'd seen the ugliness in men, and she'd made it a habit not to trust any man who wielded more power than her.

They got her body—at a price. She sold them passion. Nothing more. It was the reason she'd chosen to be a courtesan and not a man's mistress. She was beholden to no one. And chose whom she obliged in the boudoir, when, and how often.

A knock at the door halted all conversation. Joseph, the tall, slender majordomo, stood on the threshold of her antechamber after Isabelle bid him come in.

"My ladies." He gave a bow. "Forgive the intrusion, but a gentleman is here, and he is quite insistent on seeing you, Madame Carre."

Isabelle's brows rose. "Me?"

"Yes, madame," Joseph confirmed. "Though I know it's early for a social call, he won't be dissuaded from leaving. He's still downstairs and has a message he wants me to relay."

"Oh? What is the message?" It was known that neither she nor Nicole entertained any men at Nicole's *hôtel*. Who could the man be?

"He says to tell you it is raining. And since he's heard it's refreshing and good for you, he wishes to know if you'd like to join him."

Oh God.

CHAPTER SIX

Isabelle made her way across the vestibule, her heart pounding faster than the tempo of her steps on the marble floor.

She was sending Luc on his way. Promptly. This was her home. Her *son's* home. Regardless of her desire to reunite with her sister, this was no place to entertain conversations with a man. Especially one she'd coupled with this past night.

You aren't ready for this. You need more time.

More time to determine how best to assess whether she could trust him with her great secret and elicit his help.

More time to shore up her defenses.

And more time to learn how to quash the quickening in her belly caused by the mere knowledge that Luc de Moutier was here.

And he wanted to see her.

Stopping before the closed door of Nicole's salon, Isabelle took in a fortifying breath and let it out slowly. But it did nothing to quell the physical frenzy that spiked the moment she placed her hand on the door latch.

He was so very near.

Calm down… You're acting foolishly.

She wasn't the same young girl she'd once been. She was a grown woman. With a child. He was her first priority. She could—*would*—curb these physical urges where Luc was concerned. What happened last night wasn't going to be repeated.

Isabelle steeled herself, as she'd done many times when cool composure was needed, turned the latch, and walked in.

The sight before her stopped her dead in her tracks. His head was down, and he was idly thumbing through a book of poetry. His dark blond hair was wet from the rain. And so too was his doublet—defining those broad shoulders and strong arms in the most spellbinding way. Standing there in the middle of Nicole's salon in the light of day—wearing black breeches, a white shirt, and dark gray doublet—was undoubtedly the most exquisite male on this side of the sun. Unable to help herself, her gaze drifted to his sculpted chest, his hard abdomen, and his long, muscled thighs, chiseled to perfection due to his years at sea.

He was by far more muscular than the average aristo. Signs of the beautiful boy he'd once been were gone.

Before her was a man, beyond handsome, beyond seductive, with a tall, powerful body. A man who exuded an alluring confidence. With an edge of danger.

And far more devastating to behold than ever before.

She waited for the bolt of heat that shot through her veins to dissipate.

This wasn't going to be easy. It had been less than twenty-four hours since she'd been intimate with him. That was far too soon. Clearly, she was still feeling the aftereffects of Luc de Moutier.

Pressing forward, she forced out, "My lord?" Opting for a formal greeting. It would give her some much-needed distance.

Turning his attention away from the book in his hands, he looked up at her. And then he smiled. The sort of smile that reached his eyes.

Oh, those eyes…

It was impossible to count how many times she'd dreamed of them.

She'd never met anyone who had green eyes like his, their color so light, they were mesmerizing. They'd always had her transfixed and a little breathless.

Now was no exception.

He dropped the book on a nearby chair, then sauntered over. If she had any good sense, she'd stop him from getting any closer. But she couldn't drag the words up her throat. Her body already humming with awareness at his approach.

Stopping before her, he took her hand and, with a bow, brushed his warm lips ever so lightly over her knuckle before he pressed a kiss to it. Her sex responded with a warm gush.

"Good day, Juliette," he said, straightening to his full height with a gorgeous, lopsided smile. Still holding her hand, he grazed his thumb over the spot he'd just kissed. Tiny tingles sped up her arm and shot to the tips of her breasts.

How did he do it? How did he wreak such havoc on her—when no one else ever had—with the most innocuous gestures and comments?

Dismiss him, quickly.

She'd have to make it clear he wasn't to come to her home again. He'd have to abide by the same rules as every other man—regardless. Except this man was far more dangerous than other men. This man exuded the promise of sinful pleasure in intoxicating doses.

And she had Gabriel here.

Desperate to reassert some control, she schooled her features. "My lord, I'm going to have to ask you to—"

"It's raining. I can't get the image of you wet from the rain out of my head. I know how much you love it when it showers. Would you like to take a walk with me in the summer rain?"

That was the last thing she should do.

"Thank you, but no."

A slow grin formed on his handsome face. "Then I'll have to think of other ways to make you wet." Her heart lost a beat. He leaned in, and, with his mouth close to her ear, he murmured, "You look so very fine this morning. And you smell so good." He nuzzled her neck. "I want to fuck you with nothing on except satin scarves around your ankles and wrists."

Her feminine core gave a hungry clench. Every fiber in her body rioted against her resistance.

Oh, she was definitely in over her head with this man. Nicole was right when she said Luc de Moutier was a lot to handle—especially for a woman still a relative novice at bed sport. He was far too potent for her senses.

A formidable carnal force wrapped up in the most irresistible masculine packaging. Besieging her senses.

Before she could summon her voice, from the vestibule behind her, she heard, "*Maman!*" Isabelle started, jumped back away from Luc. *Oh God, no...*

Her young son raced to her and gave her one of his sweet embraces, his arms wrapped tightly around her skirts. His chin resting against her side, Gabriel's head was tilted back as he gazed at her with his usual love and adoration that was so very mutual. She put her arms protectively around him and shot Luc a quick glance. If he dared say anything she deemed inappropriate or hurtful to Gabriel, she'd have him tossed out on his highborn derrière. Nicole purposely employed a number of large male servants who could easily remove any unwanted gentleman.

But Luc didn't say a word. In fact, he couldn't have looked more stunned over the presence of the young boy in her embrace.

"I finished my sketch, *Maman*." Gabriel's smile was enormous.

She couldn't help but smile back and brushed a lock of his dark hair from his forehead. "That's very good. Now I need you to return to your rooms…"

Gabriel turned his head and gave a gasp as he noticed Luc for the first time since running into the salon—so unaccustomed to visitors. Quickly, he pulled away and gave him a bow. "Monsieur, good day," he said to Luc, looking very proud of himself for his well-executed greeting—just as he'd been taught.

Isabelle studied Luc, her maternal instincts to protect filling every fiber of her being, still unsure of how Luc would react to the boy beaming at him. Where on earth was Annette, Gabriel's nurse, when she needed her?

Luc's lips twitched in amusement, and he returned the bow. "Good day. You may call me Luc."

That pleased her little mite, evident by the way he continued to beam. "You may call me Gabriel," he said before a frown furrowed his brow. "Your hair is wet."

"It is. It's raining."

"You should dry your hair so you won't get sick." Gabriel stepped toward Luc and took his hand. "Come sit by the fire." He led him toward the hearth.

Isabelle's stomach plummeted.

"Gabriel, the marquis was just leaving. I'm afraid he can't stay." She looked pointedly at Luc. A half smile still on his face, Luc simply allowed Gabriel to escort him to the crackling fire.

"He can't leave, *Maman*. It's raining," her son reasoned calmly. "You wouldn't want him to become ill, would you?" She knew Gabriel had an ulterior motive for keeping Luc here. Truth be told, he craved male companionship. Daily. He was always seeking out the cook or the majordomo Joseph, neither of which satisfied Gabriel's need for male camaraderie. Though that didn't stop him from talking to them and his private schoolmaster, Monsieur Bernard, incessantly.

"Yes, Gabriel is correct. It is definitely raining," Luc said, concurring with his young ally. "And you wouldn't want me to become ill now, would you?" Luc settled himself down in the tall blue velvet-and-wood chair near the hearth, clearly intent on staying. Mischief openly gleamed in his eyes.

His motives weren't as innocent.

Gabriel stood near the chair Luc occupied, still holding his hand.

A lump formed in her throat. She had to get Gabriel out of the salon. And Luc out the door so she could formulate some semblance of a plan to sort all this out. She couldn't just simply blurt out, *"Oh, by the way, didn't I tell you? I'm Isabelle Laurent, your sister-in-law's dead twin. I'm actually alive and selling my body to men for money—just as I did with you last eve. Will you take me to my sister?"*

She didn't know how Luc would react. There was no reason to trust him at this point. It was one thing to give a man your body. Quite another to give him leverage over your life—and that of your child's life.

"You're a marquis, then?" Gabriel asked Luc.

"I am."

"Is it difficult to be a marquis?" was her son's adorable question.

"Some days and nights are better than others," Luc said, giving her a discreet wink and a smile. She didn't miss his double entendre.

Gabriel turned to her. *"Maman,* do you think Montague will like Luc?"

Her stomach lurched. *Montague.* Luc had her so out of sorts, she'd completely forgotten about him. Quickly scanning the room for her unruly dog, she realized that he was nowhere in sight. He had to be upstairs, asleep in his favorite spot—on Gabriel's bed.

"Gabriel, please tell me you closed the door to your rooms when you left." She held her breath, praying Gabriel would say yes. She had enough to deal with without Montague's antics and his general mistrust of strangers in the house.

"Yes, *Maman.* I did."

Isabelle let out a sigh of relief.

"But Montague isn't in my rooms. He's outside in the courtyard."

"Oh, Gabriel, go fetch him, darling. He's in the rain."

"No, *Maman*. I left the door open so he can enter whenever he wishes."

*****

Who the hell is Montague?

It was ludicrous that Luc was in the least bit bothered by the notion of another man being in attendance. But he was. Since when had he ever cared if a woman he bedded had other men? She was certainly free to do as she wished.

Yet, he wanted the aristo gone. Now. Whoever he was.

And apparently, everyone in the world was suddenly standing in the rain. Including him.

He'd ventured out into the downpour just to see this woman again. Just to learn more about the female who'd kept him up most of the night with the memory of their encounter. From her wet, snug sex clenching around his cock, to the sultry sounds she'd made, to the stunning release he'd had with her. Yet, as he glanced at the young boy still holding his hand, Luc now had even more questions about her than before.

She was forever surprising him.

A loud sound akin to a bark suddenly resounded in the vestibule. It was the last thing he remembered before a streak of white fur shot through the door and slammed into his chest, hurling him backward onto the floor while still in the chair.

"Montague, no!" came from the boy. A sudden flurry ensued. Quick steps approached him.

Briefly dazed, Luc looked up and took a moment to realize that he was staring into the brown eyes of a giant wet white beast panting above him. Water from his drenched fur dripped onto Luc's face. At least he hoped to hell it was water dropping onto his brow. Two large paws held him down.

Then the beast was gone, allowing air to flow into Luc's chest freely now.

Juliette dropped to her knees at his side. "Good Lord. Are you all right?" Warm, soft hands wiped at his brow.

He took a long deep breath, expelled it slowly, then rolled onto his side away from Juliette and up on his knees, the toppled chair between them. Sitting back on his heels, he placed his hands on his thighs and gazed back at the two horrified people in the room. The great white beast sat calmly near Gabriel, as though nothing out of the ordinary had just occurred.

Merde. This was not exactly how he'd envisioned this visit transpiring. A passionate roll on the floor with the beautiful woman in the room? More than fine by him. Being knocked to the ground by a large animal, he could have done without.

Suddenly, Gabriel rushed toward Luc, his massive pet barreling forward with him.

Oh, hell, no… Luc shot to his feet, not wanting to be knocked down by the animal again.

The boy and beast stopped before him, then Gabriel righted the chair. "Please, Luc, don't be angry with Montague or *Maman,*" the mite said. "This is my fault. I should have closed the door to the courtyard." Then he did something that took Luc by surprise. He stepped in front of his mother. A purely protective stance.

Luc's gut clenched. It was like a second blow to his body as memories of his own similar attempts to protect *his* mother from his father's wrath flitted through his mind. He hated the way the boy was looking at him now. Fear and worry were etched on his face. Before Luc could respond, Juliette was on her feet and gently pulling her son to her side. "Gabriel, no one is angry." She glanced over at Luc. "Isn't that so, my lord?" Her gaze dropped to his chest, and her lips quirked. Luc realized she was holding back her mirth. He glanced down, and there in the middle of his once white, pristine shirt was a long, muddy smear and two perfect muddy paw prints.

His gaze shot back at her, and he noticed her hand was over her mouth now, and she was trying to hold back a laugh. He burst out laughing, the situation beyond farcical. She dropped her hand and joined in, a delicate sound he very much liked.

When at last he sobered up, he moved closer and placed a hand on Gabriel's shoulder.

Montague let out a resounding bark. His large teeth showed.

Christ. He removed his hand from Gabriel's shoulder. In no way did he want to do anything to anger that large mass of teeth and sodden fur. "There is no reason to fret, Gabriel. I'm not angry at your *Maman* or," he glanced over at the animal in question, "Montague."

That made Gabriel smile. "Montague likes you, Luc. He doesn't like everyone."

"I can't tell you how relieved that makes me feel." He smiled in return. He meant every fucking word.

Montague barked again, and this time smacked Luc's thigh with his paw, leaving another visible muddy smear, even with his black breeches.

Bloody hell…

"Montague, behave!" Gabriel admonished. "We have a visitor today. You can't have all the attention always," he explained to the beast.

Of course he can. That beast is hard to miss.

"All right, my darling, we've done quite enough to the marquis and his clothing today. Please bid him adieu and take Montague to your rooms," Juliette said. "The marquis must be on his way now."

With clear disappointment, the boy bowed, bid him good day, and left with his oversized pet, quietly closing the door behind him.

*****

Isabelle grasped Luc's elbow and started across the room for the door with the tall aristo in tow. "My lord, I too bid you good day."

"What? No time to recover from my traumatic ordeal? I was pounced on by a large beast." Without turning around, she could easily hear the teasing in his tone. She had to fight back another laugh. He was so adorably disheveled at the moment. A sharp contrast to this handsome man's always perfect appearance. Even the wind knew to rustle his hair just right.

She stopped at the door of the salon and turned to look at him. Those beguiling light green eyes stared back at her, and the half smile tilting his lips instantly played with her pulse. "We both know what remedy you seek to overcome your 'traumatic ordeal.' One that will not be administered in this house." *Or ever.*

She quashed down the disappointment that spiked inside.

He chuckled softly. "I meant only to bask a little longer in your company. Nothing more, especially with your son here." That he'd care about Gabriel over his physical needs surprised her. That wasn't the typical response she'd normally get from men. Their needs were paramount at all times. Above everyone else. Always.

He then leaned in. His mouth close to her ear, he said, "And I don't consider sex a treatment, because desire isn't an illness. It's an irresistible attraction that occurs between certain individuals—like you and me. It's expressed through a variety of carnal acts for the purposes of shared intense orgasms…when you're bound to my bed." His voice took on that low sultry timbre that made her clit start to pulse.

It took her a moment to fight back the urge to graze her lips along his neck, so tantalizingly close. She took a step back. "Be that as it may, you still must go," she forced out. Opening the door, she then marched out, hauling Lord Seductive with her.

Did he have any idea of the earthshaking impact he had on a woman's senses? She was more than a bit stunned by how good-natured he was being about being knocked to the ground by Montague and having his costly clothing ruined. This former naval officer who'd once commanded scores of men, this formidable aristo whose hand was quick to the scabbard, and yet he'd held Gabriel's hand and demonstrated nothing but patience and cordialness.

He was every bit as complex, enticing, and fascinating as he'd always been.

This man who wanted her naked and bound in his bedchamber and who could possibly collapse the foundation of her carefully crafted world, if she wasn't careful.

She'd always sensed there was more to him than just the physical appeal that set females aflutter.

There was so much more she was curious about—such as what had caused those unexpected flashes of sadness in his eyes at her father's theater on those rare occasions he'd let his guard down long enough for her to glimpse them? He'd had everything a man could want. Looks. Riches. Power. What could have caused him a moment's melancholy back then? Was that sadness gone now? Or had he simply become better at disguising it over the years?

Isabelle crossed the vestibule, stopped at the main entrance of the *hôtel*, and released his arm. The solid muscles she'd felt beneath her fingers were too much temptation for her liking. "My apologies again for the state of your clothing, my lord."

"*Luc*," he said. "I much prefer it from your lips than 'my lord.'"

"Yes, well… Luc, I don't allow men in my home where my son resides. Especially men that I have…Well, I'm sure you understand."

"I do." He smiled and simply gazed at her in a way that made her want him to linger longer. Want more physical contact with him than she should. "May I ask you a personal question?"

Isabelle stiffened, a visceral reaction, concerned his questioning would be about Gabriel. She didn't try to hide him. But she didn't offer information about him either. He was part of her private world and far too young to be part of Juliette's existence. She didn't want Juliette discussing details of her son. And she suspected he was going to ask about Gabriel's father, which was none of his concern.

"That depends on the question." Her words came out sharper than she'd intended.

It didn't go unnoticed. His eyes searched hers briefly, the way she used to search his at the theater, trying to delve deeper into his innermost thoughts. Then his smile returned.

"I simply wondered…why do you have a small horse in your house?"

That made her laugh, tension melting from her muscles. Not exactly the query she'd anticipated. She had a strong feeling he'd graciously changed his question based on her curt response. He was too perfect in every way, this older version of Luc de Moutier.

"Perhaps you've hit your head too hard?" She brushed an errant strand of his hair from his brow, unable to stop herself from indulging in another touch. "He's not a horse. He's a dog."

"And a rather large one for his already large breed. Most keep such dogs outdoors where they guard the property."

"Montague doesn't mind his anomaly any more than we do. He's rather special in many ways and prefers the indoors."

"I see." There was amusement in his eyes. "Well, you may thank Montague for teaching me a valuable lesson in the follies of paying an impromptu visit to a certain beautiful woman." Smiling, he opened his doublet wide, indicating the muddy smears on his white shirt. His smile moved her to one as well. What was it about this man that had her smiling and laughing so often?

In a way no one had in a very long time.

"Just one of his many talents," she teased, enjoying the sound of his laughter once more. *For God's sake, stop flirting with him and get on with it, Isabelle!* "I'm afraid I must insist you take your leave now." She opened the door.

Just then, a loud clap of thunder rattled the skies, and the rainfall suddenly increased to a strong downpour.

With his hands on his hips, Luc shook his head. "Why am I not surprised this is happening. I can safely say that there is never a dull moment around you, *chère*."

The urge to ask him to stay was powerful. As was the desire for him bubbling in her blood. She swallowed down the words, reminding herself this was neither the place nor time to be in the company of Luc de Moutier.

Especially the way he excited her body.

"May I see you tomorrow?" he asked. "I could send my carriage."

Tomorrow was far too soon. But it didn't matter anyway. "I'm sorry, but I shall be with my son all day. And night." She'd promised him and she didn't break her promises to Gabriel.

"What about—"

"I'll be leaving the day after that and will be gone a week," she said, anticipating his next question. "The Vicomtesse d'Appel is having a fête at her château in Magon." She wasn't relishing the sojourn away from Gabriel for several days, but she'd accepted the invitation weeks ago at Nicole's behest, and she couldn't disappoint her friend by denying her request to accompany her.

It would allow her time to reassert some much-needed self-discipline where Luc was concerned and sort out the delicate situation she found herself in.

"What a coincidence," he said. "I'll be there too."

Her stomach dropped. "You will?"

Taking her hand, he bowed and pressed a lingering kiss to her knuckle, his warm lips lightly brushing against her skin. A hot pulse quivered through her core. "I will—as soon as I secure my invitation." A glint of wicked promise entered those intoxicating green eyes. "To our week together, beautiful Juliette. Adieu," was the last thing he said before sauntering into the rain to his waiting carriage.

CHAPTER SEVEN

"Darling, have you heard a word I've said?"

Nicole's voice pierced Isabelle's reverie. She dragged her gaze away from the château and back to her friend. "I'm sorry, Nicole. I fear my mind was elsewhere."

Strolling in the manicured gardens of the Vicomtesse d'Appel's château, arms looped, should have been relaxing—especially in a rare moment where she didn't have a barrage of men vying for her attention. The chatter among Madame d'Appel's guests melded with the sweet strains from the violins nearby and the trickling water of the fountains. It was late afternoon. The sun was out, and its rays gently warmed her shoulders. It couldn't have been a more perfect day. And yet she was a bundle of jangled nerves. Isabelle glanced back at the château.

Again.

No sight of him. *He isn't coming. You can relax...*

She'd arrived last night along with most of the guests. A second wave had arrived early this afternoon. Surely all those who'd been invited were present by now?

Nicole leaned into her and said, "I suspect I know what, or rather who, is running through your thoughts."

Isabelle took a deep breath and let it out slowly. "I'm being foolish. I know. It's all for naught, really. I doubt he secured an invitation in such a short amount of time. And even if he does arrive, I can manage this one man."

Who are you trying to convince? Nicole? Or you? She couldn't even think of him without a thrill racing down her spine.

Nicole simply smiled and said, "Of course you can, my dear. You can manage any man. Do not allow those doubts inside your mind to tell you otherwise."

"Am I that transparent to you? Or do you possess some magical power to read my thoughts?" she teased. God, how she deeply adored her. Nicole always understood. Always knew just the right fortifying words to say.

That drew a soft laugh from Nicole. "No magical powers. I know your thoughts because I was in your position once. Now then, I was saying that Madame d'Appel was positively thrilled when she learned you'd accepted her invitation." Nicole smiled. "Yet another example of your clear rise in influence. She doesn't invite just anyone. I am delighted for you."

Ordinarily, that would have brought Isabelle a measure of satisfaction. But not today. Today, Luc was stealing her inner peace. And he'd begun to invade her dreams. She wasn't prone to salacious dreams. Not for a very long time. Yet last night, a certain gorgeous aristo with irresistible eyes was naked in her bed. His hands and mouth grazing her skin and setting her body ablaze with desire.

A hand touched her bare shoulder. Isabelle jumped and spun to the left to find the Duc de Vannod looking as startled as she. "I'm terribly sorry. I didn't mean to startle you."

Isabelle smiled and recovered quickly, though her heart rate did not. "Good day, Your Grace."

He returned her smile and, with a bow, kissed her hand, then turned and greeted Nicole similarly. "Good day, *mesdames*, and please, I insist you call me Richard."

"Of course, Richard. It is good to see you here." She couldn't help notice that not a tingle—not the slightest stirring—had occurred when he'd kissed her hand.

And she wished that wasn't the case.

The duke was attractive, with a slender build, dark curly hair, and blue eyes. His company was pleasant. And he was as enthralling as stale bread. It should appeal to her that he didn't wreak havoc on her mind and body the way Luc did.

But it didn't.

Luc de Moutier wasn't even in attendance, though he might as well have been. His name was on the tongues of most every guest as news of his appearance at the Comtesse de Grandville's masked ball the other night was now fodder for gossip.

Especially by a number of women who'd feigned disinterest at his unexpected return. The tales they'd fabricated about the attention Luc had lavished on them the entire night had made her all but grit her teeth.

When she shouldn't care about their stories.

Or that these unmarried young women were only lying simply to elevate their popularity. But the lies about Luc bothered her more than she could comfortably admit. As did the news that the reason for his return was to seek a wife.

"He's here!" Those words came from one of the two women nearby, snagging Isabelle's attention.

The phrase rippled through the crowd around her.

Without turning around, she *knew*. Her heart had already begun to pound, hard steady thuds. Awareness shimmered over her nerve endings.

Slowly, she turned to the château. Her mouth went dry.

There at a distance, several stone steps above the throng, standing outside the large double doors of the vicomtesse's grand salon with a man of similar age was none other than Luc de Moutier. The summer breeze blew open his green doublet, pressing his white shirt and tanned breeches against his tall, muscled form. Defining his masculine attributes for her hungry eyes.

The stirring sight of a Greek god before mere mortals.

He was handsome, intelligent, with polished charm and carnal talents too dangerous for any one man to possess.

And she was gawking at him the way she used to at her father's theater, with the same breathless awe. Only now she knew just how incredible his skin felt. How his hands felt on her body. How mind melting it was to have him so deep inside her.

The murmur around her grew stronger.

And so did the fire in her blood. Now that he was here, she had to behave far more urbane about his presence than this.

Where on earth is the cold rain when you actually need it?

*****

"I just want you to know I had to agree to fuck Eléonore in order to get you this invitation," Marc said.

That yanked Luc's searching gaze away from the guests in the garden to his friend. "*Eléonore?* You mean the attractive widow who is our hostess?"

"Yes."

"And the hardship in that is…?"

"That you have reduced me to swapping sexual favors for you. I feel so used." Marc's pathetic attempt at sounding wounded made Luc laugh.

"Then I have only two words to say to you. *You're welcome.*"

At that, Marc laughed. "Yes, well, don't expect a thank-you until after I've had her the better part of this week."

Luc returned his attention to the crowd before him. The gardens stretched out as far as the eye could see. There were at least a hundred guests present.

But only one mattered to him at the moment. His eyes hunted for her.

"*No, no, no, Marc… I'm not interested in a courtesan.*" Marc mimicked Luc's voice. "*I plan on finding a bride. Being celibate as a monk. I have reformed my libertine ways…*"

Luc cast him a sidelong glance. "Are you through?"

"Probably not." Marc was grinning, clearly enjoying himself. He clamped a hand down on Luc's shoulder. Luc flinched ever so slightly, hoping Marc hadn't noticed. He knew it was merely a friendly gesture, but *Jésus-Christ*, the urge to knock his hand off his shoulder and end the touch surged inside him. "In all seriousness, Luc, I am delighted you're focused on a woman who isn't dead." Marc released his grip on Luc's shoulder.

The tension instantly uncoiled through his body. A sweet relief.

"So am I," he said. Thank God, Isabelle had begun to fade, and he was damned grateful to Juliette for it. She was a far better mental distraction. Because of her, he hadn't picked up Isabelle's journals in days. "And I haven't given up on marriage. Nor have I mentioned a thing about celibacy."

"Good. Because celibacy is damned unnatural." Marc shuddered, overly theatrically, drawing another laugh from Luc. "Look at them,"

Marc said with a jerk of his chin toward the gardens. "You have their undivided attention, my friend. You've set their tongues wagging. They're all talking about the long-lost ghost of Luc de Moutier that has suddenly materialized before them. It's a good thing that you've caught Juliette Carre's interest. That alone will open doors for you."

"No, I'm not here because I'm looking to use her to 'open doors' for me."

Marc looked at him, incredulous. "You jest, no?"

"No."

"Luc, you have had the most sought-after woman in the country— the details of which you *still* haven't shared with me—and you aren't going to use it to your advantage? It instantly elevates you in the opinions of those fools out there who are eager to reject you. Especially the men, who we both know…umm…"

"Despise me." He finished the sentence for him. "With the King's pardon, I have my family's reputation restored. And I have my former wealth once more. They'll accept me as husband material when the time comes to offer marriage and negotiate a contract. For now, I'm simply interested in the company of one woman here."

"So are many others in attendance."

It was Luc's turn to clamp a friendly hand on Marc's shoulder. "Since when have you known me to shy away from a challenge?"

"Never. Bloody hell, you managed to walk into your first masque since your return and tantalize Juliette Carre right out from under the noses of the men panting in heat around her. I can't blame you for going to all this trouble for her. She's beautiful, and the sex must have been incredible."

Luc's gut tightened. For some reason, he disliked Marc talking about Juliette the same way he'd spoken about his other paramours in the past. "There's more to this woman than physical appeal." There was something about her that made him want to learn everything about her.

One whole week under the same roof as Juliette Carre, to delight in her endearing quirks and antics. A week to entice that edible little form and show her the decadent delights in mixing sex and bondage.

Dieu, what could be finer than that?

And if by the end of the week Isabelle Laurent had been eradicated for good from his thoughts and dreams—all the better. Spotting his hostess near the bottom of the stone steps, he said, "Come, let's greet the comely Eléonore. And you can begin to thank her." Giving Marc a wink, Luc descended the steps, a smile on his face.

He couldn't wait to see what more he'd discover from his beautiful Juliette Carre.

*****

"He's a scoundrel of the highest order, I say. They should have stretched his bloody neck on the gibbet like his father," Vannod spouted as he cast an angry glance at Luc. A short distance away, the object of Vannod's disdain chatted with Eléonore d'Appel near her fountain of Venus. Isabelle had never seen Vannod, normally a placid man, this provoked.

But really, she wasn't all that surprised. All men of power eventually exposed their more hateful side. It was only a matter of time. And to what degree.

"I understand the King has acquitted him of any wrongdoing," Nicole said.

"Hmmph. That particular Moutier is guilty of plenty of wrongdoing. My cousin has a sizeable scar on his leg thanks to him." Vannod jerked his chin in Luc's direction. "The wound almost killed him. Despite dueling being illegal, everyone knows that Moutier has incited plenty of them nonetheless. I had no objection to seeing his older brother Jules regain the King's favor. He's an honorable man. I never believed the accusations that Jules de Moutier had betrayed his country or king. But his younger brother… That's a different matter altogether. He's capable of any lowly act."

An objection to Vannod's remarks about Luc surged up Isabelle's throat. She swallowed it down. She hadn't seen Luc in a long time and had even heard about his dueling from the gossipmongers in the garden and at her father's theater. Though the disparaging remarks Vannod made about Luc's character didn't ring true to her from her observations of him years ago, she had to quash the urge to defend him regardless. It could give the impression that she'd known him far longer than Juliette ever could have. How well did she know Luc anyway?

"Good day, Madame de Grammont." Luc's voice behind her made her jump. Mentally, she chastised herself. *Will you calm down.* She couldn't keep starting each time someone approached. She needed to treat him no differently from other men in her life. But Luc had never made that easy to accomplish.

Luc took Nicole's hand. "It's a pleasure to see you, madame. It's been a long time," he said with a bow and a kiss in that beguiling, polished manner of his. Isabelle was pleased by his discreetness, acting as though the encounter at the masque had never occurred.

Nicole's smile was gracious as always, giving nothing away. "Yes, it has been a long time. Though it seems like only yesterday. This is Madame Carre." She continued Luc's ruse.

His light green eyes captured her gaze. A smile graced his lips as he bent at the waist and pressed a kiss to her knuckle. It was an entirely appropriate greeting, and yet, unlike Vannod's kiss on her hand, Luc's awakened every nerve ending in her body. Making them quiver with life. "Madame Carre. A pleasure," he said.

She responded in kind.

"And I believe you know the Duc de Vannod." Nicole gestured to the man.

"Of course. It is good to see you, Vannod."

Vannod cocked a dark brow, dealt him a glare, and, after a rather awkward pause, finally drawled, "I wish I could say the same."

This side of Vannod was becoming irksome and his rudeness inappropriate at the vicomtesse's gathering. Fearing the situation would unravel, Isabelle opened her mouth to interject when Luc surprised her with a genuine laugh.

"Vannod, you're utterly adorable when you're miffed. I'm glad to see you haven't changed."

Oh dear God.

The duc stiffened. "You... You're...you're..."

"Welcome?" Luc supplied with a smile.

Vannod's face turned deep red. "Sir, do you know to whom you are speaking?"

She'd never hit anyone in her life, but at the moment, she wanted to smack Luc. If he wanted to reenter society, this wasn't the way to go about it. Though Luc had considerable wealth, the duc held significant social rank.

And had far more friends present.

At that, Luc frowned. "It appears your facilities are failing you, Vannod. Are you having trouble remembering who you are?"

Isabelle's heart lost a beat. The redness on Vannod's face had crept down his neck. He puffed out his chest and, turning sharply on his heel, stalked away without another word.

The slightest sound escaped Nicole, suspiciously like a laugh, and for a mere instant, amusement crossed her features before she schooled her expression. She tapped a slender finger against Luc's chest. "You, dear boy, are trouble. Mostly for yourself. Though you've never backed away from it before, but then, that's part of your charm, isn't it?"

She smiled with no sign of the irritation Isabelle felt, bid them a good day, and wandered toward the other guests.

"Are you *trying* to get into a duel?" Isabelle asked the moment they were alone.

"No."

"You've just insulted *a duc*," she said, sotto voce.

He shrugged. "Vannod is a coward. He'd never challenge me. And I don't intend to challenge him. I don't duel anymore." He was back to giving her one of those irresistible smiles, gorgeous green eyes aglint. The kind of smile that made being angry at him difficult.

Even when she wasn't completely over the urge to smack him.

"If you are looking to make friends here, that was hardly the way to go about it."

He leaned in and, in her ear, said, "I hate these people. I don't care for their friendship." He pulled back, gazing into her eyes once again.

There he was. That rebellious boy she'd been so desperately enamored with so long ago. The one male aristo who always seemed to be on the outside looking in. Never fitting in. Never truly part of the upper class he was born into—despite his exalted pedigree and his brave naval service to the Crown she'd heard so much about from Nicole.

There was a certain vulnerability about him, one he tried to conceal from the world. And that vulnerability was one of the many reasons she'd been drawn to him from the start.

That same Luc was back now and, God help her, even more beckoning than before.

"You're the only one whose company I crave," he said, so low, so softly that it melted her insides a little—when she didn't think words from any man could inspire soft sentiment. And the way he'd said *crave* made her sex clench.

This aristo could turn her inside out. She had to be far more immune than this.

Offering his arm, he asked, "May I have the honor?"

She took his arm and began to stroll with him down the garden path, not wanting to cause a scene. Tiny stones crunched beneath her shoes. There was no need to look around. She knew the entire throng of guests was watching them. The younger version of herself would have wildly celebrated being on Luc de Moutier's arm.

But she was much more jaded now. She'd been through much more than that dream-filled girl could have ever imagined.

"How is Gabriel?" he asked. That took her by surprise. It wasn't a question that would normally come from men of the upper class. They wouldn't ordinarily voice concern about a boy who wasn't even close to his social standing. His query was touching. And perfect.

A little too perfect.

For years she'd built Luc de Moutier up to be incredible in every way. When would he inevitably disillusion her? When would he show his true unkind nature that was so prevalent in his gender and social class and finally crush to dust all the foolish notions and fantasies she had about him?

When would she see what Vannod and his other peers saw?

"Gabriel is fine." She smiled and nodded politely at the elderly Comte and Comtesse de Gigot as they passed by. Once out of hearing range, she added, "Please don't use my son to ingratiate yourself with me. Flowery words are fine, though I have heard them all. But I don't want you using my son in the hopes of sexual gain." There. That should do it. That should evoke some sort of fiery response, show the temper he and everyone else mentioned he had. No doubt some cruel commentary would spill from his perfect lips for good measure.

Finally ending her infatuation with him—for good—and prove he wasn't trustworthy.

He stopped abruptly and faced her. But anger wasn't what was in his eyes. His brows knitted, and a look of hurt, one she'd remembered from long ago, surprisingly flashed back at her. It was like a blow to the belly. "You think I'd use a young boy to seduce you into more sex?" He sounded incredulous.

Suddenly, she was unsure of her actions. "Men have done worse." She offered that bit of raw truth. "Men also try to bed me simply to elevate their status among their peers—since I am, at the moment, the current coveted courtesan. And we both know you could use some help there. Especially after your encounter with the duc."

Are you mad? She'd never behaved this way. Of course men used her. She was *a courtesan*. She hadn't cared about being used before. It shouldn't matter if this aristo had or was as well. Yet it bothered her.

More than she wished it did.

His brows shot up briefly, then he rested his hands on his hips, tilted his head, and studied her in silence for a moment. Then another. And another. She glanced about, unsure what to do.

At last, he said, "I wish to apologize for my peers. I'm sorry, Juliette. Clearly, they have made a bright, passionate, beautiful woman mistrusting of men. And who can blame you given that lot?" he said, jerking his chin in the direction of the guests behind her in the garden. "But let me make something very clear. I don't lie to women. I won't lie to you. I don't—*won't*—use anyone or anything to manipulate a woman into having sex with me. If it's not something we both crave, a mutual carnal attraction that's hot and intense," his voice dropped an octave, "*just as it is with us,* then I'm not interested. I don't need to use a child to get sex. My concern for Gabriel was genuine. And I don't need to bed anyone to elevate myself. My title, my wealth, and my years of distinguished service to my country and King speak for themselves. Anyone who wishes to dismiss any of that wouldn't be someone whose opinion I'd give a fuck about."

No temper. No cutting words.

He even offered an apology.

Good Lord, what was she to make of that? He was either as close to perfect as any mere mortal could be. Or he was far better at concealing his character than most.

"You are the reason I'm here, Juliette. *I want you...*" The soft, low delicious way he said that sent a bolt of lust rippling through her senses. He gave her one of his beautiful smiles. "I want to make you come for me—hard—again and again. I want your little clit in my mouth and to hear you scream my name in pleasure. I want you naked and bound as I bury my cock inside you. And, *Jésus-Christ,* I want to taste that mouth of yours in a long, lush kiss more than you could ever imagine. There are many decadent delights I'd like to share with you— if you would allow me to. I know there are other men here who want you too. But if you choose me to be your lover, I'll bring you to a level of sexual bliss you've never known."

Had the sun suddenly become hotter? Her blood was rushing through her body like liquid fire.

Unable to speak, she shook her head no and gave him a rueful smile as another couple walked past. But when she went to reinforce her physical action with words, what tumbled out of her mouth instead was "We'll see…"

We'll see? She wanted to kick herself.

He chuckled. "I see how it is. You want to make me work for it. Fair enough. I'm most enthusiastic about the challenge." The promiscuous promise that gleamed in his eyes spiked her fever further. He offered his arm once more just as a small group of guests wandered by, their chatter drifting in and out of their space in the gardens.

Isabelle took his arm. This was quite the dilemma. She needed to be around him to see if there was a way to reach her family. But remain immune to his seductive charm. It was time to steer this conversation away from sex.

For the sake of her sanity.

"I feel it is my turn to apologize. I'm sorry for my earlier accusations. They were horribly inappropriate and rude. I have tried to keep Gabriel from this part of my world. He is innocent and too young. I hope you understand."

He still sported a lopsided smile as they walked on, deeper into the gardens and farther from most of the guests and the vicomtesse's château. "No more talk of Gabriel…for now."

She cocked her brow and gave him a look of warning. His lips twitched in amusement. "Except to say, I think you are an excellent mother. He is a lucky boy and a charming child."

"I am the lucky one. And thank you."

"I do wish to know more about him."

Isabelle stiffened. She could feel her defenses begin to rise. "Why?"

"Because he's a part of you. Because I don't just want you. I like you—very much. And I'd truly like to learn more about you." He leaned in toward her ear. "I want to know all your secrets," he gently teased.

That made her uneasy and nervous. What would he truly do if he knew who she really was? *How's that for a secret?* Would he turn on her as Roch had?

"No more talk of Gabriel," she said, wanting to change the subjects about her son and her secrets.

"All right, then. What about Montague. May I inquire about him?"

That made her laugh. "Yes, Montague is fine."

"Wonderful. How is that white horse you live with?"

She laughed again. "Dog," she corrected.

"If you say so." He shrugged, mirth etched on his handsome face. "Has he ever eaten any of the staff?"

Another laugh. "Montague is a dear, sweet dog. All staff members, and their limbs, are very much intact and unmarred."

He chuckled. "I and, I'm sure, your staff are happy that's so."

She enjoyed this side of him. The banter was endearing. It wasn't often she had the luxury to converse with a single person. There was usually a group of men competing for her attention. Instead, at the moment, she had just one sinfully seductive lord who made her burn for him in a way no man ever had. And whose appealing charm was on full display. She could easily stroll through the gardens for hours on his arm like this, discussing subjects of little consequence. But she had a beloved sister she wanted to see again.

She decided to probe guardedly.

"Tell me something about yourself, Luc. I know little about you. Tell me about your family."

At the word *family*, she felt a tightening of the muscles in his arm.

"I'm sure you've heard a great deal about them from others."

"I'd rather hear about them from you. I understand you have a brother?"

"I do."

"Where is he? I don't believe I've met him."

"He's in the West Indies with his wife."

Isabelle's heart began to pound at the mention of her sister. "He's married? What is she like?"

"Sabine? She's lovely. Very bright. Fiery. She's just what my brother needs." He smiled. "I very much like her."

Her heart constricted. A lump formed in her throat. Somehow, she managed to ask, "Do they have children?"

"A daughter. Perhaps more now."

A daughter! "Wh...What is her name?" She prayed he didn't hear her voice crack.

"Isabelle."

She froze in her tracks. Overwhelmed with emotion.

"Is something amiss?" he asked.

She looked down, unable to make eye contact with him. Fearful he'd see the tears in her eyes. She blinked them back quickly.

It took her a moment before she could speak. She had to swallow hard twice before she could say, "I…I think I have a pebble in my shoe."

He lowered himself down onto his haunches and looked up at her. "Which foot?" His hand was already slipping under her hem.

"The left," she said randomly.

Warm, strong fingers wrapped around her ankle. He slipped her shoe off, gave it a gentle shake, then placed it back onto her foot.

Leaving her body tingling in the wake of his touch.

He rose to his full height. "Better?"

It was. His touch had helped blunt the initial stab of anguish the news of her niece had caused. But the longing was still so fierce, she wanted to race to the West Indies, throw her arms around Sabine and her child *right now*. And never let go. "Yes. Thank you. How old is your niece?" Not the smoothest attempt to steer the conversation back to her family, but she didn't care. She wanted to devour all the information about her sister and daughter she could.

He frowned, clearly confused. "Why?"

"I'm simply curious," she said with a practiced nonchalance. "Does she look more like her mother or her father?"

He shook his head with a soft laugh. "Just when I think I know just what we'll talk about the next time we meet… You are many things, but predictable is not one of them. To satisfy your curiosity, Isabelle would be about two years of age now. All I know about her is that 'she is as beautiful as her mother'—a quote from my brother. I've never seen her. Jules left France with Sabine three years ago with no intention of ever returning. However, this year, he did return unexpectedly to help out a mutual friend who also lives in the West Indies. Jules wasn't here long and was anxious to return home to his wife and child—which he did with the balance of Sabine's family and our mutual friend Simon on one of Simon's privateer ships. I don't expect either Simon or Jules will return again."

The ground fell out from under her feet. She took a quick step back just to balance herself. "*Never?*" The single word rushed out on a breath.

"Never."

"But…but… You can't! I…I mean… He's your brother. Your kin. If he won't return here, you—you must visit him."

"My brother and I have always led very different lives—from boyhood. I know he's happy, and that's enough for me."

"But you will never meet your niece! Or any of his other children."

"That is regrettable, but there isn't anything I can do about it. You need a ship to get there. I'm no longer in the King's navy or a privateer for France. And it's too far to swim," he added with a small smile, clearly trying to leaven the conversation.

She was reeling. For years, she'd quietly kept the hope alive that she'd see her sister again. Through many deep, dark moments, it had kept her spirits up. This was almost too cruel.

"Do you know what island they're on?"

"Yes."

"Then surely there's got to be a way to get there. What about some other ship bound for the West Indies?" She tried to keep the distress from her tone.

"The war between France and Spain is over. The King's ships no longer sail to the West Indies as they used to, to attack Spanish silver fleets returning from New Spain. And given the sheer number of cutthroats in that area, the only safe passage to the West Indies is on a fully armed warship. Anything else is highly risky and foolhardy."

Her chest was tight. As was her throat. Maintaining her composure had never been more hard-fought. She wanted to crumble to the ground but locked her knees and battled back the urge. There was more to this than he was saying. Something in his eyes, in his tone— ever so subtle—told her so. "You don't *want* to visit him in the West Indies, do you?" The words tumbled from her mouth uncensored.

For the briefest instance, surprise flashed across his features, telling her in an instant she'd been accurate in her hunch. He tightened his jaw and looked away. When at last he returned his gaze to her, he gave her a firm "No."

"And you didn't much care for his last unanticipated visit, did you?"

"No, I didn't. In truth, I wished he hadn't bothered."

"Did you have an argument?"

"No. We've accomplished what we'd set out to do together—clear our names and regain favor with the King. Now that that's done, I don't want to ever see him again. And he knows it." His words were firmly unequivocal. For the first time ever, she saw a coldness in his eyes.

Her heavy heart plummeted. Of all the hardships she'd endured since her family had lost everything, she'd never felt more dispirited in her life. And given the hell she'd been through, that said a great deal.

"Ah, there you are, my beauty!" Auguste, Marquis de Prost, had arrived sporting a large smile. He took her hand, bowed low before it, then pressed a kiss to her knuckle. At least a dozen years her senior, he had dark hair and dark eyes, with a pleasing enough frame and face. And had at least three mistresses when last she heard. He'd been sniffing around her skirts for some time now.

His younger brother, Frédéric, Comte de Meslon, stepped out from behind him and kissed her hand too. "Good day, Madame Carre. You are without a doubt the loveliest thing in this garden." Married and smarmy, he had no chance at all despite his many attempts to bed her.

"Thank you," she offered politely, though Meslon's praise was overdone.

"Moutier… " Auguste nodded to Luc. "Quite the stir you've caused with your return. You've been gone a long time. I understand from the Duc de Vannod that you are unchanged in your…er…*charm?*"

Frédéric laughed at his older brother's little gibe. Luc surprised her by joining in. He placed his hand on Auguste's shoulder. "I'd like to say I'm glad to see you, Prost, but I promised the lady I wouldn't lie."

That sobered the men. Luc then nudged them out of the way and took her hand. "I'm also going to promise the lady I'll cause her no trouble." He leaned in and brought his mouth near her ear. "You deserve far better than these two artless fools. Let me be the man who fulfills your every sexual desire. Day or night." Pulling back, he bowed and placed a kiss to her knuckle. "I thank you for the lovely stroll, madame. Until later…"

Then walked away.

Suddenly, she was surrounded by more male admirers, realizing that they'd stayed away due to Luc. Intimidated by him. She walked along the path, affixing a false smile to her face as they vied for her attention, regaling her with stories and gossip she barely heard and couldn't care less about.

She was at a loss.

Trapped in a gilded cage.

Was this truly to be her life? Alone to raise her son, apart from her family? Never to see Sabine again? With no way to tell them she was alive?

She simply couldn't—*wouldn't*—accept that.

Something was pulling the brothers apart. Scouring her memory, she tried to recall all the tiny tidbits she'd learned about Luc while in the employ of his father.

The coldness in Luc's eyes flashed in her mind. Followed by the memory of the sadness she'd seen in his eyes at her father's theater. What had caused that sadness? And all the anger that followed?

She had but a few days, to the end of the fête, while Luc was readily available to her, to unravel all this. It could set matters right in her life. And perhaps even in his.

All she had to do was learn *his* every secret.

Oh, and keep the sinfully gorgeous Lord Seductive out of her bed.

Why don't you add learning to fly to that list while you're at it?

CHAPTER EIGHT

"You know if you continue to cast glares at the men around her, you're going to cause Vannod to piss himself."

Luc ignored the comment Marc murmured in his ear. And his snicker. He was too busy trying not to gawk at Juliette across the room. It took all his concentration and willpower.

He'd been seated at the opposite end of the grand dining room during supper, forced to make idle conversation with the ladies to his left and right—Marie, Comtesse d'Oise, and Anne, Duchesse de Clermont. Their flirtatious commentary and the unnecessary press of their breasts against his arms as the young women leaned into him to speak told him in no uncertain terms he had an open invitation to their boudoirs. Both were eager to be taken. Suggesting he have them at the same time wouldn't have been met with any objections from either woman. They obviously cared little that their ancient husbands were close by. Not that either the duc or the comte noticed what their wives were doing.

Their focus was on the other women in the room—the duc in particular lavishing his attention on Nicole de Grammont.

Inarguably, both ladies were lovely. While his former self would likely have indulged in what one or both were offering, he'd politely excused himself. His interest was in Juliette. *Dieu*, this unbreakable pull he had to her had him following her around the countryside.

In a deep green gown with a tantalizing scoop to her décolletage accenting her gorgeous breasts in the most mouthwatering way, she had every man surrounding her riveted, as always, hanging on her every word. Bedazzled by her every smile.

He wasn't touching her. Wasn't physically near her. Yet his body was on fire for her. His cock stiff as steel. The pressure in his prick was so great, it was driving him to distraction. He wanted to march across the great salon, through the crowd, past the dancers dancing the *menuet*, and fist her beautiful hair adorned with small green bows, tilt back her head. And claim her mouth.

Spectators be damned.

Instead, he stood near the wall, affixing his shoulder to it, battling to control his gaze, fearing if he didn't, he'd start panting for her like a dog. What the hell was wrong with him? He couldn't make any sense of his reactions lately. He wasn't acting normally toward women at all.

First, he was obsessed with Isabelle.

Now Juliette.

And *Jésus-Christ*, he liked this woman. A little more than he should. A little more than he was comfortable with. He liked the easy rapport between them. Liked how she could easily make him smile. And that he could draw smiles from her as well. Loved the intensity of the carnal fire they ignited in each other.

If he'd been uncomfortable about how strongly Isabelle had been affecting him, he'd managed to meet a woman who'd completely eclipsed her—in his thoughts. In his desire. *Merde*, she'd banished Isabelle to the far fringes of his mind.

She was just as witty. Just as beguiling. A living, breathing siren he couldn't resist.

And Juliette seemed to have the very same uncanny knack Isabelle had. She was just as attuned to him as Isabelle had been. He hadn't intended to talk about his final conversation with Jules. It unnerved him that anyone could decipher him with such ease.

Who the hell *was* this woman?

"Tell me everything you know about her?" Luc caught himself looking at Juliette again before dragging his gaze back to Marc.

"You mean Juliette?" Marc's lips twitched as he made a poor attempt to feign ignorance.

Luc pushed himself off the wall. "Yes, you know that's who I mean." Unsettled by Juliette's astute perceptions, he wasn't in the mood for Marc's ribbing tonight. "What do you know of her background?"

Marc chuckled. "I see we're going to set the matter of looking for a bride aside for now. Just as well. You have managed to antagonize a number of the men here. You do know that the men make the decision to grant you permission to marry the bride of your choosing, no?"

"Back to Juliette."

"Ah, yes, all right, Juliette Carre... Well, she arrived several months ago. A friend of Nicole de Grammont. Through Nicole's introductions, she's become a darling of all the major salons of Paris. She's well-read. Well educated in various languages. Came from Venice, I believe."

"Venice?"

"Yes, Venice," came a distinctly female voice from his left. He shot his gaze in that direction.

Juliette was standing there. Smiling.

Dieu. She'd caught him discussing her.

"I'm flattered by the interest, my lord." As she still graced him with that smile that had captivated him from the start, he was moved to one as well. He was going to say something about unwanted formality, when she turned to Marc, who quickly took her hand with a bow of his head and a kiss.

"Madame Carre... Allow me to introduce myself, as my friend here has such terrible manners."

"She already knows that, Marc," Luc said, making light of himself. He was rewarded with a delightful laugh from his dark-haired beauty. Lord, he loved the sound of it. Almost as much as the sound she made when she came. "Juliette, this is Marc d'Emery, Marquis de Vigneau."

"It is a pleasure," Marc said, fawning over her hand again as he bowed, then kissed it a second time.

And oddly, that irked him.

"I do believe the guests here ought to be rather grateful for your attendance, my lord," Juliette commented to Marc.

His brows furrowed in confusion. "Grateful for my attendance, madame?"

"Yes." She leaned into Marc and, sotto voce, said, "Are you not the reason our hostess is sporting such a radiant flush to her cheeks?"

That made Marc grin like a fool. "I am not one to brag, madame... Yes. Yes, I am."

Juliette laughed softly again.

And that irked Luc too. *Enough*, he mentally chastised. He wasn't the possessive type. And he didn't want to be.

Juliette's beautiful, big dark eyes swept to him. "It's rather hot in here. I would so enjoy some fresh evening air. Would you be so kind as to escort me for a stroll outdoors?"

A bolt of lust licked up his spine. *Oh hell, yes.*

Just when he thought he'd have to approach her to coax some time alone with her, she came to him. He was the most fortunate man in the room—not something he could often say in his life. Together, under the night sky with this sensuous, highly responsive woman. The mere thought made his heart hammer.

He offered his arm. "There's nothing I'd rather do." Well, there was one thing. And it involved having her naked, bound, with a sheen of sweat covering her lovely body, after he'd rocked her sweet form with several strong orgasms.

She took his arm and murmured parting pleasantries to Marc. Luc escorted her through the grand salon. Just about every pair of male eyes was on them.

Fully aware she'd chosen *him* over them and their company.

And as Luc walked toward the doors that led to the gardens, a sense of bliss seeped deep into his very marrow, the likes of which he'd never known.

And everything at the moment felt so very right with the world.

*****

You can do this. You can keep him and your desire for this man at bay...

Isabelle had repeated those two sentences at least twenty times since stepping into the darkened gardens with Luc. Her pulse raced. Her nerve endings hummed with awareness. The casual conversation they made as they walked through the gardens was a sharp contrast to the havoc Lord Seductive wreaked inside her.

This isn't the greatest obstacle that's ever been placed in your path. But that thought immediately rang hollow. Luc de Moutier was the only man who'd ever stolen her breath away. His effect on her had always been more potent than all other men combined.

The moon slipped in and out from behind the clouds, casting its silver light again and again. God, he looked so good. Smelled so delicious. The scent of his soap drifted to her on the warm wind, tantalizing her heightened senses. She cursed her luck at being placed so far from him in the dining room. She could have attempted to draw more information from him safely seated in a room full of people. Instead, she'd have to do so alone with Luc de Moutier.

In the moonlight.

Her body had already begun to rail against her plan to abstain from him. She wanted to throw her arms around him, bury her face in his neck. And inhale his scent deeply.

You want more than that. You plainly want him—buried deep inside you. Just as before.

He stopped, and she realized that they were a good distance from the château now. In fact, the river that dissected the vicomtesse's lands flowed directly before them.

Moonbeams sparkled on its surface.

He removed his doublet and placed it on the grass, then sat down beside it and held out his hand. "Come sit with me." His voice was soft and low and so wickedly appealing. A feral need unfurled in her belly.

Don't do it. Don't do it. Don't do it, a voice chanted in her head.

She smiled, intent on steering Lord Seductive in a different direction from the carnal one he was silently suggesting. "Let's continue our walk. Wasn't the pheasant delicious?" She turned and began walking along the river. "I read a book about a pheasant once. It was rather comical. Do you enjoy reading, Luc?" She stopped and realized that he wasn't by her side, as would have been the case with any other man if she'd declared a desire to continue to stroll.

She turned around and was astonished that he still sat in the very same spot. Smiling. Looking suspiciously amused. Though it was dark, she was certain she saw his lips twitch.

He patted the spot beside him on his doublet.

That was an unmistakable invitation to sit.

Clearly, he wasn't moving. *He thinks you're making him "work for it,"* as he'd put it. This was a fine time to learn he wasn't the kind of man she could lead around by the nose as she did with all the others. Every man at the vicomtesse's château who was trying to bed her would eagerly do whatever she asked.

Except Lord Seductive.

Briefly, she cast a glance at the château in the distance. Nicole was back there. As was Serge, the large servant who normally accompanied them when they traveled. She could run back there now. But she wouldn't. She'd mute her base needs and focus on the task at hand—getting information from Luc and ultimately reuniting with her sister—if miracles still happened.

She took in a fortifying breath and let it out slowly.

Miss Moth, may I introduce you to Mr. Flame...

She began the walk back to Luc, feeling she was losing ground with every step. *Let's face it. You're a courtesan who isn't very wanton. Except when it comes to this man.* That unruly wanton he inspired inside her was presently battling against her restraint with a battering ram.

Fighting to be freed.

When she reached him, he offered his hand again. She took it and sat beside him on his doublet. Tiny tingles raced up her arm. Touching him was a luxury all its own.

"You didn't bring me out here to discus candied fruits and how delicious the champagne and pheasant were. Now that you've got me here alone, what are we going to do?" She didn't miss the suggestion in his tone.

"Talk," she said, keeping her tone light. Thankful more than ever for the acting skills she learned long ago.

He cocked a brow. "*Really?* About what?"

"About you. I enjoyed our conversation today and—"

"No."

"Pardon?"

"No," he repeated. "I don't want to talk about me."

Just keep him talking... You can steer the conversation back to him. "Then what would you like to talk about?"

A slow smile formed on his handsome face. He rose onto his knees, and before she realized what he was about, he undid his cravat and pulled his shirt over his head in one fluid motion, tossing them onto the grass.

Isabelle blinked. Words evaporated from her mind. *Dear God...* Every muscle and sinew on his strong shoulders, arms, and chest were bathed in silver light. She allowed her eyes to devour every delectable exposed inch of his form. Her sex clenched hungrily.

He curled his fingers under her chin and tilted her head back. His warm mouth grazed up the side of her neck to her ear. And gave her earlobe a sensual bite.

She lost her breath.

"Juliette," he murmured. "In case it isn't abundantly obvious, I've been walking around hard for you since the masque. I'm open to a conversation of a more carnal nature—like how many times shall we make you come for me?"

Say something. Quickly.

"Luc, why don't we get to know each other a little better—"

He brushed his lips back down her neck. Then, finding a sensitive spot he seemed to instinctively know existed, he drew on her neck with a soft sublime suck. She closed her eyes briefly and swallowed down her mew of pleasure.

"Venice!" she said a little too loudly. "Let's talk about Venice. Earlier, you were asking your friend about my time there. Why don't you let me tell you about it? Ask me anything. What do you wish to know?" She knew plenty about Venice thanks to members from her father's acting troupe she was raised around. She could speak about it convincingly.

And she needed something—*anything*—to distract her from the temptation of Luc de Moutier.

"What I wish to know is whether or not you want me to suck those pretty nipples pressing against your gown." His mouth moved to her throat. She fisted the grass on either side of her, her breathing becoming rapid and raw.

Her breasts were achy. Her entire body rioted for him. The feel of his mouth against her skin was nothing short of inebriating.

She suddenly found herself on her back staring up at him, realizing she'd done so of her own volition. "Damn that wanton," she whispered.

He pressed his palms down on the grass near her shoulders.

Not touching her.

Not straddling her.

Simply sporting that smoldering smile that was so Luc. And so dangerous to her resolve.

"What did you say?" he asked. Slowly, his tactile gaze moved down her body and back up, and she felt his regard right through her clothing, like a hot caress over her skin. She couldn't hold back a squirm.

"I…umm…rather…" Moisture pooled between her legs. She squeezed her knees together. The pulsing of her clit was a horrible distraction. *You should stop this. Don't do it.* Dear God, she wanted him so badly... Her last amorous encounter with him was more heaven than she ever thought she'd experience.

"What say you, beautiful Juliette? Are you going to surrender yourself to me?"

Say no! But she couldn't drag the word up her throat. She looked away, trying to muster the willpower she needed. Her clothes felt too confining. Too hot. She wanted to tear them off. She wanted his cool skin against her feverish body more than she wanted to breathe.

"Let me show you the heights we can reach together. Let me bind your wrists..." he said softly.

That was a sobering sentence.

"No!" shot sharply from her lips.

*****

Luc saw some of the sexual abandon dissipate from her eyes, and he cursed his blunder. He was too eager. Too damned desperate for her. He was far better at moderating himself during sex—except when he was with this woman.

She'd grasped his wrists as if to keep him from reaching for his cravat.

"Easy. It's all right, *chère*. This is about losing ourselves in some sexual oblivion. I won't do anything unless you give me leave to do so. I won't force anything on you." He pulled a hand off the grass. She squeezed his wrist in protest. "It's all right..." he repeated, and caressed her cheek with the backs of his fingers, her quick breaths warming his hand. "I'm sorry some piece of *merde* hurt you. Destroyed your trust. But I'm not like him. I'm not like any man you've ever met." That bit of raw truth slipped out unintentionally.

There were certain events in one's life that seeped into the deepest crevices of your soul. And altered who you were. Forever.

He took her hand and brought it to his prick straining inside his breeches. "This is what you do to me. I want to fuck you. Make you come hard." He stared down at her lovely face, needing her more than he'd ever needed or wanted anything else. "No binding this time, you have my word." Yes, he said, *"this time."* Because he sensed that sooner or later, her desire and curiosity would get the better of her.

He waited, doing nothing more than mentally willing her to trust him and acquiesce.

Her lips were parted. Her breasts rose and fell with her quickened breaths. An eternity seemed to pass. Then her fingers wrapped around his hard shaft. And she squeezed. His eyes practically rolled back in his head. He immediately swelled in her hand to painful proportions.

Oh, that was definitely a yes.

"You're all mine..." he growled. Reaching under her gown, he yanked her *caleçons* off, tearing the drawers slightly with his urgency.

He had her legs spread in an instant. Kneeling between them, he cupped her sex under her skirts and began massaging her mound, coating his fingers with her juices. He watched her reactions. Lips parted. Eyes closed. Her breaths choppy.

Then he drove two fingers into her slick core.

She arched off the ground with a cry—the sultry sound making him seep some spunk. She was so wet, so soft. Exquisitely tight. Her snug clasp around his fingers was driving him out of his mind.

In the distance, he heard thunder rumble in the sky. He shoved thoughts of possible rain from his mind. He wasn't stopping now. He'd waited forever to have her again. Nothing was going to ruin this.

But Juliette had noticed the sound too. Her delicate brow furrowed as she looked up at the sky. Locating that sweet spot inside her vaginal wall, he curled his buried fingers and pressed, making her cry out for him again. She squirmed. Clearly, no one had ever showed her how to enjoy the intensity of it. The surprised, hungry daze in her eyes was as adorable as it was inflaming.

Both this time and the last.

Luc silenced the niggling questions that flitted through his mind about this woman and how extensive her sexual experience ought to be. He had her undivided attention now. And he couldn't wait to bring her into new, uncharted sexual territory.

"Focus, right here, *chère*..."

She writhed against the sensation, her breaths shallow and short, no longer caring about the sky or the second thunderclap overhead.

He eased the pressure and began lightly thumbing her engorged little clit, adding more familiar sensations so she wouldn't squirm away from the slow circular strokes he was plying to that sensitized spot inside her sheath.

Her squirming lessened instantly.

She began to moan, each delicious sound reverberating through him down to his aching sac. "Press against my hand. Don't try to pull away from it." But her eyes were shut, and she responded with more wiggling. More little moans.

"I…I can't… I'm going… I can't…" Each incoherent phrase was uttered on a pant.

He smiled, despite the state he was in. "The sensations are intense, aren't they?" He pressed a little harder on the textured spot inside her core, strengthening his strokes.

She squeezed her eyes shut with a whimper and nodded.

"Good. You'll get used to it. This is the level of intensity you can expect with me."

With his hand under her skirts, he couldn't see a damned thing. And while he had a break in the clouds overhead, he wanted to see her sex. He wanted to see her entire alluring form that right now was on fire for him. Grabbing the hem with his other hand, he impatiently tossed it back without missing a stroke inside her cunt and to her clit.

His hand glistened with her juices, and her hips still wiggled erratically. His mouth watered. "Juliette…fuck my hand. You can do it. Thrust into it."

But his beauty wasn't listening, too engulfed in the keen sensations inside her tight, sweet sex.

Keeping his strokes steady, he lowered his mouth onto her swollen clit and sucked.

Her hips shot straight up, a sharp mewl escaping her throat, the action allowing him to push his fingers against the overwrought spot harder, sending a sharp spike of sensation through her cunt. Just as he wanted.

Her gorgeous derrière fell back down onto the ground. Her legs were shaking. Her fingers were digging into the grass. And she was back to writhing. "Luc…*please*…"

"Oh, I'm going to please you. I'm not even close to being finished with you," he growled. Her taste in his mouth drove him wild. She tasted so good. The most delicious aphrodisiac.

Fuck. He had to have more.

"Do it again," he demanded. "Fuck my hand." This time, he dipped his head, hovering his mouth over her clit. Close enough for her to feel his breath. Without touching her. "Thrust your hips up. Put your pretty clit in my mouth. You know you want to."

She didn't hesitate, despite knowing the spike of sensation she'd get from his buried, busy fingers, and arched hard toward him. He rewarded her with a deep suck and another intensified stroke inside her sex before her hips fell back down. Hungrily, she began thrusting her hips at him again and again. He suckled and lapped at her clit each time she met his mouth.

He had her craving each new heightened shot of pleasure inside her sheath now, greedily thrusting for more. And he reveled in it, inebriated by her taste and the erotic sight of her undulating hips. *Dieu*, this was heaven and hell. His need was unbearable. He was so damned hard, he felt light-headed.

Another thunderclap resounded overhead. The clouds temporarily blotted out the moonlight casting them in darkness. He cursed. Rain was coming. Soon.

And he had to have her.

He gave her one last suck, then removed his buried fingers and all the sensations he'd been plying her with.

"No!" Her protest came instantly.

"We're not done," he assured. "Take these clothes off. I'm seeing all of you this time." With practiced haste, he began stripping away her clothing. She sat up to help, her urgency causing her fingers to fumble. He brushed them aside. "Let me." He pulled her gown up over her head and pressed her onto her back. But he stopped short of freeing her arms from the gown. Before she could react or even notice, he tossed off the remainder of her undergarments, then slowly slid her final article of clothing, her chemise, up her soft form to tangle with the gown around her arms.

The clouds above moved, casting moonbeams onto her beautiful body, naked except for her stockings and slippers, aglow in silver light. Her arms caught up in the voluminous material were over her head, making her breasts more pronounced. Her nipples were taut little berries, needing to be sucked.

Just then, she tried to pull her arms loose from her clothing. He stopped her. "Don't. Just stay like that."

He saw her objection cross her features, and before it came out of her mouth, he gently pressed her arms back onto the grass and, bending over her, kissed the sensitive spot under her ear. "You can easily pull your arms loose if you really wish to. There is no need for alarm. I didn't hurt you the last time when you allowed me to pin your wrists. I won't hurt you this time either." He cupped her breast and gave her nipple a sensuous tug. She gasped. "Trust me, Juliette…just as you did before." He gave her tender teat a pinch. This time, she arched as she sucked in a sharp breath. "Your gorgeous cunt needs my cock."

"Your cock needs me too," she shot back, delightfully saucy despite her pants.

He smiled. "Damn right it does. Let's end this sweet torment for both of us. Tell me you'll keep your arms just as they are the entire time." He dipped his head and sucked her nipple into his mouth. *Merde.* He was going to start begging if she didn't agree soon. And he'd never begged. Not once in his life. Not even when he was a boy did he beg for his father to stop.

Her moans were burning through his blood. He turned to her other nipple but stopped just before drawing it into his mouth. "I'm going to need an answer. I'm going to need to hear you say yes." He gave her nipple a luscious suck.

"Yes!" She arched off the grass. "I'll do it… I want you *now!*"

She was so frantic and frenzied. He was undone.

Opening his breeches, he lowered himself on top of her. He wedged the crown of his cock at her entrance. "I'm not going to be gentle," were the only words he could force out. His shaft never felt as heavy or as hard as it did when he was with this woman.

Her eyes were closed and her face turned. Her response was a soft whimper and a nod. He hooked her leg over his arm, angling her hips to his liking for the deepest possession, and drove into her. Feeding her his full length.

His groan eclipsed her cry. Pleasure slammed his senses. She was clenched around him so tightly, he could feel his prick pulse. And he had no idea if the throbbing was coming from her or him. He buried his face in her neck and fisted the grass near her head with his free hand, the pleasure so keen, he could barely contain the urge to let go— when self-control had never been a struggle during sex before.

Vaguely, he heard another distant clap of thunder. A bead of sweat rolled down his back just as the first drops of rain hit his skin—the cool droplets that only added to the dazzling sensations swamping his body. He withdrew slightly, then tunneled back in. Testing his restraint.

She squirmed under him and thrust her hips, trying to grind against him.

A delectable little plea for more.

He withdrew with a slow, muscle-melting drag, then thrust back in. Then again, and again, increasing his speed and intensity with each downstroke. "This is what you want, isn't it? My cock inside you." His voice was so rough, it didn't even sound like his own. She moaned her approval. Pressing his palms on the ground near her hip and head, he lifted his chest to watch the siren of his fantasies. To let the cool raindrops hit her skin. With her arms above her head, her breasts were lifted so gorgeously.

Rain began to fall on her face, on those lips he was so starved for, on her beautiful tits. Water drops rolling across her skin, dripping from her nipples. She looked so damned good. She felt so incredible. And she didn't object to the rainfall. She closed her eyes and surged up to meet his every fierce plunge. Matching his hunger with her own.

He fucked her for all he was worth, relentless rapid thrusts stroking her sex, his angle making contact with her clit each time. The moment he felt the fluttering inside her sheath, he knew she was about to come and braced himself for her release, pinning down her gown that was twisted around her arms.

She bucked beneath him and screamed his name, her snug sheath tightening around his shaft as waves of stunning little spasms coursed along his thrusting cock. He gritted his teeth, fighting to hold back his orgasm until the final contraction clenched his length.

Semen barreled down his cock. He jerked himself out, crushed her to him, groaning long and hard against her neck. Each spurt of come shot from his prick in a powerful rush. Ecstasy swirled up his spine, flooding his system. He held her tightly, still coming in mind-numbing jolts, until the final draining drop.

His heart pounded. His breathing labored. And his muscles had melted to nothing. *Jésus-Christ*, he'd had good sex before. His carnal encounters were always intense.

But sex with this woman took it to an entirely different level.

Euphoria hummed in his blood.

The rain had diminished to a fine mist, lightly teeming down on them. He lifted his head and looked down at her. Even in the faint light, he could see she was just as overcome by their encounter as he was.

He forced his lax muscles to move, shifting his body partially off her. He brushed away a strand of her dark hair from her face, then snagged the first article of clothing he could find, her *caleçons*, and wiped his semen off her belly and thigh before cleaning himself. Tossing it to the side, he pulled her arms free from the gown and chemise and gently massaged them.

"Are your arms sore?" he asked.

*****

Isabelle shook her head. Her breathing slow to return to normal, she struggled to find her voice. Her sex was still lightly pulsing after the deluge of erotic pleasures he'd flooded her with. Without a doubt, this man was dangerously gifted in the art of pleasure.

She was deeply sated, soaked from the rain. Utterly wrung out.

She wanted to curl into him and drift to sleep, regardless of the weather.

He nuzzled her neck. "I've ruined more of your clothing. I'm going to owe you an entire wardrobe soon." His breath was warm against her rain-soaked skin.

She didn't care about her clothing. And she couldn't seem to muster any remorse over the encounter she'd just had with Luc. It was incredible. Beyond exhilarating. Once again, she felt such deep bliss. Such deep peace.

And so vulnerable to him that slowly, steadily, panic was beginning, shredding away the rare sense of contentment.

He caressed her breast. She flinched, her nerve endings feeling raw and overwrought.

"Too sensitive still." He smiled. "You look so beautiful. Have you any idea how breathtaking you are?" The soft way he said that made her heart flutter. And for tender emotions to surface. Familiar emotions she'd once harbored for him.

And that frightened her more.

Desire and soft sentiments clouded one's judgment. She couldn't seem to rein in her hunger for this man. But any romantic feelings were out of the question.

Especially since she didn't know if she could trust him with the truth.

She'd seen what aristos were capable of, their unconscionable acts during the *Fronde*, the civil uprising that had devastated everyone outside the upper class and cost her family their theater. Their world. Then there were the aristos who'd been part of her life, like Leon de

Vittry, a longtime friend, practically from childhood, who'd managed to conceal the twisted evil he harbored inside—for years.

And Roch, whose initial benevolence had been so convincing, she'd placed not only herself but, more importantly, her son in harm's way.

Dipping his head, he pressed his warm lips against her throat and lightly drew her cool, wet skin into his hot mouth with a soft suck she felt all the way down to her toes.

Leave! screamed the voice of reason. Her treasonous body was already beginning to rebel against her. Again.

"I would love to stay here and have you again and again. *Dieu*, I've never found the rain more appealing than when you are in it."

Isabelle pushed firmly against his chest. "I have to go." She managed a smile. She needed to leave. To shore up her defenses that were far too easily decimated by this aristo.

His brows rose in surprise, but he sat up, allowing her to do the same. Disappointment was easily readable in his eyes.

"You don't have to leave," he said as she stood and began donning her drenched clothing.

"I do, I'm afraid. It's raining." She seemed to always be leaving him in this sodden state.

His smile returned. He looked up at her, still seated on the grass, his wet sculpted chest bare. His breeches open. And with the rain beginning to diminish, the clouds departing, the light of the moon illuminated that impressive part of his male anatomy he used with such masterful skill. She had to force her eyes to remain on the task at hand—dressing herself.

"A beautiful woman once told me the rain is good for you."

"Everything in moderation." Her wet fingers fumbled with her ties. *Damn it.*

He leaned back on one elbow, the moon casting shadows on the dips on his abdomen.

His smile grew to a grin. "I prefer excesses in certain things in life. Like sex. You. Sex with you."

He drew a smile from her, despite the urgency she felt to flee. She had the distinct impression he wasn't trying to be engaging—as most men did. This was simply his natural charm and seductiveness.

"I thank you, but we are soaking wet, and I'm in desperate need of a warm bath."

He opened his mouth.

"Alone," she quickly added, reading his next tempting offer.

With a soft laugh, he rose to his full height and sauntered over to her. His breeches were still open, the wet fabric molded against his thighs and narrow hips.

A devastating image to behold.

She quickly shot her gaze to the river, far less inciting to her senses. "Would you kindly assist me with this gown?"

"It would be my pleasure." He moved behind her. His fingers brushed against her back as he helped with her clothing. A tiny thrill flickered inside her.

His fingers brushed her skin again and again as he completed the task at hand. Forcing her to fight off salacious thoughts she needed to quell. And if his tantalizing touch wasn't enough, she couldn't get the image of his open breeches out of her mind. He was close enough that she could reach behind her and wrap her fingers around that glorious shaft of his. The urge was beyond fierce.

"There. All finished," he murmured in her ear.

She swallowed hard and brightened her face with a smile before turning to him. It took every bit of self-discipline not to ogle his body. Or his sex, now protruding from his breeches.

Proof that his desire had spiked, like hers, at their proximity.

She stepped back and grabbed his shirt off the ground. "You should dress." Firmly, she pressed it against him. The sooner he dressed, the sooner she might regain her faculties.

He cocked a brow, and his lips twitched in amusement. "Are you sure, Juliette?"

No. "Yes."

He waited what was probably a moment but felt more like an eternity, then pulled his shirt over his head and down his torso. The wet fabric immediately molded to his chest like a second skin. He tucked in the shirttails, and they stuck against his newly stiffened cock. Every inch of his erection was there for her viewing pleasure. A sudden bolt of raw desire shot through her blood.

He might as well have kept his shirt off for all that it concealed.

"All right, then! Let's be on our way, shall we?" she said, spinning away, then quickly marched toward the Vicomtesse d'Appel's château, her slippers making odd sucking sounds as they stuck to patches of mud along the way. She couldn't get away quickly enough. That shrewish wanton within her was now shrilling in protest against her departure. "We can enter the château through the kitchen and make our way to our respective rooms from the servants' stairs." It took exactly two more heartbeats to realize he wasn't by her side.

She turned around, one of her long curls smacking against her face and sticking to her cheek. Peeling it away, she saw, to her utter frustration, Luc was still in the same spot, his hands resting on his hips. And he didn't look as though he was going to move anytime soon.

CHAPTER NINE

Good Lord. Why on earth is it so difficult for this man to just follow?

Isabelle stalked back over to Luc, exasperated.

"Why are you always running away after sex?" he asked when she was close enough to hear. That question stopped her abruptly, several feet away. He didn't allow her to think of a response. He continued, "What are you so afraid of?"

"I'm not afraid."

"Then come to my rooms with me." He approached and stopped before her. "Allow me to show you more pleasures. I'll have dry clothes brought to my chambers and a hot bath to warm you." He ran his knuckles down her cheek. "Then I'll warm you on a soft bed, with some silk ties."

Hunger roiled through her in a hot wave.

She took a quick step back, unable to quell the quickening in her pulse.

"I wouldn't keep asking if I saw complete disinterest in your eyes," he said. "That's not what I see. It isn't that you're not interested or curious. Because, by your body's reactions, I see that you are. Who hurt you? It was a man—a member of the aristocracy. Isn't that so?"

*****

Luc waited. And watched. She didn't respond. Silently, she simply stared back at him, keeping her secrets.

He pressed on. "What did he do?" They were both drenched and in need of some dry clothing. In need of a bed. But damn it, he wanted to know, hating the notion that anyone would harm this woman in any way—because he knew, down to his marrow, that he was correct. Everything told him so.

Again, she offered no answer.

And for a moment, he thought she wouldn't respond at all. But then she shook her head. "Not just one."

That hit him like a blow to the gut.

"Who?" He'd see to it that he paid each one a visit. But her only response was to shake her head again. *Damn it.*

"Was one of the men Gabriel's father?"

"No," she said, quick to defend him. And that uncharacteristic possessive feeling rose back up in him.

"How many men?"

"Two."

"What happened?" He caressed her soft cheek again, his heart constricted by the tears he saw form in her eyes. "It's all right. Tell me, *chère.*"

"What happened is that I learned to be cautious with highborn men. I swore after surviving the clutches of both those men, I would remain in control of my life. No one would govern over me. And no one would ever be allowed to get close enough to me where they could harm Gabriel."

Anger scorched through his veins with an intensity he hadn't experienced in a long time—hating it with all his being that anyone would cause this woman distress. Gently, he curled his fingers under her chin and tilted her head up. "I understand your anger at the people who hurt you." More than she could ever imagine. He'd harbored rage for so long, it had become lodged in his soul. Taking years to master. "I told you before, I won't lie to you. I won't hurt you. I'm not like them. You can trust me," he urged.

She looked him straight in the eye, her spine stiff, her lovely smile gone. "All words I've heard before. I have a son. His welfare is not something I'll risk. Not for anything or anyone. Not even for my own wants and desires."

Once again, he marveled at her. His own mother hadn't been able to protect him. Her spirit had been broken under his father's tyranny. He'd often volunteered to take the abuse meant for her. Whatever this woman before him had endured, it hadn't broken her. Her defenses were in place for the sake of her son.

And he couldn't fault her for that—though he wished she'd tell him more. Trust him more.

In no way had he given up on learning all the many facets that made up Juliette Carre, but he wasn't about to demand answers. Nor interrogate her. That would only make her run from him or shut him out completely. And that was the opposite of what he wanted.

He leaned in and pressed a soft kiss against that sensitive spot under her ear. He loved her little gasp. "I'll earn your trust. And a kiss from your beautiful mouth, Juliette. But for now, let's get you to your rooms, dry clothes, and that warm bath you crave."

There were certain people he had no patience for. Juliette wasn't one of them. She was worth the trouble and the time it would take to gain her trust. To be a confidant. A friend and lover. The more he learned, the more he liked her. She was loving and loyal to her son. Full of endearing little peculiarities. Sensual and so deliciously sensitive to his touch.

Always full of surprises.

Moreover, this woman was an impressive actress. She might have fooled the others, but she hadn't fooled him.

Because he was certain of one thing.

Juliette Carre was no seasoned courtesan from Venice.

*****

"Surely you jest," Isabelle said, unable to hold back a soft laugh.

Luc's amusing take on *A Lady's Dilemma* was the reason for her mirth.

The popular novel was frequently discussed at all the salons around the city and published anonymously—as many of them were.

She'd walked all the way back to the outside doors leading to the kitchen, engrossed in the subject of Luc's favorite novels. And some of his least favorite. She was delighted to learn he was such an avid reader. Together, they strolled through the busy kitchen, their clothing ruined from the rain, as the staff raced about. Yet the rapid movements and chatter around them faded into the background as Luc's comments on the novel had her laughing again and again.

"No jest. It was awful," he insisted.

"Oh, come now," she said. "You can't tell me you didn't at least enjoy the merchant and his wife in that book? They offered a delightful bit of comic relief."

"The cat was my favorite character because he didn't speak. It was a relief from the tedious dialogue."

That drew another laugh from her. She was thoroughly enjoying this new side of him she'd just discovered. They'd reached the servants' staircase and made their way up to the next floor.

"What about the duc? He was gallant and brave. Did you care for him?"

"A fool," he said.

They stopped at the top of the stairwell, before the door leading to the corridor of the second floor. "Don't tell me—you liked his horse."

"Of course." He smiled. "*Because he didn't speak.*" She finished the sentence with him in unison and joined him in a laugh.

She watched as Luc opened the door and peeked out into the hallway. "It's empty. Which room is yours?"

"Third to your left."

He took her hand and laced his fingers with hers, then proceeded into the hallway. Holding his hand as she walked with him felt so natural. And right. As though he'd been hers for years.

In a way, she supposed, he had been.

The younger, naïve version of herself had been so in love with him, and though they'd never even spoken back then, being with him now felt wonderfully familiar. When she'd had many dreams of moments like these with him in the past. When everything else in her life was one new obstacle after another.

They stopped in front of her door. She turned to him and smiled, feeling a little awkward and far too aware of his proximity to her body and her bed beyond the door.

"Thank you for escorting me to my rooms."

He had the most infectious smile. The moment it appeared and reflected in his eyes, it broadened hers to a happy grin. He really was like a balm at times that seemed to coat all the disquiet and worry she harbored inside. And she relished that.

"Thank you for a delicious evening." He curled his fingers under her chin and tilted her head back.

She closed her eyes and braced herself for the thrill of his mouth against her skin. A sensation she couldn't get enough of. He didn't disappoint. The light brush of his lips up the side of her neck tantalized her nerve endings, sending ripples of pleasure quivering down to her core.

"I'm going to think of you as I lie in bed," he said in her ear. "I'm going to luxuriate in the memory of your body covered in raindrops, your arms over your head. I'm going to imagine you feverish for me. Ready to take my cock again." He gave her earlobe one of his sensuous little bites. It snatched her breath away. "…And how good it feels to be inside you." Her heart was already racing. She squeezed her eyes shut and put her hands behind her back to keep from reaching for him. Concerned that if she touched him, she might not let go.

"I hope you'll think of me too, Juliette. I hope you'll allow yourself to imagine what it would feel like to relinquish complete control to me during sex. To be bound for my pleasure…and yours." That was the last thing she'd allow herself to imagine.

A loud thud and a cry stopped the heated moment cold.

Isabelle snapped her eyes open and saw a servant down on the ground, folded linens scattered on the floor beside her. She realized instantly the servant had slipped on the wet wood. Water that had come from her soaked gown.

Isabelle dashed from her spot between Luc and her door to the woman on the ground. Falling to her knees, she quickly helped the servant to a sitting position. "Are you all right?"

"Yes, madame. I'm sorry to have concerned you," she said, distracted. Her gaze darted about at the linens she'd dropped, some of which were now wet. She was about Isabelle's age, slender. And distressed.

Being familiar with the duties of a servant, she felt instant compassion for the woman's predicament. She didn't know how sharp Eléonore d'Appel was with her staff for minor infractions, but something like this would have been harshly dealt with by Charles de Moutier in his household.

"Let me help you up. Then we'll attend to the linens," Isabelle said as she stood and reached out a hand to aid her to her feet.

The servant finally dragged her attention from the linens on the floor and met her gaze.

She let out a shriek.

It took Isabelle two heartbeats to change from surprise over her reaction—to recognition.

Her heart dropped to her stomach. This was no ordinary servant. She was a former servant of Luc's father. One Isabelle had worked with many years ago.

Delphine...

Seated on the floor, her mouth agape, Delphine looked at her as though she was seeing a ghost. "You're...you're...al—"

"Allow me to assist." Luc reached down and pulled Delphine to her feet before Isabelle could stop her words.

Delphine tore her gaze from Isabelle to Luc. She let out another shriek and jumped away from him—bumping into Isabelle.

Luc met Isabelle's gaze, bewildered over Delphine's behavior.

"M...my lord, my apologies," Delphine began her babbling to her former master's son. "It's...*you*." She snapped her head in Isabelle's direction. "And...And YOU."

Isabelle threw her arm around Delphine's shoulder. "I think she may have hit her head. She seems confused," she said to Luc. "I'll attend to her in my rooms. Good night." Then she whisked Delphine away before she could utter another word.

Matters just became more complicated.

*****

The moment Isabelle closed the door of her antechamber, she pressed a finger to Delphine's lips to silence her. Though her eyes were wide, she remained quiet as Isabelle listened to the sound of Luc's footsteps in the corridor diminish to nothing.

When she was sure Luc was gone, she removed her finger and, taking Delphine's hand, pulled her into her bedchamber, closing that door as well. They were far enough away from the hallway now to have a private conversation without being overheard.

She took a deep breath and let it out slowly. This wasn't going to be an easy conversation to have.

There was a very different woman standing before Delphine from the one she'd known years ago.

Isabelle Laurent was now a mother and a courtesan.

Delphine remained transfixed by her, her mouth agape. She reached out tentatively and touched Isabelle's cheek as if to see if she were real.

"Yes, Delphine, it's me, Isabelle." Clutching both her hands, she squeezed them and smiled.

Delphine's eyes filled with tears. "You're…you're *alive!*" She threw her arms around her and hugged her tightly, then pulled back to gaze at her once more, still in obvious astonishment. "H…How can that be?"

"I know this is all a shock. And the story is rather long and complicated. In short, Leon de Vittry, Baron de Lor—a man who pretended to be a friend to my father and my family for *years*—harbored a dark madness no one knew existed. He hurt many people. Murdered others. He tried to silence me when I'd discovered what he was about—his twisted plans. He set the servants' outbuilding I was in at the Moutier château ablaze. I managed to get out. I managed to save Virginie's baby." Isabelle's throat constricted. "But not Virginie." Those words were painful to utter, even after all these years. Images of that horrific day flashed in her mind—the inferno blazing high in the sky, as Gabriel, but a few weeks old, lay so quietly in her arms as if he too was too terrified, too in shock to cry. "The building was engulfed by fire so quickly. I couldn't find her in the smoke. I managed to locate Gabriel, and we ran from the building. But I couldn't go back for his mother. Moments after Gabriel and I got out, the roof collapsed." Her throat felt as raw now from emotion as it had that day when it was scorched by smoke and heat from the flames.

"You mean the body they found was the village girl who used to come begging for food?" Delphine asked, incredulous.

"Yes. I told her what time I'd be in the outbuilding that day. I always gave her something to eat. She was a widow with a baby and no family."

"What…What happened to the babe? Why did you not come back and tell us you were all right? Did you tell your sister? They buried the village girl's body thinking it was you."

"I knew they would. I simply couldn't let anyone know I was still alive. That would have placed people in danger, including my family and me. Leon wouldn't have stopped until I—and everyone who he believed knew the truth about him—was dead. I had to have him think he'd succeeded in killing me. As to Gabriel, that adorable baby boy had absolutely no one. He was, at that moment, as alone in the world as I. I've raised him myself. He's my son." Her heart swelled at the mere mention of the most important person in her world. "We have a new life, and I have a new identity."

She'd refused to change the name Virginie had given her son.

It was her way to honor her.

"Oh my…" Delphine yanked a handkerchief out of her bodice and dabbed her tears, then blew her nose. "That's so very touching…" Another loud blow of her nose. "So, so touching what you did for that babe." She composed herself after a loud sniffle and a final blow into her handkerchief. "This is all so incredible." She looked down.

"I know. It is quite a lot to digest." Oh, there was so much more. But some things didn't need to be retold.

Delphine's head shot up as if she'd just recalled something important. "I saw you with Monsieur de Moutier! Isabelle, he was all you ever spoke of… And you were just…well, rather he was…" Her cheeks reddened. "I mean, you were both…"

Delphine had a habit of babbling when she became excited. Or nervous. And she was more often than not in one state or the other. Isabelle sat on the edge of the bed and pulled her friend down beside her. "I believe you're searching for in flagrante delicto," she supplied. There wasn't going to be any way around this. Delphine was about to learn just what her new life entailed.

Delphine blinked, staring back at her.

"In an amorous situation," she said, trying again.

"Oh yes! *That!*" Her gaze swept over her from head to foot, puzzlement entering her hazel eyes. "And why are you dressed this way, in all this finery? And why is it all wet?"

Delphine had been the only person at the Moutier château who hadn't laughed at her girlhood affinity for Luc. Or mocked her dream of winning the heart of Charles de Moutier's youngest son, when at the time, she was nothing more than one of their servants.

As sweet and exuberant as Delphine was, she was also at times forgetful. Isabelle wanted to remind her that once, finery was what she always wore—albeit not in wet ruins like the gown she presently had on, but instead said, "My new identity is Juliette Carre."

Delphine shot to her feet. *"The courtesan?"*

Calmly, Isabelle pulled her back down to a sitting position on the bed. "Yes." Her heart was starting to pound. Her stomach began to tighten back into a knot—the usual feelings that barraged her since the day she fled from the fire. The wonderful lassitude that Luc had inspired was clearly beginning to dissipate. Besides Nicole, this was the first person who knew the old Isabelle.

But this wasn't Nicole, who was urbane about such matters.

She wasn't sure of the possible condemnation she was about to receive. She couldn't help but think of her sister and wonder what Sabine would say about the acts Isabelle was willing to perform for funds.

"You…you…copulate with these men?" Delphine's voice had dropped to almost a whisper, though they were alone in the room. Her eyes couldn't be open any wider.

"Those of my choosing, yes." She shifted, feeling more and more disquieted.

"I've heard the aristos talk about you. About Juliette Carre. You are highly desired."

"Yes, that is rather a must in being a courtesan."

Delphine let out a shriek—making Isabelle jump—then laughed and clapped her hands. "Why, that's wonderful!"

"Wonderful?" Not exactly the word she would have used.

"Yes! You have all these powerful aristos fawning all over you. Do you know they argue with each other over who is most deserving of you?"

At least she was performing this courtesan role correctly.

Delphine didn't grant her time to reply. "Do they adorn you with expensive gifts and funds?"

She shifted at the mention of payment for her services. "I wouldn't do this if it wasn't providing funds for Gabriel and me. I intend to make certain that his future is secure. He will want for nothing. And he will not be vulnerable to poverty and know the horror of it. Nor be at the whims of wealthy men. That is why I need you to keep my secret. Isabelle Laurent is dead. Do I have your word?"

"Of course!" Delphine was back on her feet and pulled Isabelle to hers. She moved behind her and started undoing her gown. "You needn't worry about my saying a thing. I'm so glad you're alive and well, *Madame Carre*. And I'm glad you are able to take some of these aristos' wealth for yourself. You deserve it. And so does your son. Now, let's get you out of this wet gown before you catch your death."

Isabelle's pulse began to relax, as did her stomach, as she realized just how much it had meant to her to have her friend's acceptance of her new persona. She was glad she'd found Delphine again. Another ally. Someone she could trust in a world full of disloyalty and malicious schemes. She heard loud sniffling behind her. Turning her head, she saw that Delphine was weeping again.

"Delphine, what is the matter?"

"You...you were with Luc de Moutier. How incredible is that? You made your dream come true."

No, I haven't, she wanted to say, ignoring the twinge in her heart. Not in the way she used to dream about them together—where she had his love and his body.

But she had gotten one thing right in her old romantic fantasies. Being with Luc *was* incredible—her beautiful aristo outcast.

Once again, he'd taken her with her arms above her head, not allowing her to touch him.

And she was determined to learn why. She wanted—no, *needed*—to know each and every one of his hidden secrets before she could ever entrust her and her son's safety in his hands. Before she could ever reveal her own secrets. She couldn't allow herself to be fooled again.

Bad enough she'd made three reckless wishes once.

She wouldn't allow herself to make another major mistake after placing her trust in Vittry and Roch. Both still gave her nightmares.

Her wet gown flopped to the floor. She stepped out of it, standing in her wet undergarments. Delphine picked up her gown.

"Oh, you don't have to do that." Isabelle grabbed hold of the skirts.

Delphine gently swatted her hands away. "Nonsense. I want to. And it would look rather odd having you do it." She smiled and walked away and draped it over one of the chairs. "I'll attend to it, and it will be as good as new."

"Thank you... Delphine, I have some questions I must ask you, if you don't mind."

Her friend approached. "Of course. What would you like to ask?"

"Why do you suppose Luc didn't recognize you just now? You'd been employed at his father's château long before I arrived."

Delphine shrugged. "I only saw him there once. Briefly. He's forgotten, I suppose."

"Just once in all those years? He never returned home during my employment there, but I thought perhaps prior—"

"Everyone knows he and his father didn't much care for each other."

"Yes, I'd heard that many times. But *why*? What happened between them?"

Delphine looked uneasy, shifting her weight from one foot to the other. "I don't know if any of it is true..."

Isabelle's stomach began to tighten again. Her friend's sudden unease was palpable.

"What is it, Delphine? Tell me."

"I heard, mind you, people can often exaggerate—especially since the late marquis was so despised by his staff..."

"Out with it, please." The suspense was becoming excruciating.

"I heard that the late marquis would drag his son into his *cabinet* and...well..."

"Well, *what?*"

"There was much screaming. Not the angry sort. The sort associated with pain being inflicted. Some say they'd hear heavy lashings—always for minor infractions. Always just to his youngest son. That is, until the boy stopped screaming even when the lashing sounds could be heard. I was told he learned not to cry out anymore. Also, he'd often take beatings to spare his mother."

A wave of revulsion oozed into her stomach. *Dear God...* She didn't want to believe any of this had actually happened to Luc. That this was nothing more than venomous talk among servants, most of whom had despised Charles de Moutier. But she'd seen firsthand how heartless he was with his staff.

And, yet...his own son? Could he truly have misused him so barbarously? She couldn't imagine inflicting any abuse on Gabriel. Ever.

She was sickened, furious, heartbroken for Luc, and incredulous all at once. Yet, of all the talk among the staff about the late marquis, if all this happened—repeatedly—why had no one ever mentioned or hinted at the abuse?

"Why didn't you tell me this before?"

"I didn't know. I'd only learned about it from the cook one night when he was into his cups. I heard the same thing from another member of the staff several months later. This happened after you left."

"How...How long did they say this went on?"

"Until his mother, the marquise, fell ill and died and he was big enough to fight back. He began engaging in fisticuffs in taverns. And in duels. I'd heard that one day, he came to physical blows with his father. Pummeled him well, then left to join the King's navy."

Was this the reason for the sadness she'd seen in his eyes years ago? Could this be connected to the falling out Luc had had with his brother?

Though she'd learned that Luc certainly wasn't the only man who indulged in erotic bondage, she couldn't deny it had overwhelming appeal to her now. Especially after tonight. She was sorely tempted to surrender to the restraints he wanted to use on her.

But was his attraction to it only about enhancing sexual play?

Or had his body been so mistreated that he didn't want it touched?

She had to know, from his lips.

*****

"Luc!" Hearing his name called out behind him stopped Luc in his tracks. He sighed and placed his hands on his hips. It was late afternoon. Eléonore's salon was beginning, and he was anxious to see Juliette.

He knew he'd find her there.

Given her love of literature, she was sure to join in on an intellectual gathering where people came together to discuss and debate philosophy, religion, politics, books, and grammar. Where she was regularly invited, not for her vocation but for her extensive knowledge and wit.

Salons had never been of interest to him in the past. Mostly because he didn't like those in attendance at the more prestigious ones where the aristocracy were in greater number than the literati. But last night, he'd thoroughly enjoyed debating with her about books.

Hell, he'd enjoyed every moment in her company.

His bright and beautiful faux courtesan.

A woman hiding behind a façade named Juliette Carre who didn't even realize just how intensely sensual she really was. How sensuous she was during sex. He loved expanding her sexual horizon, more than he could ever admit. She was pure delight at every turn.

And a mystery he couldn't wait to unravel.

Marc caught up to him. He clamped a hand onto Luc's shoulder good-naturedly with a smile. Once again, Luc had to tamp down the wave of revulsion that roiled through him, every fiber of his being screaming for him to knock the hand away.

"Where are you off to, my friend?" Marc asked.

Dropping his hands from his hips, Luc jerked his chin in the direction of the double white doors at the end of the long window-lined corridor and stepped back casually, breaking Marc's touch. "To Eléonore's salon."

"I'll walk with you. I have something to tell you. You are going to thank me." He seemed pleased with himself.

"Oh?" Luc slowed down his brisk pace so he wouldn't have to listen to Marc's ribbing about the reason for his rush. He'd run right into Marc last night on his way back to his rooms—soaking wet, sporting what must have been a big, foolish grin on his face—fresh from his encounter with Juliette.

It took Marc half a moment to decipher what he'd been up to. And with whom.

"What am I going to thank you about?"

"Well, since the only people you seem to be charming here are Juliette Carre and your female dinner partners, I thought to help you out by having a lengthy talk with the Marquis de Nort about you."

"Why would that make me thank you?" Damn it. It was going to take forever to get to the salon at the leisurely pace Marc walked.

"Because the man has no fewer than four daughters. Two of marriageable age."

"So?"

His brows shot up. "I thought you were looking for a bride. He's interested in speaking to you. If you don't challenge him to a duel or offend him—and you happen to find one of his *attractive* daughters to your liking, who, by the way, don't talk about their footwear—you could possibly begin contract negotiations to wed one of them."

This subject didn't hold the same appeal it once had.

"I appreciate your efforts, Marc. Truly, I do. Perhaps another time."

Marc stopped dead in his tracks. "You jest."

Luc kept walking. "No, I don't."

His friend raced up to him. "You're going to snub the man?"

"No. I'll speak to him. Just not about marrying one of his *attractive daughters who don't talk about footwear.*"

Marc laughed and shook his head. "All right. I understand what's happening here. And I can't blame you for your lack of interest in Nort's daughters. Not when you have Juliette Carre. Bloody hell, there isn't a man present who doesn't envy you at the moment for your success with her."

"Success? She's not a contest. She's a woman." An extraordinary one, full of delightful surprises, with whom he was having spine-melting sex.

"One you're too silent about. Come now, Luc. Provide details. Something. Anything. Have some mercy. I doubt she'll ever favor me as she favors you. Allow me to live the experience through you. How good is the sex?"

"How good is the sex with Eléonore?"

"Stop trying to change the subject. Or I may decide I don't like you anymore." Marc's smile nullified the threat and made Luc laugh.

"The crowd of people who don't like me is rather large. You'll only melt into a sea of faces." They stopped before the doors at the end of the hallway with Marc chuckling.

"My friend, you can't afford to lose me. I might be the only man in the entire realm who still tolerates you."

Luc smiled. "I think you're correct on that score." Though, now that he was back among his peers, that notion didn't at all bother him.

Just as he was about to put his hand on the door latch, Marc said, "At least tell me… How does she like your particular sexual propensity?"

He knew he was asking about sexual bondage. Images of last night, Juliette's trembling body glistening with raindrops, her arms above her head tangled in her gown as he fingered her to the edge of release, flitted through his mind. His cock stiffened in an instant. Mentally, he cursed. Walking into the salon with a stiff prick was the last thing he wanted to do.

He turned to Marc, his friend's expression etched with anticipation of his next utterance. "I haven't really taken her that way."

Marc blinked. Surprise, then shock crossed his features.

Luc sighed. He needed a moment to cool his blood so he could walk into the room and not look like a rutting roué, but the subject of taking Juliette bound wasn't likely to help in that regard.

He should have simply kept his bloody mouth shut.

"What on earth does that mean? *Not really taken her that way?*"

"It means exactly what I said. I haven't had her bound. She said no."

Marc's mouth fell slightly agape, and his eyes were so wide, it was almost comical. "And...And you didn't...*walk away*?"

"No."

Marc's mouth opened wider. Then he threw back his head with a loud guffaw. "Oh, this is too incredible..." More laughter. It took him long, annoying moments before he sobered up, adding, "This is unbelievable. *You?* You *didn't*..." That prattle was followed by some snickering.

Well, he'd needed a cooling effect, and Marc had provided just enough irritation to take the edge off.

"What are you carrying on about?"

"You *never* take a woman who's not willing to be bound when fucked."

"Clearly, that's not true. There's Juliette." If truth be told, no one was more surprised than he at the fact that he'd had her twice—two utterly delicious carnal encounters—with the full knowledge that she wasn't truly restrained during any of it.

He couldn't tell Marc that that wasn't even the most unimaginable part; she'd touched his back, and he hadn't even noticed.

Marc shook his head, still snickering. "For you to forgo a sexual practice you enjoy immensely, an integral part of how you fuck, she must be incredible."

"She most definitely is."

"It must be her vast carnal experience."

"She most definitely isn't."

Marc frowned, confused. "She isn't what?"

"Vastly experienced in sex."

"What are you talking about? She's a courtesan."

"She may be a courtesan. She may be highly sought out. But she's not as experienced as is being suggested about her."

"But...you said she was incredible during sex."

"She is beyond incredible during sex. The best I've ever had, in fact. But she also has only a basic experience in the carnal arts—a fact you'll *not* tell anyone," Luc warned.

"Of course not. I'd never betray your confidence, but..." Marc rubbed the back of his neck. "*Dieu,* Luc, I can't believe this is true. How can she be practically a sexual novice? All the talk about her... And her family... She comes from a long line of Venetian courtesans. Not to mention she's a friend of Nicole de Grammont."

"Madame de Grammont has many friends. That means nothing. I'm certain not every woman she socializes with has an advanced knowledge of sex. You've mentioned Juliette hasn't been in Paris long, but from what I've gathered, the Marquis de Cambry is the only other man here who's had her. As to her background, I don't know a thing about her family or where she comes from, but I will. There's nothing I'm looking forward to more than to learn every detail about her." Except, perhaps, getting her alone in a bedchamber, near some silk or satin ties.

And permission to kiss her mouth to hot oblivion and back.

He couldn't take the smile off his face. The mere thought of her did that to him. She made him feel joyful while setting his body on fire at the same time. And he loved that combination—more than he could ever admit. His every nerve ending was already humming in anticipation of seeing her. He wasn't going to barrage her with the questions he had about her. He knew she wouldn't be receptive to that. He'd take it slowly, relishing the notion of getting to know more about her a little at a time. It was like savoring the unwrapping of an unexpected present, anxious about what surprise awaited him.

Luc opened the door and walked in. Eléonore was the first woman he spotted among the various groups clustered about the room, and he forced his legs in her direction first, rather than look for Juliette, wanting to bid his hostess a good day and afford her every regard she was due. Her invitation to her weeklong gathering, regardless of any amorous arrangements she and Marc might have made, was sincerely appreciated.

Eléonore smiled at his and Marc's approach. Luc made light chatter with her and the group of mostly ladies surrounding her, making certain not to get too involved in their debate of the Spanish classics. Not when he'd rather be in the far corner of the room where he'd located Juliette, dressed in a mouthwatering, gold-colored gown. As usual, Vannod was there. And she had him and other men and women in her group captivated by whatever commentary she was making.

So much for hoping his unruly cock would behave. Not even seeing the way Vannod leaned into her from time to time could redirect his heated thoughts. Marc dove into a discussion of one of the sonnets by the late Spaniard Miguel de Cervantes and moved to stand next to Eléonore, immediately enthralling her and the group. Allowing Luc a gracious exit.

And he couldn't be more grateful to Marc, knowing he'd done so purposely to help him.

Luc approached Juliette's group, intending to keep the promise he'd made to her the other day not to cause her trouble by purposely rattling or verbally sparring with Vannod—or the idiot brothers Auguste and Frédéric he just noticed were also in her company.

"Marquis de Fontenay, how good to see you." Juliette smiled. It made his heart race. "Please join us, won't you?" Luc relaxed his shoulders, not realizing he'd tensed as he approached.

He had an easy rapport with women. A casual approach to any affair. And it wasn't as though lust was foreign to him. Hell, he loved the feeling of desire coursing through his blood when a woman he wanted was near. But this woman and his attraction to her was on another, entirely new level of intensity altogether. What this woman could do to him with a glance, a smile, a word was fiercely unraveling. Worse, he was beginning to have those odd tender feelings Isabelle alone had inspired with her journals.

And he had no idea what to do with them.

Or how to tame this interest he had in Juliette.

All he knew for certain was that he wanted more of her. *Dieu*, he wanted to take her to his private rooms and have his fill of her. After just two carnal encounters, he had a fear deep down inside he'd never had before. That he might not ever get enough of her.

She, and not Isabelle, had taken over his thoughts and erotic dreams.

He greeted the ladies, followed by the men in the group, before turning his full attention to Juliette, ignoring the icy reception he got from his male peers.

"We're discussing various Italian poets. Do you read Italian poetry?" Juliette asked him. Her genial regard of him immediately caused the palpable tension in the group to diminish. Though the men were still glaring at him with disdain, the women's expressions were of curiosity at his response to Juliette's query.

He positioned himself near friendly faces, standing between the Comtesse de Gigot and her daughter, Béatrix.

"I've read some." It was an understatement. His education had been his childhood escape. Something he deeply treasured. His time with books—as many as he could devour—and with his tutor, the kindly Monsieur Henri, were the happiest moments of his boyhood.

Rebuilding the costly libraries in his châteaus that were plundered while in the Crown's possession had been a priority during the renovations. Though most things confiscated had been returned, he estimated he was still missing at least eight hundred volumes. And that pained him.

"Italian poetry?" Vannod scoffed. "A barbarian like you?" He practically spit the words at him.

Luc knew he was referring to his former habit of engaging in fisticuffs and duels. His time privateering probably fit into that category in Vannod's opinion as well. He could have congratulated Vannod for demonstrating a rare instance of courage—since Vannod bloody well knew he'd dueled over lesser offenses and that his skill with weapons far exceeded Vannod's—a man who'd never once sullied his lily-white hands in the service of his country. But instead, he chose more gracious words. "Yes, even a *barbarian like me* has been known to enjoy a sonnet or two."

"Do tell, which Italian poets have you read?" the Comtesse de Gigot asked, the older woman looking up at him genuinely curious.

"Well, let me see. There's one that stands out to me. A poetess named Isabelle," he said, smiling at Juliette. Oddly, he thought he saw her flinch. "Or rather *Isabella di Morra*," Luc pronounced in Italian. "To be more accurate."

"Oh!" The comtesse clapped her hands with excitement. "I have read her work! Such a tragic figure. And such scandal, if what her brothers accused her of was true. Have you read any of her sonnets, Monsieur le Duc?" she asked Vannod.

Luc felt a measure of satisfaction at the renewed glare he got from Vannod. Here the poor duc was trying so hard to impress Juliette—his sac likely blue by now as he still waited on her. And Luc knew the answer, given the look in Vannod's eyes, before he was forced to admit to it.

"No," Vannod said, quietly miffed.

"What about you, Madame Carre?" the comtesse asked. "I know her work was popular in Venice. Since you're from there, have you had occasion to read her sonnets?"

Merde. He'd forgotten that part. He too had heard about the late poetess's popularity in Venice. Though Luc was more than a little skeptical of Juliette's Venetian origins, he would never have purposely placed her in jeopardy of having any deceptions come to light.

Especially before this lot.

"Yes. I've read her work." Juliette's friendly smile faded slightly. "It's somber and rather heartbreaking."

Luc was impressed. She did know of the poetess and was familiar with her sonnets. Just when he was beginning to believe she might not be from Venice at all... The mystery of the woman before him only continued to grow and puzzle him.

"I gather you don't care for her sonnets, then?" he couldn't help but ask, genuinely interested in Juliette's opinion.

"It isn't that I don't care for them. I think she was extraordinarily talented. I'm happy her sonnets didn't die with her. But it's hard on the heart to read them. There's a great deal of sadness and feelings of isolation in them."

Those were the very reasons he'd identified with the sonnets—so different from the writings of another woman named Isabelle. One who was in no way morose. Whose journals came to life. Written in a distinct, engaging style he'd come to adore, it depicted a woman full of passion and wit. Bright, brave, astute, and compassionate. A positive force he'd have loved to have known in his life.

And likely the reason he was so drawn to Juliette, who had the same qualities.

"Tragic? Scandal? How was Isabella di Morra tragic and scandalous?" The questions came from the comtesse's daughter, Béatrix.

"She was the daughter of a baron, I believe," Luc responded. "Her father abandoned his children, and her cruel brothers kept her mostly isolated in a castle where she wrote. Her only friends were a neighboring couple—a handsome former soldier and poet named Diego and his wife. When her brothers suspected Isabella of an affair with Diego, they murdered their sister, her tutor, and later Diego too."

The comtesse nodded. "Yes. That's right."

"Oh my... How sad and scandalous." That came from Béatrix. The other men, Vannod, and the buffoon brothers looked annoyed and bored. Clearly, intellectual gatherings such as these were something they considered tedious. He suspected Juliette was their only motivation for being in attendance.

And she was the only one whose reaction Luc cared about.

He met her gaze. In those big beautiful dark eyes, a smile shone back at him that matched the one on her lips. She seemed pleased, and delighted that he knew the story behind the poetess.

"And you, sir, what do you think of Isabella di Morra's work?" she asked him. "Do you care for it?"

"I do. I think there's a little bit of Isabella di Morra in all of us."

Her smile didn't slip, but there was a brief flash of sadness in her eyes before she gave him a small nod, telling him she very much liked and agreed with his response. *Dieu*, his affinity for this woman was far deeper than any other he'd ever bedded. For her sake, and hers alone, he'd just admitted to having similar emotions to the Italian poetess. Something he'd never have done for anyone before. The way she was looking at him with appreciation and pleasure left him feeling as if warm, sweet nectar had just melted over his insides.

"Not me," Frédéric said, his obnoxious voice piercing the moment. "I can achieve gaiety easily with but some good wine and the company of a beautiful woman." He smiled at Juliette. She didn't even glance his way. Her gaze was still affixed to Luc.

And it made him happy.

"If you like stories with damsels and castles, Monsieur de Fontenay, you really should read *The Princesses' Adventures*, if you haven't already," the comtesse said. "Everyone is talking about them and wondering who the brilliant author is behind the anonymous volumes. The third novel is due out very soon, I suspect. I cannot wait to see what the sisters will do with their princes next."

Reluctantly, Luc dragged his gaze away from Juliette. "*Princesses' Adventures* with sisters?"

"Yes. Have you read them?" the older woman asked.

"No. I haven't."

"Well, you should. The princesses are twins and get into quite the intrigue and trouble just to win the hearts of their princes."

That sounded so very much like the books Isabelle mentioned in her journals. The plot was identical. His interest was piqued. "Do you have a copy of the first volume, Comtesse?"

"I do." Juliette spoke up. "I'd be delighted to lend it to you."

CHAPTER TEN

Luc slammed the door shut to Isabelle's private rooms.

A half smile tilted his mouth.

She knew what was coming, and there wasn't a fiber in her being that could muster the will to stop it. The aching need had been building at the salon and as they made their way to her rooms.

Only this time, it included a longing in her heart, so similar to the way she'd felt all those years ago.

When she couldn't allow him to matter that way to her again.

Realistically, any permanent romantic relationship between them was laughable, whether she divulged her secrets or not. She wasn't her sister. She'd chosen a different path. *Let's face it. You are hardly marriage material for a man in the aristocracy.* Not even the most celebrated courtesan of all, Nicole, had managed to do for herself what she was able to accomplish for her children—marry into nobility. And just when Isabelle was beginning to think she had an understanding of this aristo, he unbalanced her yet again. It took a certain depth and sensitivity to appreciate the heartbreaking words of the late Italian poetess Isabella di Morra.

It took someone who'd known pain.

It wrenched her heart to think of what he might have suffered at the hands of his father. She wanted the pain erased. His and hers.

Even if it was for but a brief interlude.

The fire this man ignited made the entire world melt away.

He hoisted her up off her feet, bracketing her legs around his hips, and shoved her up against the wall. "Beautiful Juliette, you need to be fucked…by *me*. You need *my* cock," he murmured against her neck before pressing his lips to it.

There were so many reasons she should simply hand him a copy of her first *The Princesses' Adventures* volume as she'd promised and stop this amorous encounter. Pain-soaked discussions needed to be had. But as his mouth trailed across her skin, sending ripples of pleasure shimmering down her neck and through her system, she shoved away all reason. For now.

Instead, her response to his blunt comments was to arch into the hard bulge in his breeches pressing so deliciously against her sex. He rolled his hips, plying her clit with the most perfect stroke. Her gasp mingled with his groan.

She fisted the shoulders of his doublet.

Any final thoughts of resisting dissolved into the ether.

She'd read once that strength came from knowing one's weakness. And hers was Luc de Moutier. He always had been. He didn't know how many times thoughts of him had bolstered her—during those dark days with Roch, isolated and afraid, with a young child.

Her Fair Prince…

She wanted—*needed*—him. With shocking desperation.

She kissed a path up his neck and drew on his warm skin. His low groan was a heady rush.

"Not here. On your bed," she heard him say as he pulled her away from the wall and walked toward her bedchamber, her body wrapped around him. Pressed snugly against his solid shaft, each stride he took caused a scintillating friction against her already soaked sex. By the time he'd reached the foot of her bed, she was starting to squirm.

He dropped her onto it. She landed on her bottom with a small bounce, her heart now thudding harder in her chest.

Anticipation roared through her senses.

Riveted, she watched him strip off his doublet and drop it to the floor, his smoldering eyes wreaking havoc on her. He untied his cravat next and tossed that on the bed beside her.

The one article of clothing that was weighted with sexual suggestion. And a multitude of questions.

Opening his breeches, he pulled out his shirttails and discarded his shirt onto the floor in one fluid motion of utter mouthwatering masculine grace.

He wrapped his hand around his erection protruding from his breeches and squeezed. "You have no idea what you do to me."

Oh, she had some definite inkling.

Especially if it was anything resembling the carnal chaos rioting inside her.

That cravat on the bed was tempting her sorely—the pull growing stronger with each sexual encounter they shared. Luc had been affecting her most of her life. And she *needed* to touch him. Needed for him to accept—no, *want*—her touch.

She rose from the bed and took his hand. "Allow me." There was curiosity in his beautiful light green eyes as he let her turn him around and seat him on the edge of the bed. She lowered herself onto her knees and pulled off one boot, followed by the other. She sat back on her heels to admire the man before her.

Far more exquisite than any statue or painting of any Greek god she'd ever seen.

She couldn't fathom what she'd done so right in life—when she'd chosen all the wrong paths, made all the wrong wishes—to deserve these experiences with *this* man. The very man of so many long-held dreams.

Regardless of what the future had in store, she had this moment.

Right now.

A rare chance for her to make some exquisite memories to help squeeze out all the bad ones that replayed in her mind again and again. It had been years now since the silence stopped being quiet.

He watched her intently for her next move. She didn't hesitate. Reaching out with both hands, she placed them against his solid chest. His skin was warm, inviting. And she could feel the quickened beats of his heart, racing her own. She grazed her hands downward, relishing every delicious dip and ripple of his abdomen, his muscles flexing and tightening under her fingertips. She wasn't sure if he'd stop her at any moment, more than a little surprised and elated over the fact that she was touching him at all.

And for the first time ever.

Perhaps she was mistaken about him in this? Perhaps Delphine was wrong about the stories of his childhood too? And that thought elated her further still.

Reaching his generous sex, she wrapped her fingers around its base, then stroked him to the tip and back down. Briefly, he closed his eyes, his Adam's apple bobbing as he swallowed. Oral pleasure was something Roch had demanded often. Until this day, this moment, she'd considered the act distasteful, had hated every minute she'd been made to gratify Roch this way. But with Luc, it was different.

She wanted him in her mouth.

She *wanted* to taste him. To be the one bestowing pleasure the way he'd bestowed it on her with mind-melting skill.

Ignoring the soft feelings clustering in her chest, she dipped her head and swirled her tongue slowly around the crest of his cock. At his low groan, moisture pooled between her legs.

His fingers tangled in her hair. Fearing he'd stop her, she plunged him deeply into her mouth and began strong, slow sucks, her tongue stroking the sensitive underside of his prick with each plunge and drag. To her delight, it drove him to distraction. His head fell back, and he hissed out an expletive between clenched teeth. Being in command of his pleasure was a heady rush. She kept to a steady pace, savoring him. Sucking him. Teasing him with her tongue. Relishing the low groan that rumbled from his chest.

Without missing a stroke, she slipped an arm around his waist, pressing her palm and splaying her fingers against his strong back.

Suddenly, she was staring at him at arm's length—no longer touching him at all. It took three beats of her rapid heart to realize he'd yanked her away, his grip firmly on her shoulders.

Her eyes widened in surprise. Clearly she'd been mistaken in her perception that things were going well. "I'm sorry. I've done something to displease you."

He dragged in a ragged breath, then expelled it slowly. "No." He cupped her face and pulled her near until his forehead touched hers. "You haven't done a thing to displease me. You are incredible. More than any man deserves. Including me." His soft voice, his tender words, all wrapped around her heart and squeezed. "*Dieu*, I need to be inside you," he whispered, then trailed his mouth along her jaw to her earlobe and gave it a sensuous bite.

Her sex clenched hungrily.

He reached beside him and picked up his cravat, his other hand still cradling her face. "I want you to trust me. Allow me, Juliette…" She knew exactly what he was asking of her.

She shook her head. "I want to be able to touch you." Voicing her own wants during sex was still so new. And she liked it. He was the first man with whom she'd felt able to do so. She'd stopped acting like a courtesan with him practically from the start. Truth be told, she'd stopped acting like a courtesan—period. He was the only lover she wanted at the moment. An arrangement based on mutual desire. Without financial transaction. And though she hadn't lost sight of her responsibilities of providing for her son, she had to see this matter between them through.

Because she wanted—no, *deserved*—to experience more of the way he made her feel.

Because there might be the chance, no matter how small, to see Sabine again.

A small smile formed on his lips. "You have touched me—more than you know."

Again she was aflood with emotion. And it frightened her. She couldn't allow it to lower her defenses. No matter how he affected her, she'd remain in control of those emotions.

She pulled back, out of his hold on her cheek. Needing some distance. Needing to reassert control over her heart—even if that meant sabotaging this glorious moment. "You want to bind me and take me, but this…" She pulled the cravat from his hand. "This isn't just a sex game to you, is it?" His body changed immediately. Every beautiful muscle before her tightened. And the softness that was in his eyes clouded.

She didn't let that stop her. "Perhaps it's a way of maintaining a level of detachment. It's a way to keep anyone from touching you during carnal encounters—both physically and emotionally, isn't it?"

He shot to his feet with a curse, making her jerk back in surprise. He stood several feet away from her now, his hands on his hips, head down as he stared at the floor. Isabelle rose and braced herself, unsure what was about to happen next. Was that infamous temper of his about to make its appearance at last? It was best she saw it now, in its full glory, when she could summon protection. Where she could get to safety. Before she'd even attempt to convince him to take her to her sister, she needed to know what she and Gabriel could face trapped on a ship with him for months.

"Tell me, Luc," she pressed.

He lifted his head and stared back at her. She couldn't read his eyes or the expression on his face.

"We've already discussed this. I enjoy it. I enjoy fucking a woman who is willing to indulge in it."

"There's more to it than you're saying."

He blew out an exasperated breath. "*Merde.* Juliette, perhaps I do like a certain level of detachment during sex. Is that any different from you not allowing a man to kiss you?"

She didn't so much as flinch when she responded firmly, "Yes. There is a difference. You don't have my...*vocation.* My time, body, passion are all for sale." *Except with you.* "I've chosen to withhold one thing that is not for purchase—that's permitted only when I choose and with whom I choose."

An utterly beguiling smile slowly formed on his lips, and he tilted his head, a lock of dark blond hair falling against his brow.

"I'd like to be chosen," he said with far too much devilish charm.

Damn him. How does he do that? How did he combine the most perfect smile with the most alluring timbre in his voice? She felt a smile tugging at the corners of her mouth, a little exasperated at how easily he disarmed her.

Focus, Isabelle. You might as well continue what you've just started. Even if at the moment she wanted to run into his arms and forget their pasts.

"We're not talking about kisses now. We're talking about you." She tried admonishing him, but she was having a difficult time not reacting to that infectious smile.

"I prefer to talk about kissing you."

"I'm sure you do."

"What are you afraid of? That if I tie you to that bed, I'll fuck and kiss you mindless?"

God...yes. There was definitely that.

He'd already more than proved he knew how to drive her to sexual delirium.

"Because if that is what you're worried about," he continued, "you have good cause for concern. I've already planned how I'm going to bind you, take you, and the first thousand deep kisses—when you give me leave, of course."

A feral need slammed into her senses, practically shifting the ground beneath her feet. Without a doubt, Lord Seductive was in top form, at his finest, and he was causing her to melt. Soon she'd be a helpless puddle on the floor.

She took a step back, needing more space and cleared her throat. "You and I live by a different standard of rules. Your gender and your class give you superiority. You can do practically anything you want to whomever you want with impunity. My rules are there for my safety and that of my son. I avoid vulnerability at all cost whenever I can."

He gave a nod. "I understand. Gabriel is at the center of all your decisions. And I admire how you love and care for your son. But I wish you to understand this: the rules I live by, I've broken for no one—*but you*. I don't engage in sex with a woman who doesn't share the same sexual proclivity I do. I don't dance, but that first night, I danced—just to meet you. I wouldn't normally come to a sojourn like this. I prefer to limit the time I spend with many of those in attendance here. And again, I came here to spend time with *you*." He raked a hand through his hair, then softly laughed and shook his head. "Believe it or not, I'm much more aloof than this. And if you want honesty, and if you think erotic bondage makes you uncomfortable, know that *this*—whatever this is between us—is making me uncomfortable because I'm so bloody well drawn to you. Fascinated by you. Attracted to you—if this vastly uncomfortable erection doesn't make it obvious. And if that weren't enough, today at the salon in front of Vannod, Prost, and Meslon, I admitted to something I've never admitted before."

"What is that?" Her words slipped past her lips on a soft breath. She was a little unbalanced anew. He was chipping away at her safeguards with his every utterance.

"That I have emotions—though I think I'm safe in assuming they're still very much skeptical about that," he said, still sporting one of his knee-weakening smiles. "*Ma belle*, we have a bed and the desire between us that's intense enough to burn this château to the ground. You don't want me to tie you up. You're not ready for that—fine. To hell with it. Forget it. But don't stop. Don't pull away."

She glanced over at the bed, then back to him. That was the crux of the matter. There was actually a part of her that didn't want to simply forget it. That wanted to give in to his request and surrender to him completely. "I want to trust you, Luc…"

For so many reasons.

He studied her silently for a moment. "What did those two men do to you? What did they do to make you so leery of men in my class?"

Normally, she wouldn't answer that. And though it shouldn't matter what he thought, she wanted him to understand she had good reason to fear. "One of them tried to...kill me. He was someone I'd known a long time." Nightmares of being in a burning building with Gabriel and Virginie still plagued her.

"*Merde!*" The word exploded from his mouth in shock and anger. He walked up to her and grasped her shoulders. "*Jésus-Christ*, Juliette, tell me who he is, and I'll make sure—"

Isabelle shook her head and cut off his words. "He's dead. And so is my late husband, who also pretended to possess decency but harbored none."

"Husband," he said. "You were once married, then?"

It was just easier to call Roch "husband" than to delve into the details of his grand ugly ruse and what a fool she'd been ever to believe a word he'd uttered. She was about to lie about her "marriage," but then, "Yes and no," left her lips. And again, she'd no idea why she wanted to tell him anything about her past at all.

His fingers captured her chin so she couldn't look away. Those light green eyes held her gaze, as though he were trying to read all the thoughts in her mind. "What does that mean?"

"It means I was once a great fool. I was led to believe we were properly wed. It was all a sham. An unlawful union. And a living hell. The man who wed us was no real priest at all." She could feel her insides beginning to quake with fury. At Roch.

And herself.

"Was this in Venice?"

Mentally, she flinched. She'd told many lies about her fictitious past. But lying to Luc felt different. Each time it felt...harder. Wrong.

And so she said, "No." Giving him the truth without negating her tale about her Venetian roots.

"And this man *wasn't* Gabriel's father?"

"No." That was all she was prepared to say on the subject of her son's sire, because she guarded everything about her precious little boy—fiercely.

Luc drew her into his arms and pressed his cheek against her hair. "I'm sorry someone tried to harm you. That they put you through any misery at all."

His arms around her felt warm and strong enough to stave off the rest of the world. So good. Too good. The sort of feeling a woman could easily grow used to. Crave, even. And for the very first time since leaving home all those years ago, she felt almost…*safe*. Her arms wound around him of their own volition.

He pulled back, breaking their embrace, and curled his fingers under her chin once more. "I understand why you would be cautious. Those men should have been trustworthy. They violated that trust profoundly and perversely. Your trust matters to me, Juliette. Tell me, what about *me* frightens you into not bestowing it?"

How to begin to answer that?

"I don't have the luxury of placing my complete trust in any aristo. I have Gabriel to think about… You are also bigger, stronger, and with a self-admitted temper." *And thus far, you've been too incredible to be true…*

Too close to the girlhood dreams I've had of you to be believed.

"You think my temper might flare when I have you bound and could hurt you." It was a statement. Not a question.

"It has crossed my mind."

He raked a hand through his hair, then returned his hands to his hips. "I'm certain the rumors don't help. The duels I used to fight. My killing my cousin."

Isabelle's heart lurched. "You…you…*w-what?*"

"Oh, you haven't heard about that? That's surprising. I would have thought Vannod and the others would have delighted in telling you all about it. Or at least their twisted version of the truth."

A slow cold fear began to congeal in her blood.

FOOL!

This was the reason she shouldn't—couldn't—lower her guard with this man. Or any other. He almost had her convinced.

She took another step back.

He looked down and softly swore again. When he met her gaze again, it appeared to be unguarded. Without artifice. "You're looking at me as though you think I'm going to lunge at you and slay you where you stand. I've told you before—and it is the absolute truth— I've never harmed a woman. There is no woman who has ever suffered at my hand. I challenge you to find one. Or even a rumor of one. There isn't anything you can say or do, bound or unbound, that would make me harm you, Juliette."

"Even if…" Her words croaked out her throat, barely audible. She swallowed and tried again. "Even if I were to accept that you'd never harm a woman, what about someone like Gabriel? Given your animosity toward men, how long before you see him as no longer a boy but an adversary? How long would someone like him be safe near you?"

Even though Luc had no idea she was contemplating a ship voyage with him, and even though men didn't normally interact with their paramour's child—especially one they hadn't sired, Luc's accidental meeting of Gabriel notwithstanding—her fears for her son's safety were valid. Particularly when the man in question struck fear into a number of his peers.

He was seasoned in dueling, a master with weapons.

Her little boy grew a little every day.

He nodded. "That is a fair question. I would expect no less from a devoted mother. The answer is, he would *never* be at risk from me, no matter his age, for two reasons: one, he matters deeply to you. I would never wound you, whether we continue this affair or not. The second is, I'm no longer the man I once was. Yes, there was a time I was full of fury. It took little to unleash it. If that were still the case, I would have slammed my fist in Vannod's arrogant jaw by now. Being in the King's navy changed me—for the better. I was the commander of a number of ships. There were several hundred men under my command. Their lives depended on me and my orders—a sobering responsibility I *never* took lightly. They trusted me in every battle we fought and we fought hard together. I had their respect, and they had mine. Then I was arrested and wrongly accused of treason—like my brother and Charles—and brought back to Paris. Being held prisoner in a cell, faced with the possibility of an execution before a cheering crowd, with nothing to do with my time but think caused me to reflect on my life. I'd been stripped of my officer's commission in the navy. My family labeled traitors. My service to my King and country tarnished by false charges. And I decided that if by some miracle I walked out of that prison alive and to return to society, I would not allow myself to become the man I once was around my peers—brash and volatile. Not ever again. I chose to abandon the anger I'd harbored and seek and embrace inner peace. I continue to choose it now." A small smile formed on his lips. "And I appreciate and relish all exquisite moments in my life, like those I've had with you, because I choose to experience pleasure over ire."

*****

What the hell are you doing? Luc was astounded at himself. Things he'd never told anyone, would never tell anyone, were falling out of his mouth. Yet, he couldn't seem to stem the words.

Had Isabelle's effect on him somehow changed him around women?

Or was he only going to behave this way around those who reminded him of her? It was obvious that part of Juliette wanted to run from the room. His idiotic slip about his cousin was the root cause. He was used to people fearing him. During his combustible youth, he'd even liked it.

It kept people at bay.

But the thought of any woman, much less *this* woman, fearing him, fearing for her son's safety because of him, didn't just bother him.

It gutted him.

Her beautiful dark eyes gazed at him. Her breathing, though soft, had quickened as she stood there, clearly contemplating what to do.

He reached out and cupped her cheek. She lurched at his touch.

"Easy," he said softly, cradling her face in his palm. "We're not strangers. We've been alone together before. We enjoyed each other's company, and the carnal pleasures we've shared have been nothing short of spine melting. You're safe with me. Your son has nothing to fear from me. And before you ask about the incident with my cousin, I will tell you that he died because of our duel. He was a good deal older than me. It was many years ago. Before the navy. His wound festered for a few days before he succumbed to his injury, and he damned well deserved to die. In fact, I've no doubt he's burning in hell."

He hadn't talked about Bastien de Bellac—ever. He shouldn't have spoken of him now. Just the mention of Bellac was causing myriad emotions to gather inside him.

"What on earth does that mean, Luc? Why would you be filled with so much anger? Why would your cousin deserve to die?"

He mentally chastised himself. *This is why you keep your mouth shut. Offering information only leads to questions.* And though this maddening affinity he had for her was strong, there were some things he couldn't—wouldn't—talk about.

In fact, he could feel his throat tightening, his body silencing the horror, as the sounds of Bellac's chilling laughter mingling with Charles's echoed in his brain.

Memories he'd learned to crush through the years.

Luc shoved them from his thoughts through force of will now and pulled Juliette into his arms once more. Burying his face in her hair, he took a moment to let the sweet scent of lavender from her soft tresses infuse his senses. Her body stiffened against him, and he knew he had to give her some sort of response. Briefly, he squeezed his eyes shut and steeled himself, determined to keep those unwanted images confined to that black hole deep inside his chest that had been created long ago.

It stored every horrible moment of his life.

Luc pulled back and looked into her eyes. "I suppose it's a situation much as you've described. He was someone who should have possessed decency but harbored none. He was evil." *And so was that fucking demon who sired me.*

"What did your cousin do?" Her tone was so gentle and soft. He was amazed that even so much as a sliver of him wanted to tell her the ugly truth. He easily quashed that infinitesimal urge.

He shook his head. "It doesn't matter. The duel was fair. He lost. He's gone."

Good riddance…

"Duels are illegal. Yet you were able to fight in so many without ever being arrested before the treason charges," she stated, underscoring her previous comment about the impunity men in the noble class had when it came to breaking the law.

A mirthless smile formed on his face. "Charles's influence was able to keep me from arrest then." The piece of *merde* was quick to act— not for Luc's sake, but out of fear Charles's twisted little secrets might be brought to light by the state of Luc's body.

She gazed at him intently. He couldn't read her expression. He had no idea what she was thinking or what she was about to say next, but an uneasy feeling came over him. There was something in the way she was looking at him…

"Did your father harm you when you were a boy, Luc?" Her question was but a whisper, but it might as well have been screamed out.

He stepped back.

His ears instantly started ringing.

"Why the hell would you say that?" The words shot out his mouth, uncensored.

He was instantly furious at himself for not simply denying it by saying, *No!*

But no one had ever asked him that question. Not even his own brother. Charles's treatment of Jules had been benevolent, hiding his malevolent nature from Luc's older brother.

And so had Luc. He'd never told Jules about the extent of their father's mistreatment of him.

No one knew, except Charles and Bellac.

And they were both dead.

"I'm sorry. You have such contempt when you mention your father. Always refer to him by his Christian name. I thought perhaps…" Her words trailed off.

And he was grateful.

He simply couldn't talk about this. Couldn't dwell on how accurately this woman had deciphered the truth.

Merde. He'd already said too much. Given away too much. This subject was excruciating. Especially when her words were tinged with anguish for him. When there was the hint of tears in her eyes.

To see it tightened his very entrails.

In certain ways, she was a kindred spirit, having had her own experiences with human heinousness.

And he hated that for her.

He hated it as much as having the hatred for Charles and Bellac surging inside him—when he no longer allowed himself to feel this level of loathing.

He couldn't remember the last time he'd felt like this.

Luc turned away from her and stalked over to his clothing on the floor. She gasped as he snatched up his shirt. He didn't need to look back at her. He already knew what she was reacting to.

His back.

In all its mangled glory.

Fucking beautiful, isn't it? The surface of his back was covered in long scars and raised welts.

He had his usual explanation ready. The lie he'd retold multiple times of being in battle, being captured by pirates and lashed. Lord knows he'd fought enough of them in the West Indies to know firsthand how depraved they were.

Just like the two dead members of his family.

It wasn't difficult to convince past mistresses that the tale was true.

The lightest stroke brushed against his back. He practically jumped a foot and spun around to find Juliette right behind him, surprise etched on her face. Her hand was raised slightly, having just touched him.

"What the hell are you doing?" *Damn it.* He hadn't even heard her approach.

"You." She swallowed as her surprise turned back to anguish. "You couldn't feel my touch, could you?"

Fuck. Fuck. *FUCK.*

CHAPTER ELEVEN

"Clearly, that's not the case," Luc countered, fighting down the bile threatening his throat.

"I was touching you for several moments, with no reaction."

"DON'T DO THAT! I don't like my back touched!" He was all but bellowing at her. *Merde. Calm down!*

His heart was pounding. His breathing came short and sharp. He hadn't been this overwrought in years. And he wanted none of this on display before Juliette.

Before anyone.

Luc sucked in a breath and expelled it slowly, beating back the raw emotions rioting inside him. "There are areas on my back I cannot feel. And other areas I can. I have some permanent injury from my capture by cutthroats, all right?" Well, at least that was calmer.

Not bloody much.

She remained silent and composed in the face of his discomposure. But the expression on her face told him she didn't believe his pirate tale. She damn well saw through his lie.

Though he wasn't easily rattled, that shook him to the core.

She shook him to the core.

She was able to see through the veil he concealed all things he wanted hidden. A veil others never saw through.

He needed to leave the room. Now.

He intended to throw on the shirt fisted in his hand. But instead, his legs lowered him to the floor of their own accord. Knees bent, his back resting against the bed, he settled his arms on his knees, tilted his head back, and closed his eyes. Then he did the one thing that always brought him peace.

He envisioned his beloved sea.

A calm ocean. Rolling waves. Its soothing sound. Its cool mist against his face. The gentle rocking of his ship.

There was nothing on earth like it. Nothing as soul quenching—except when there was perfect passion between him and a woman. The likes of which he had with one confounding, dark-eyed, dark-haired female who was twisting him inside out.

A rustling sound followed by a light press against his side and hip made him open his eyes. He found Juliette sitting beside him on the floor, her legs straight out before her, pink slippers peeking out from her skirts.

There was a certain warmth in her eyes, and she gave him a smile. It was one of those smiles of hers that always seeped into his chest and melted a part of him deep inside he didn't know could even be affected.

"You're going to wrinkle your gown," he told her softly.

"In case your memory is faulty, sir, I am in the habit of doing far worse to my gowns in your presence."

That pulled a smile out of him.

"You've looked gorgeous each and every time," he said, with the utmost sincerity.

"So have you."

He could feel his agitation begin to quell. It was incredible, really. But just being here on the floor with her like this was helping to beat back his demons. It was surprising. A relief. His heart and breathing were returning to normal.

"I'm sorry, Juliette. I shouldn't have raised my voice. I dislike any sensation against my back."

"I'm sorry you had to sustain such injury." Her voice lowered to all but a whisper when she said, "You didn't deserve it…"

His chest tightened. Another jolt of tender emotions lanced through him. Another comment no one had ever uttered to him before. He couldn't count the number of times his father and Bellac had told him he'd deserved every lash on his back.

Every blow to his ribs.

Every beating he'd endured.

He turned away from her, leaned his head back against the mattress, and closed his eyes. There was no way for him to respond to that. A knot had just formed in his throat and made it impossible.

He heard her move, and the press of her body was now gone, much to his regret.

Her hand landed gently on his arm.

He opened his eyes to find her on her knees at his side. She sat back on her heels. There was no mistaking it. Compassion shone in those big dark brown eyes of hers. Not the sort of look he got from, well...*anyone.* He'd never inspired compassion in anyone before. Except in a dead woman's writings in her journals.

Jésus-Christ. He had truly found Isabelle's incarnate. Women he'd had in his life were genial. Accommodating. Desirous of his company—for the purposes of sex. But none of them ever looked at him the way this woman was looking at him. Gazing deeply. Seeing beyond the sexual surface.

And he was astounded that he hadn't walked out of the room under such scrutiny.

"Though you're not obliged to tell me anything, Luc, I'd very much like to hear about what happened to your...in your past."

He laughed scoffingly.

"Are you afraid I'd betray your confidence?"

"I'm not concerned about you betraying my confidence." He trusted her, even though she didn't trust him. "I've told you before. I don't give a damn what people think of me."

"Then tell me about your past."

"It's the last thing you want to hear."

"Let me be the judge of that. It's the reason for the bondage, isn't it?"

He sighed and raked a hand through his hair. "Partly." It was his way of changing the horror of bondage—when he'd been tied up and beaten—into something purely pleasurable. Passionate. Wonderful. "I also like it. Very much. And you will too."

"Luc—"

He sat forward and slipped a hand behind her neck, her soft curls tickling his hand. "No more..." he said, eager to push away the ugliness of this subject. Wanting instead to revel in the woman before him. "Let me remind you how good it is between us." Luc pulled her closer, and thankfully, she didn't pull away.

If only this was no more than good sex between them. But there was more. Much more. And he didn't know how to grapple with it. Or sort any of it out.

He resorted to what he knew. What was familiar. What made sense.

He dipped his head, then grazed his mouth along her jaw to her neck, stopping at that sensitive spot just under her ear, and lightly sucked her warm skin between his lips.

She gasped, a sensuous little sound that sent a bolt of lust through him. That delicious fire that always smoldered between them instantly ignited into flames. He could feel her pulse racing beneath his mouth. He could hear the quickened breaths from her lips.

Dieu, those lips…

The ones he was starved for. Having them around his cock earlier had all but caused his eyes to roll back in his head. It was time he reminded her that she'd trusted him with her sweet form before, and that he knew how to give her what she needed and wanted.

And he needed and wanted *her.*

He rose to his feet, then swept her up into his arms and deposited her back on the bed.

His heart pounded for an entirely different reason now. His body clamored to possess her. But he forced himself to stop and wait.

"Unless you object, we are going to proceed with what we started—without bindings." He searched for any sign of reluctance.

There was none. Just a warm, willing woman, the only one he couldn't seem to get enough of, awaiting his next carnal move. "No objection." She said it softly, yet it roared through his system.

Luc lowered himself beside her, and without wasting a moment, he stripped off her clothing with practiced haste, sucking, licking, kissing her exposed skin, wanting to taste every inch of her. Loving her every little mewl and moan she couldn't contain. Loving how eager she was to help.

Loving how her fingers fumbled because she was so flustered and famished for him. Her bodice was open. The gorgeous breasts before him made his mouth water. But it wasn't enough. He wanted her naked. Her skin against his. Nothing between them.

He was back on his feet at the end of the bed, yanking off the last of her clothing, then his own, tossing them to the floor in a heap.

He gripped his cock and squeezed, trying to combat the pressure inside his prick. The head of his sex was already wet with pre-come and his sac was so full. Yet he couldn't drink in her beauty enough. Lying on her back, she watched him with those fathomless eyes. Her cascade of dark curls was puddled around her head, her perfect tits rose and fell with her rapid breaths, and she had the most adorable little curve to her belly.

He grabbed her ankles and yanked her to the end of the bed. She squeaked in surprise, finding her legs apart and suddenly dangling over the edge. Leaning over her, he braced a hand against the mattress near her head. With his other hand, he stroked his fingers along the folds of her wet sex.

Her eyes fluttered shut. She tilted her chin up, her lips parting with a soft gasp. She was so damned sensual. He forced himself to mute the urgency thundering inside his veins as he scored his fingers along her slick folds again and again, teasing her clit with the occasional light pinch just to make her moan for him. Her hips jerking upward toward him, begging for more. Her little bud was so swollen with need, glistening with her juices.

And he wanted her wetter, wilder.

She wiggled, urging him on. "Luc…"

He liked how breathless his name sounded.

"Not yet…" He rewarded her little clit with a stronger pinch before driving his fingers deeply into her core.

She cried out, her sex soaking his hand further. Just as he wanted. He homed in on that ultrasensitive spot inside her vaginal wall, curled his fingers, and began to ply it with short, sharp strokes. Making her buck and fist the sheets. Her sweet tight sex seeped more moisture onto his hand.

He told her how good she felt around his fingers. How beautiful she looked. Soothed her with words while heightening her hunger with his hand. And he told her how hard she'd come for him.

Then he withdrew his wet fingers and was immediately met with dismay—a sound of frustration shot out of her throat. He smiled and massaged her sex again, instantly easing her agitation. "I promise, we are far from done." Spreading her essence, he coated every pink inch of her pretty cunt watching as she closed her eyes and bit her lip. Then he pressed a slick finger firmly against her puckered little hole. Her eyes flew open, and this time, she jerked back in sharp surprise. He knew right there and then, that sweet puckered hole was untried and untouched by previous lovers.

And that only reinforced his suspicions about her.

He gripped her hips, pulling her bottom back to the edge of the bed once more.

"Tell me you want me." His breathing quickening by the moment. Her wet sex beckoning him fiercely.

"I want you." No hesitation. Just a breathless affirmation. It spiked his fever.

"I'm burying my cock deep inside you. You're going to take all of me, aren't you?"

She nodded, unable to speak. He flipped her onto her belly, availing himself of her pert derrière for his viewing pleasure. Her hips rested on the edge of the bed. She rose up on her elbows, looking back at him with a critical eye. He tightened his hold on her hips and wedged his cock at the opening of her warm, wet cunt.

"You trust me to give you pleasure, don't you, Juliette? Because you know I know what your body needs." *Jésus-Christ.* Her moist heat cinched around the crown of his cock was driving him mad.

She looked away and hung her head, her breaths as rapid and raw as his. He could feel her body trembling between his hands. And though it was soft and shaky, he heard distinctly, "Yes..." Then the most luscious, "*Please...*"

He drove the whole length of his stone-hard prick into her. Pleasure slammed into his system. His head fell back briefly as he steadied himself against the stunning squeeze of her tight, wet sheath. She had him throbbing in an instant.

The pulsing sensation was exquisite.

The tall bed just the right height for his body. And this dark-eyed beauty, this woman who had him so undone, was perfect. His perfect match.

He dragged his cock almost completely out, then rammed back in deep, his groan blending with her moan. He drove into her again and again with solid, rapid thrusts, stroking her soft snug sex with his heavy cock. Basking in the flood of sensations radiating along his length. His hand still slick with her juices, he moved his finger back to her puckered hole and pressed, breaching it just with the tip as she jerked with a mewl.

And clenched her inner muscles, dragging a raw growl of bliss from his lips.

"Just relax. *Trust me…*" he managed to say between pants, and sank in to his second knuckle, then the third. He could feel his own plunging cock on the opposite side of her inner flesh. This was without a doubt a new experience for her, the way she was tightening around his finger, tightening around his cock, clenching her vaginal walls and squirming that beautiful bottom, not knowing how to absorb the novel sensations flooding through her sex.

She was so snug. The pleasure was almost too much to bear. He rode her for all he was worth. Working her with his finger. Lost to the maelstrom of stunning sensations rushing through him.

*****

Isabelle trembled. Every fiber of her being quaked. And the bud between her legs throbbed so hard, she could barely stand it. She couldn't move. Couldn't speak. Fisting the counterpane between her fingers in a white-knuckle grip, she could only muster feral sounds the likes of which she'd never heard from her mouth before. The sensations were overwhelming. Her sex had never felt so full. The new sensations were a deluge on her senses, currents of powerful pleasure flooding her body. And she had no desire to maintain any control. No desire to do anything other than surrender to the only man who could drive her to delirium. She couldn't muster shock or objection over what he was doing. She was simply suspended in euphoria, reveling in his every thrust, gluttonous for more. Pressing her forehead into the mattress, she braced herself for the climax that was rushing at her, feeling her release mountaining inside her, growing bigger. Faster. Stronger by the moment.

Ecstasy slammed into her, reverberating through every nerve ending in her body, knocking a scream from her lungs. Her inner muscles wildly contracted around his length, his finger.

Luc.

Curling her toes, she rode through the orgasm, through every fierce clench and release of her vaginal walls. And each glorious thrust he gave her. When the final flutter inside her sex faded, he reared, yanking out his finger and cock. His hard body came down on hers, pressing her into the mattress. He crushed her to him and buried his face in her neck. He groaned, long and deep, as warm semen coated her back. His body jerked, then shuddered until he'd drained himself dry.

She felt flush from the top of her head to her toes. Her muscles were so lax and heavy, her body so spent, she didn't want to move. She remained slumped against the mattress as he pressed a kiss to her shoulder and rose. Immediately she mourned the loss of his body. The divine feel of his skin against her.

Once again, a warm, serene, contentment blanketed her.

It was a feeling like no other.

And there was just one reason for it: this one man she'd dreamed about most of her life. She closed her eyes and listened to the sound of pouring water and soft splashes as he washed himself. She knew she should join him. With her torso on the bed, her feet on the floor, she should at the very least change positions from this rather awkward one.

Isabelle pressed her palms down on the bed, intending to push herself up off the mattress and force herself to stand, when a cloth swiped against her back. She gasped at the coolness against her heated skin.

Suddenly, there was a dip in the mattress near her shoulder and his handsome face appeared inches from hers as he leaned over her, bracing a palm against the bed. The small smile on his lips reflected in his eyes. There wasn't a single male in the entire realm more beautiful than Luc de Moutier.

Or more shattered as a young man.

The pirate story was a lie. They both knew who'd brutalized his back, but the devastated look in his eyes when she'd pursued the subject shredded her heart, made her hurt for him, and stopped her from pressing him further.

"I'm sorry the water isn't warmer," he said, washing her back with the wet cloth in slow, wonderful strokes. This thing he did, this endearing act after every carnal encounter, only melted her insides more. She wanted to put her faith in him. She wanted to blurt out the truth of who she was. And that frightened her as much as the flood of romantic feelings she was having toward him.

The protective wall around her was getting harder and harder to fortify.

He walked away, then returned and stroked the wet cloth over her sex. The soft, cool sensation along her flesh was so exquisite, it drew a soft moan from her throat. He tossed the cloth away and scooped her up in his arms. Sinking one knee into the mattress, then the other, he lowered her onto the bed, stretching out beside her on his side, propping himself up on his elbow.

He gave her one of his stomach-fluttering smiles.

And to her utter mortification, face-to-face with him now, she blushed. Thoughts of what he'd just done to her swirled in her mind.

He slipped his fingers under her chin. "Are you blushing, Juliette?" His smile had grown, and he looked almost...proud at himself for producing the effect.

That only heated her cheeks more. She rolled onto her side and slipped her hands under her cheek and took in her Lord Seductive. "No," she said. A blatant falsehood. And she returned his smile, unable to stop herself. *Who could resist a smile as infectious as his?*

He chuckled and gently ran his knuckles down her cheek. "I'm not used to seeing it and I like it."

"I'm not used to a man like you."

He cocked a brow, amusement shining in his eyes. "What exactly is a man like me?"

She propped herself up on her elbow, matching his pose. "Are you shamelessly looking for compliments on your carnal skills again?" she teased.

He affected a look of utter innocence. "Of course not. I simply want to make certain I hold true to the title you gave me—*Lord Seductive*." He grinned.

She laughed, adoring his banter.

Adoring him.

Careful...her heart warned. She'd built this very man into a fairy-tale prince over the years. Male perfection. Above all others. He was even one of the main characters—one of the princes—in her novels, *The Princesses' Adventures*. She had to hold on to her heart. She couldn't afford to make any missteps. Once revealed, something couldn't be unrevealed.

"Rest assured, you still hold that title, sir."

He slumped back into the pillows. "Thank God," he stated dramatically, then propped himself back on his elbow, her laughter blending with his.

He leaned in and pressed a kiss near the corner of her mouth, so enticingly near. Once again, she was struck by an overpowering urge to turn her face and meld her lips with his. Dying for a taste.

When he pulled back, he said ever so softly, "You want to know my secrets. But you have some of your own, don't you?" Oh, she wasn't ready to respond to that. She held her tongue. "Tell me something else about you. Something I don't know."

"You know everything you need to know." *At least for now.*

"What about the man who sired your son? Was he a good man?"

"I am not comfortable talking about Gabriel."

"All right, then, what about your rules about bedding married men? Why avoid them?"

"It's less complicated that way. No angry wives."

"Did your husband have an angry wife when he led you to believe you were lawfully married?"

Isabelle looked away, contemplating whether to answer, then offered, "Yes. She threw Gabriel and me out of our home in the middle of the night before his body was even cold. I'd only learned she existed a week prior to his death." Roch's deceit and what he'd put her through, thinking she was his wife, still caused a knot of cold anger to form in her belly and the last thing she wanted was for Roch to destroy this moment of quiet bliss. "That is all I'm prepared to say," she added, "until I learn more about you."

He studied her quietly for a moment but said nothing.

And she knew that he was contemplating how many more of his secrets he was willing to divulge. Her heart began to pound, willing him to talk, and afraid of what he might say.

"It's been years since the King reinstated your fortune, title, and lands. Where have you been during your absence?" she prompted.

"Renovating my châteaus that had fallen into disrepair while in the hands of the Crown. I've done extensive changes, wanting each one to be very much my own—both the interior and exterior."

She didn't need him to say that he wanted to wipe away all traces of his father. She could easily discern that without any words. "Are they done? I'd like to see them sometime."

He smiled. "I'd love to show you." He became quiet again, then he brushed a lock of her hair from her brow. Again she waited, giving him time to speak. Sensing his desire to say more.

He looked away and trailed a hand down her arm with a soft caress. "You asked me a question earlier. About my back…and Charles."

Her stomach clenched.

"I told you I'd never lie to you, Juliette. But I did. It isn't something I do, except when it comes to…this subject." He still didn't make eye contact. He simply trailed his fingers back up her arm, delighting her skin with his touch—all while holding her in suspended anticipation.

Anxiously, fearfully, awaiting his next words.

He swallowed as though there was an obstruction in his throat keeping him from speaking. "In truth… Charles was a monster. And so was my cousin Bellac. My back is their handiwork…dating back to a time when I was too young to fight back."

She'd worked for Charles de Moutier, knew him to be vile, but didn't know anyone was capable of this kind of depravity against their own little boy.

With invited assistance.

The terror Luc must have felt at their hands was unfathomable.

Hearing it felt like a fresh blow to her chest. She was winded as horrifying images of Luc as a young boy being abused assailed her thoughts. She blinked back the tears, wanting to be strong for him. Wanting to hold him.

She took in a quiet breath to settle her emotions before she asked, "Was that the cousin who died from injuries in the duel with you?"

Still no eye contact. But he gave her a nod.

"That's why you challenged him to a duel, then? Because he…he…" She couldn't get the words out. They were soaked in such malevolence. And she feared voicing them would only hurt him more.

He met her gaze. He'd schooled his features, hiding the anguish she knew was behind his beautiful eyes. He shook his head.

Surprising her.

No? What on earth did that mean?

Luc sat up and scrubbed his palms up his face, stopping over his eyes. Almost as though he was trying to blot out scenes from the nightmare he'd endured. "That's enough, Juliette. I've already told you more than anyone else."

She was overcome and undone by him. A tear slipped out of her eye, and she quickly swiped it away before he saw. She wanted to weep, but that would serve only her.

Not him.

She sat up too, just as he rose from the bed. He began to dress. Her heart dropped. She didn't want him to leave upset.

Or to leave at all.

She leaped off the bed, threw on her chemise, and approached him. He already had on his breeches and boots and had just donned his shirt when she touched his arm.

"I'm sorry, Luc. I didn't mean to hurt you with this discussion… I'm sorry…" she simply repeated, hating the notion she might have added to any of his inner pain.

He took a step toward her and cupped her cheeks. "You are not the one who hurt me. You have nothing to apologize about. I am not leaving because of you. I simply must leave."

That scared her. "What…what will you do?"

A rueful smile canted the corner of his mouth. "I am not going to duel or engage in fisticuffs, if that's your concern. That is exactly what I would have done in this situation long ago." He leaned in and pressed a soft kiss to the corner of her mouth. "I'm going home. You can find me at my *hôtel* in Paris awaiting you. But know this: if you come to me, it's because you are willing to trust me. To be as candid. If you are not ready to trust me with your secrets, then come to me and trust me with your body. That will be a start."

With her cheeks captured in his palms, she couldn't look away. Her heart was pounding, the words, all of them that revealed her hidden truths were swirling in her throat. She was too emotional. Her thoughts too disordered to think. Speak. To make decisions that could impact more than just her life.

"*Dieu*, you are so beautiful, and I don't damn well understand this connection I have with you," he murmured. "You are more heaven than I ever expected."

"So are you…" slipped past her lips, unguarded.

Her heart ached for him with the same intensity it used to years ago. She wanted to throw her arms around him, bury her face in his chest, and never let go.

Be careful! Remember Roch. Remember Leon. Don't trust. Don't trust. Don't trust.

The small smile on his face grew slightly. "I am vastly pleased you think so. I have been honest with you, *chère*. We both know there is still much you have yet to divulge. And though carnal encounters with you are incredible, we both know you aren't a Venetian courtesan. It's very likely that your real name isn't even Juliette Carre."

Her heart lost a beat. She stiffened. Before she could respond, he placed a finger against her lips. "You're going to have to trust me. The next time we are together, you're going to have to come to me and place your faith in me on some level—*any level*—you haven't been willing to before. And don't ask me why. Because I don't understand any of this. But for some reason, it matters a great deal to me. In many ways, you remind me of someone whose journals I've read."

"Journals?" was all she was capable of, barely a whisper, the knot in her throat was so big.

"My sister-in-law gave me her sister's journals. Sabine's sister, Isabelle, is buried on one of my properties, and you are similar to her."

He'd read her journals? *All* her intimate thoughts of him?

He released her cheeks, ducked his head, and pressed a warm kiss against the sensitive spot below her ear. The sensation was divine. She closed her eyes briefly and swallowed.

Scooping up his doublet from the floor, he walked out of her bedchamber and across the antechamber.

Say something! her heart screamed. But the words were stuck in her throat. Emotions barraging her. She followed him into the antechamber.

He stopped. He stared at the ebony side table, then walked to it and picked up the book there. Opening the novel, he read the title page. "This is the first volume of *The Princesses' Adventures* you were going to lend me. Thank you. I'm looking forward to reading it." With that, he left, closing the door behind him.

Wait... If he's read your journals, any entries on your desire to write a book about princesses and the Moutier brothers... Her heart lurched.

She darted to the door and threw it open, despite being in just her chemise.

Luc had disappeared into the servants' stairwell.

CHAPTER TWELVE

"Damn it, Marc. I tell you she's alive!"

Calmly, Marc folded his arms, not looking the least bit convinced. Luc let out a sharp breath and walked over to the desk in his study at his *hôtel*. He opened Isabelle's journal, flipped several pages, until he found the entry he was looking for.

"Here." He spun the journal around to face Marc and pointed to the lines in the writings. "In this very sentence, Isabelle discusses how she and her sister want to write stories about two princesses, Sabine and Isabelle, who meet and capture the hearts of two princes, Jules and me."

Marc peered at the journal.

Luc grabbed another of Isabelle's journals on his desk, slid the first one aside, and placed the second down. Flipping several pages, he located the relevant entry. "And see here." Again he spun the journal around to face Marc and pointed to a paragraph on the page. "Right here, she speaks of having begun to write the very tales about the princesses and the princes. And here is a novel." Luc grabbed the book Juliette had lent him that had been resting on the corner of his desk and held it up. "This is the first volume in *The Princesses' Adventures* series—published after Isabelle's death—about two princesses—*twin sisters*—who fall in love with two princes who happen to be brothers."

Marc's brow furrowed. "How very odd…"

"Precisely!"

"Yes, it is most peculiar that Isabelle would ever consider you princely material." Marc snickered.

Luc rested his hands on his hips. "You are not taking this seriously."

Marc openly chuckled now. "Because it is preposterous. Isabelle wrote about an idea that another author published years later. So what? There are many who have written stories about princesses and princes. *The Princesses' Adventures* is written anonymously. It could be anyone."

"It's her." He wasn't wrong here.

"It's likely an old man or an old woman with naught else to do with their time. Or perhaps someone who knew Isabelle from the theater and used her idea after her death."

"It isn't simply the same idea. It is the same writing style and the same voice in both *The Princesses' Adventures* novel and Isabelle's journals. *Everything* is the same."

Marc sighed. "I think this is wishful thinking."

"It isn't wishful thinking. Isabelle Laurent wrote *The Princesses' Adventures*." He'd read the entire volume in a day, riveted by every word. Stunned by the similarities. By the fact that Isabelle's voice was coming off the pages.

Making his heart soar.

Since finishing the novel, his mind had been awhirl over the probability that Isabelle might actually be alive.

Jésus-Christ. Alive!

He'd already sent his personal secretary, Pascal, out to purchase the other volume published in the series.

"How on earth do you suppose she could have escaped the fire in your servants' outbuildings? And whose body is then buried on your property if not hers?" Marc countered.

"I don't know." Both were valid questions he had no bloody answers to.

Marc pulled *The Princesses' Adventures* novel from Luc's grip and flipped it open to the first page. "This book was published by a foreign publisher. It doesn't have the seal from the Royal Censor as all domestic books do."

"Yes, I know. And it means nothing."

"It means, if this were Isabelle, which I'm certain it's not, she isn't even in France."

"Many who wish to avoid having to obtain royal consent in order to publish their books will falsely name a foreign publisher." He'd heard of several writers doing just that. And it made it more damned difficult for him to uncover the truth.

"The only way to prove who really wrote this is to determine the author's identity," Marc said.

"And you're going to help me."

"How?"

"You and I are going to frequent all the popular salons in the city. We are going to approach everyone in attendance from aristo to literati. Someone has got to know something about who truly wrote these *Princesses' Adventures* volumes. Or where they were actually published." Lord knows there were publishers throughout the city willing to publish anything, even falsifying the name of a foreign publisher, for the right price.

"I'll approach anyone you want, but I'm only fucking women I'm attracted to for you." Marc smiled good-naturedly. "And if you happen to be tired of the gorgeous Juliette Carre—"

"*No!*" Luc mentally cringed.

He hadn't meant for the word to come out quite so sharply. The last thing he wanted to do was to endure Marc's ribbing over just how enthralled he was with the dark-haired beauty.

And she too occupied his thoughts. It had been eight days since his return from his sojourn at the Vicomtesse d'Appel's château. He thought, rather, he was hoping—all right, perhaps more than mere hoping—Juliette would have come to him by now.

She hadn't. And he damn well missed her.

Hating it that she was still leery of him.

He'd never tell Marc that he'd stopped himself from going to see her multiple times over the last few days—because Gabriel was there. And because he'd promised her he wouldn't intrude upon their home again.

When he wasn't fending off tormenting thoughts that she might have turned her attention to Vannod, or the others panting after her, he'd begun to entertain the notion that perhaps Juliette Carre was Isabelle.

Now *that* was wishful thinking.

"Well, well, well…" His friend was back to snickering. "I don't believe I've ever known you to be possessive."

He hadn't been. Ever. What exactly this was that made him long to see her, spend time with her, and, God help him, want her all to himself, was something he didn't want to name. Wasn't even certain he could name, having never felt like this before.

The emotions he felt for Juliette were so similar to the way he felt about Isabelle.

Merde, he'd melded the two women into one.

Luc glanced down at Isabelle's open journal. His eye caught an entry he'd all but forgotten about until he'd reread Isabelle's journal the other day. Now it niggled at the back of his mind.

...I should never have climbed that tree. Sabine warned me that the branches were unsafe. Why didn't I heed her warning? Father often chastises me for being too impulsive and ungovernable. I cut my side and above my right knee. And it hurt!

Had the fall left scars? Though ludicrous, he'd mentally retraced every inch of Juliette's body but couldn't recall ever seeing any scars. Then again, he'd never had her completely naked until their last encounter. Now he cursed himself for not remembering the journal entry then.

And not paying more attention to any markings on her sweet form.

But he hadn't stopped there. He'd tormented himself further by replaying every moment they'd spent together, analyzing everything that had happened, everything she'd said to him—in a way he hadn't had cause to before. The man who'd tried to kill her, whom she'd *"known for a long time,"* he was now seeing that in a different light. *Dieu*, was that just some horrible coincidence? Or was this actually Isabelle talking about Leon de Vittry?

What about the bizarre way she'd reacted that first night she'd seen him at the masque. Was that any kind of indication that the two women were one and the same? Was she startled because she had, in fact, recognized him?

Fuck. If Juliette was indeed Isabelle, wouldn't she trust in him more? And why not let him kiss her? She'd wanted his kiss so desperately. Had her amorous feelings—all her feelings for him—faded over time?

And how the hell could that thought hurt as strongly as it did?

This battery of speculations only underscored just how far gone he was with the maddening fixation he had for both women.

Between the mystery behind the author of *The Princesses' Adventures* and the complexities of Juliette, he was losing his mind.

And a good deal of sleep.

"Focus, Marc. Duchesse d'Allain's salon is in a few days. We're going to attend." He hoped Juliette would be there. *Hell, what you really want is for Juliette to come to your home and trust you—with her body. Her secrets.*

And that part inside every human's chest that poets write about...

He squelched that last notion. It came to him with more and more persistence. What on earth did he even know about the heart? Or love?

Or how to manage it?

Marc shook his head, smiling. "I cannot believe you want to attend all these salons and chat among your peers for a mere ghost of a woman. I would have thought that the fair Juliette would have made you forget all about Isabelle Laurent."

She had for a while. Now they were both haunting him.

"I need to see this through," was all he was prepared to say. *Admit it. You want to meet the only woman, other than Juliette, who could see into your soul.*

And still want you.

Or at least he thought so. Yet, Juliette was nowhere to be found. Damn it, what more could he do to earn her trust?

"Maybe going to the Duchesse d'Allain's salon will do you some good," Marc said. "You can perhaps broach the subject of wedding one of their two daughters. Sophie is still available—eager to impart her knowledge of footwear. And there is also Bernadette." He grinned.

"Forget that. We are focused on the author of *The Princesses' Adventures*. We will not stop until we find out who she is."

He wouldn't rest until he found Isabelle.

*****

"All right, darling. You've been preoccupied since your return. Will you go see him or not?" Nicole asked from her seat on the settee in Isabelle's private rooms.

Squeals of laughter and the occasional bark echoed in the courtyard, drifting up to Isabelle's antechamber on the second floor as, with a smile, she watched her son play with Montague. Perfectly matched with boundless energy, Gabriel and their beloved pet wouldn't tire any time soon.

She turned to Nicole. Her friend's green and yellow taffeta gown was perfectly arranged about her legs. As usual, the epitome of elegance and beauty.

Stepping away from the window, Isabelle approached Nicole, glancing briefly at the crackling fire in the hearth. Three notes were presently burning within its lambent flames. They'd been awaiting her upon her return from the Vicomtesse d'Appel's château. One had arrived only this very morning. Notes that were anonymously written. And becoming uglier with each one.

Calling her a filthy whore.

Another accusing her of possessing the dark powers of an evil succubus, casting spells on men, distorting their minds with the carnal cravings she incited.

She'd no idea whose disdain she'd garnered, but someone—since the handwriting appeared to be the same in all the notes she'd received thus far—despised her. The majordomo, Joseph, had been the one to receive the missives. She intended to get to the bottom of this by questioning him at length.

The horrible notes simply had to stop.

Shoving away thoughts of the missives, she focused on Nicole's question. Her dear friend was asking about Luc, a subject that was equally troubling.

In a different way.

She'd spent every waking hour since her return with Gabriel and Montague, playing, reading, regaling him with stories, especially his favorites, but the subject of Luc intruded repeatedly. Her precious little mite was constantly asking about his friend Luc and if he'd visit soon. And was she sure he wasn't visiting today?

It didn't just disappoint Gabriel when she'd answered that it wasn't likely he would.

She felt bereft too.

Even though she'd made Luc promise not to come to her home. Even though she had a standing—powerfully tempting—invitation to visit him at his *hôtel*. Anytime.

"I wish to see him," she admitted to Nicole. "But it means…well, he'd like me to…" She glanced at Delphine, who was in her bedchamber a short distance away, placing her gown in the armoire. Delphine had turned up at her door two days after Isabelle had arrived home from her sojourn, having quit her employment with the Vicomtesse d'Appel and asking to work for her. Isabelle was delighted to make her her personal maid. Delighted to have her friend, someone she knew and trusted, back in her life.

And she also knew Delphine well enough to know she was presently eavesdropping.

Nicole gave her a small smile. "Ah, I believe I understand. It means he wishes you to explore his particular sexual practices with him when you are with him next. No?"

A sudden *clunk* from the bedchamber grabbed Nicole's and Isabelle's attentions. Delphine had dropped a pair of shoes. Her eyes were wide, her cheeks red.

Isabelle hadn't offered details of her encounters with Luc. Nor had she broken Luc's confidence by relaying the information he'd disclosed about his past. Not to either Nicole or Delphine. Unlike with other men, what she shared with Luc felt…special. Private.

Cherished.

But Luc's penchant for erotic bondage was widespread knowledge.

"Delphine, I know you are listening," Isabelle called out to her friend. "You might as well come into this room where you can hear better."

Delphine placed the shoes into the armoire and scurried into the antechamber. "Well, if you insist…" She curtsied to Isabelle, and to Nicole added, "*Madame*, thank you again for allowing me to work here."

Nicole gave her a nod, then turned to Isabelle again. "Do I have it right, then, about his wishes for your next amorous encounter? Is that the reason you are reluctant to see him?"

"It isn't just that, though that is part of it."

"Then what more does he want?"

"He has read my journals—*Isabelle Laurent's* journals." A small squeak of surprise came from the corner of the room where Delphine stood. Isabelle continued, ignoring her little outburst. "I don't know which journals. For all I know, Luc has read them all. I've kept many through the years. I left some at home, and others I began while in Charles de Moutier's employ—though I am convinced Leon stole those."

Nicole furrowed her brow. "I'm afraid I don't understand. What do your journals have to do with any of this?"

"You wrote about your feelings for him!" Delphine blurted out excitedly. Both Nicole and Isabelle cast her a glance.

"Pardon me…" Delphine slapped her fingers over her mouth to silence her lips.

"Yes, that is true, Delphine. I wrote about my feelings and desires for him, all my observations of him—my every intimate thought I had of Luc de Moutier over the years," Isabelle concurred, a little embarrassed that he'd been privy to every private amorous thought she'd had of him. Though she couldn't recall every entry she'd written, given how long ago it was, she knew that some of those journal entries had been vastly carnal in nature. She'd been as ravenous for him back then as she was now.

Perhaps even more so now that she knew just how good his touch felt.

How good it felt to be with him.

"And when last we parted, he told me that I reminded him of Isabelle Laurent. He is already suspicious that my real name isn't Juliette Carre. I'm not sure I'm ready to entrust him with the truth."

It was a relentless battle.

The thought of seeing Sabine, seeing her little girl, only intensified the pull.

The urge to divulge everything to Luc was escalating.

Yet, all she had to do was look at her son's face, and she retreated well behind defenses. Afraid to take the risk.

Nicole rose and approached. She slipped an arm around her shoulder. "And what of the sexual wishes he has? Are you inclined to trust him in that regard?"

A bolt of raw heat lanced into her belly at the mere mention. She tried to tamp down the reaction. "I am not certain…though perhaps I am more inclined to trust him in his proclivity with bondage than I am to offer my real name." Especially if she took one of Nicole's trusted large male servants with her as added protection.

Delphine let out a joyful squeak with a clap.

Isabelle and Nicole cast her yet another glance. She dissolved her smile, dropped her arms to her sides, and became suddenly fascinated with an errant thread on her apron.

"I take it that you have an opinion on the matter, Delphine?" Isabelle asked.

"Well, I do, actually…"

"And are you going to share it with me?"

"Of course! I think you should trust him. You should allow yourself to enjoy every aspect of him. There aren't many men like the Marquis de Fontenay, and you have dreamed of this man most of your life. He was all you talked about at the Moutier château. He was what you've wished for."

That word "wish" made her flinch, as always.

"I'm not that person anymore. I don't wish for things. I create my own future, and Gabriel's too—with determination. And an abundance of caution." Her reckless, impetuous days were behind her.

Long ago, she'd wished for three things—and they'd leveled her world.

She'd wished to leave the farm her family had been forced to move to after losing their theater and town house in Paris—and that set an unfortunate series of events in motion that took her away from those she loved to this day.

She'd wished to live in the Moutier home, and that almost got her killed by Leon.

She'd wished to be irresistible to men, wanting to catch Luc's eye. And that too went horribly awry. She'd caught the eye of a man like Roch.

"Darling, I understand your reservations in trusting men of the aristocracy. And I know that what Roch put you through must have been horrible…"

Isabelle nodded. "Once he convinced me that I could trust him and learned my real name, he used it as leverage against me to force me to 'marry' him. To make me stay. Threatening that he would make certain Leon de Vittry and his men learned I was still alive. I was subjected to daily lashes of his vicious tongue. To his volatile moods, especially when he was well into his cups. All of which only came to light after our sham of a marriage ceremony. And as desperately as I wish to see my beautiful sister, have her back in my life as well as her little girl, Isabelle, I *must* think of Gabriel. I managed to shield him from Roch, but I swore I'd never, *ever* allow myself to be in such a vulnerable position again. Or permit anyone to have leverage over me the way Roch did. Offering my identity to Luc—or any man in a position of privilege and power—puts my son's future at risk. I thought I could trust Leon. I thought I could trust Roch. I have made errors in the past. I cannot make one now."

It terrified her to the marrow. Could she really jeopardize everything and reveal all? And what if Luc refused to help her reach Sabine? He would then have information and leverage over her to use any way he wished.

Nicole dropped her arm, nodded in understanding, and sat back down. "And so Luc de Moutier has not earned your trust."

"It is complicated. He is complicated." *And beautiful. Intelligent. Intense. Disarming and always surprising.*

He was also battered, yet somehow he didn't break. And that, dear God, *that* weakened her resolve—along with everything else about him. When he made himself vulnerable to her about painful events in his past, when he held her, kissed her body, made her laugh, discussed and debated his take on novels and poetry. It was in those moments—rather, in just about every moment she'd spent with him, he managed to cleave away at her resistance. "It isn't just a matter of trust. He makes me feel…"

"Love?" Nicole offered.

Isabelle sat down. "I don't know." *Liar!* "Gabriel is my priority. I cannot afford to be in love with any man. He is not my prince, and I most certainly am not his princess," she said, referring to her books. She tried to ignore the instant stab of pain she felt in her chest. When she saw him next, which was inevitable, what would she do?

How much of her book and her journals had he read by now? He was an avid reader with a keen mind.

Had he been able to decipher from his readings that Isabelle had authored *The Princesses' Adventures* volumes?

She hoped not.

*****

God save him from curious virgins.

The smile Luc had affixed to his face was becoming more and more difficult to maintain. The Duchesse d'Allain's youngest daughter, Bernadette, was a little too flirtatious.

Standing a little too damn close.

Here he thought he'd have to spend his time tactfully avoiding the Duc's eldest daughter, Sophie. But Sophie had set her sights on

another. Luc had been relieved to learn that the marriage contract between her father and the family of Robert de Travers, heir to a duke-
dom, was presently underway.

Discreetly, as Luc commented on his take on *The Princesses' Adventures* novels to the grouping of four before him, he inched away from
Bernadette, moving closer to the elderly Comte d'Ailly beside him.
There was no bloody way he was going to do a thing that would give
Bernadette's father an excuse to haul him to the altar. The grand salon
was filled with aristos and literati alike. The intellectual elite were clustered in groups about the room, discussing literature and politics.
Grammarians in several of the groupings enthusiastically debated
words and phrases.

He'd arrived an hour ago and had already circulated through half
the room. It wasn't difficult to find groups that were discussing *The
Princesses' Adventures*. Having devoured both volumes in the series, he
now understood their popularity and appeal. They were as engaging
and riveting as Isabelle's journals. He'd reread—yet again—every single entry in her journals. And he was absolutely certain that Isabelle
was still alive—somewhere—and the author of the popular books.

"Who do you suppose wrote these books?" Luc asked casually. "If
I had to wager a guess, I think a woman wrote them. What do you
think, Comte d'Ailly?"

"I think that's something everyone would like to know," the older
gentleman responded. "The novels have caused quite a stir. There's
been much speculation about the author, but no one really knows. If
I had to venture a guess, I think the author is likely a woman too."

"I don't believe women should write books," Bernadette interjected. "I think they should marry, bear heirs, and serve their husbands
well." She beamed at him.

Dieu...

"Respectfully, I disagree," the Comtesse de Gigot said. She and her
daughter, Béatrix, had been the very women who'd encouraged Luc
to read *The Princesses' Adventure* novels in the first place at the Vicomtesse d'Appel's salon. And they were presently both frowning at Bernadette. "I don't see a problem with women writing and publishing
their work."

"Neither do I, Comtesse," Luc agreed wholeheartedly, hoping his
position would irk Bernadette, if not discourage her overt attention.
"Do you think the author of these novels is a woman, madame?"

"I do," the comtesse concurred.

"As do I," Béatrix said. "Most men use their names, especially if they were to author such a popular set of books. Women tend to publish anonymously."

"And do you believe the author to be a foreigner, as the publisher suggests?" Luc's question was to the group as a whole.

But it was the comtesse who responded promptly. "Oh, not at all. I think she's French."

He liked her answer. In fact, he was rather fond of the Comtesse de Gigot and her charming daughter. He was glad these knowledgeable women agreed with him on both scores.

He'd sent his secretary, Pascal, out on a mission with a sizable purse to bribe anyone he had to in order to learn which Parisian printer was printing the books. Money was no object, because every fiber inside him told him that Isabelle was hiding somewhere in France.

He glanced over at Marc. He was at the opposite side of the room, in obvious discussion with a number of ladies and lords. He hoped to hell he was having more success finding out information on the enigmatic author.

There was a slight stir at the entrance of the grand salon that caught the corner of his eye. Dragging his attention there.

Standing with Nicole de Grammont between the tall white-and-gold double doors, dressed in a gown of light blue, with matching ribbons in her hair of dark cascading curls, was Juliette. A radiant smile on her face, adorable dimples and all.

Breathtaking to behold.

She'd sucked the air from the room. And his lungs.

His heart began to thud in his chest. His throat. Reverberating throughout his body, down to the tip of his cock.

Dieu. This woman had the power to shake the very ground under his feet just by entering a room.

The two women stepped down into the sunken salon and were instantly enveloped by a group of men. Luc rooted his feet to the floor so that he wouldn't make a fool of himself by marching across the room, knocking the others out of the way, and hauling her into his arms, bellowing, *Mine!* like some sort of madman.

He'd listened for any rumors that she'd taken a new lover since they'd parted. He'd cursed his decision to leave matters between them the way he had, and he intended to rectify the situation.

He'd actually come today wanting to see both women, Juliette and Nicole—for different reasons. Nicole was a woman many confided in. If anyone could uncover the name of the author of *The Princesses' Adventures*, Nicole de Grammont could.

Her help would be invaluable.

As to Juliette, well, he simply wanted her. Not just physically, though Lord knows he was famished for her. If what the two aristos had done to her made it impossible for her to surrender to him the way he wanted, so be it. He'd forgo his sexual practices.

Only for her.

Especially if it meant she'd be back in his life.

*****

"He's looking at you," Nicole discreetly whispered in Isabelle's ear. "He has the look of a man who wants to devour you."

The information was unnecessary. Isabelle could feel the heat of Luc's gaze on her from the moment she'd entered the salon. She smiled at something the gentleman before her said, though she'd no idea what. And she couldn't recall his name. Her eyes were drawn to only one man in the room. The man was tall and well muscled, with a slight smile on his handsome face.

Beautiful and beckoning.

Her Lord Seductive—on every level. Emotionally and physically.

He didn't seem to even realize just how many women in the room were casting longing looks his way. She'd only just arrived and could see several. Including the young blonde-haired woman standing beside him.

Yet, he only had eyes for *her*.

A younger version of herself would have fainted to the floor if he'd looked at her like this back then. As it was, her knees felt weakened by the intensity with which those intoxicating light green eyes gazed at her. She was so relieved. *He's here...*

He inspired an array of emotions.

And one was a rare sense of joy. She had a smile on her face she couldn't contain.

What would she have done if she'd never set eyes on him? How would she have endured Roch's sexual encounters? Or her limited sexual encounters since becoming Juliette if she hadn't had Luc to envision in her mind?

He was the subject of every romantic thought and wildest fantasy she'd ever had. Hadn't she wondered numerous times what it would be like to completely surrender to him? Holding nothing back. A raw passion she once imagined but now knew was real.

She gave him a smile and a nod.

He returned the gesture in kind.

She'd made a decision about her Lord Seductive. One that she'd come to after many long hours, both days and nights. One that hadn't come easily to her.

One she'd decided she was going to act upon—with some precautions in place.

She excused herself from the aristo before her, possibly cutting him off midsentence. She wasn't sure. Wasn't paying attention. Then she stepped around him and boldly moved through the crowd toward Luc.

His smile grew, and he turned fully to face her, taking a step away from the group he'd been standing with.

Her excitement mounted with each step she took.

It felt as though they had the attention of everyone in the room. And she didn't care. Everyone already knew they were lovers.

By the time she reached him, a raw hunger surged through her system.

She stopped inches from him, standing a tad too close, and looked up into those inebriating eyes. "My lord, it is good to see you."

He took her hand and pressed a kiss to her knuckle. "It is good to see you too."

"I have an important question."

"What might your question be, madame?"

"I wish to know if you happen to have any silk scarves in your bedchamber that I may use?"

Surprise crossed his features. His eyes then darkened with a feral need that spiked her fever. A slow, sinfully seductive smile formed on his lips. "In fact, I do. They are waiting there—just for you."

Lust licked up her spine.

If she could entrust her body to him this way and walk away feeling safe, then maybe she could trust him with her secrets. She would regain her sister back in her life. And Gabriel would gain an extended family, one who'd love and adore him as she did, that he didn't have now. And yes, there was the factor of the anger Luc could feel at being deceived all this time, but she'd only tell him the truth when she felt he'd truly understand why she'd withheld it in the first place—for her son's sake.

"I have some stipulations," she said.

His devastating smile never wavered. "Whatever you need to feel safe."

Dear God, she had such an untamable need for this man. "I'm going to bring Serge and Yves with me. Men in Nicole's employ." They were two of Nicole's largest men who, when necessary, would accompany her to her amorous encounters. They were precautions she'd brought with her today in case she'd be returning to Luc's *hôtel* after the salon.

"As long as they're not in the room with us, I have no objections. I'm not interested in voyeurism with your staff. Or sharing the view."

"No voyeurism," she assured. "And I'm not interested in sharing the view either. I'll meet you at your *hôtel* in an hour." She winked at him, turned on her heel, and walked away, feeling ridiculously happy. And oddly light—now that her decision had been made.

And it felt so right.

Moreover, she felt less fear, more in control than ever.

Her entire body was humming with anticipation.

"Madame Carre." A male voice broke through her thoughts and halted her steps. She glanced to her side and saw that the duchesse's majordomo had approached. He extended a hand toward her with a note. "Forgive the intrusion, madame, but I was asked to give you this note."

She frowned at the oddity of someone sending her a note at the duchesse's salon. "Thank you." Taking the missive, she opened it and read the one and only line.

Meet me in the library.

Her stomach plummeted. This wasn't a note from a lover, an admirer, or even a friend.

The handwriting was identical to that of the vile missives she'd been receiving at her home.

Its author was here.

And wished a private audience.

CHAPTER THIRTEEN

"What is it?" Nicole asked the moment Isabelle had managed to excuse her from the gathering of men around her friend.

Standing in the vast foyer now, Isabelle handed her the note. "I've just received this."

Nicole glanced down at the missive, then back up at her. "An admirer?"

"No. The opposite, in fact. Do you recall the nasty letters I've been receiving?"

"Yes. Of course."

"This is the same handwriting."

Nicole's brows shot up. "What are you going to do?"

"Take Yves and Serge to the library with me and put an end to these hateful missives for good."

Nicole nodded. "I have on occasion received similar horrid letters before, but no one was so bold as to send me one at a salon. Or any gathering of any kind. Do you wish me to come with you?"

"No, but thank you for the offer. I don't want to upset this individual more than they already are. Clearly, they don't care for courtesans, and I fear that having both of us in their presence might make matters worse. I wish to disarm their wrath. I'll have Yves and Serge stand outside the library doors."

*****

Isabelle placed her hand on one of the door handles of the library's tall white-and-gold double doors. Having no idea who was behind the notes or the door, she paused to take in a quick fortifying breath.

She wanted to be with Luc.

Not with this repugnant individual.

Get this over with…

Squaring her shoulders, she opened the door, walked in, and closed it behind her. The sound caused the woman at the window to turn around.

Isabelle went stock-still.

She'd seen this woman just one other time. Yet, she'd never forget her.

Roch's wife…

Pierrette, Vicomtesse de Roch, smiled. It was mirthless. Void of any pleasantness. Just as it had been the night she'd visited Isabelle and thrown her and Gabriel out onto the street. Though she was petite, with chestnut hair, hazel eyes, and only about ten years Isabelle's senior, Pierrette somehow managed to fill the room with a certain heaviness that made her presence loom larger.

Dread seeped down into Isabelle's marrow. Her mind and pulse raced.

"Madame de Roch, how unexpected." Her voice was calm and cool. She'd be damned before showing Pierrette just how distressed her appearance made her.

Of all the people who could have written those notes, this was the one person malicious enough to upend her world.

Pierrette gave a nod. "I suppose it is a surprise to see me here. I don't travel."

Yes, she'd learned of this fact from Roch. When he'd finally revealed his duplicity, he'd complained of his wife's reclusive ways. She didn't attend social gatherings. She detested Paris. Pierrette remained at her château, preferring it to their *hôtel* in the city and ventured only as far as the edges of the vast lands upon which the château was situated.

Pierrette approached.

The rustling of her yellow taffeta gown as she walked was the only sound in the room.

Stopping before her, she said, "I should say it's a surprise to see you here in Paris too, *Augustine*."

Isabelle fought back the shudder that name evoked now. It was the name she'd adopted when she went into hiding to protect her and her then infant son from Leon de Vittry and his goons. It was the name that had passed through Roch's lips, both in rage and in lust.

Even when he'd learned her real name.

And she hated it that she'd had to take on so many aliases. Now more than ever. Just when she thought she'd distanced herself from a horrible period of her life, someone from her past—a past she'd wanted buried and gone—walked into her present.

Just how much havoc was this woman about to wreak?

"What are you doing here?" Isabelle asked. There was nothing about Pierrette that made her feel at ease.

"Well, you recognize me. That's something." Pierrette smoothed her skirts.

"How can I forget? Our last meeting was rather memorable." Isabelle kept her tone even. The less she riled this woman, the better. "What is it you want? There are others who await me…"

Her smile was more a smirk. "Of course, there are, August—I mean, *Juliette*. Still captivating men—just as you did my dear husband, Aubert. You have quite a gift."

She didn't so much as flinch, even though her heart now pounded with hard thuds. Her mind raced, trying to anticipate what was about to happen. And what to do about it. "Madame, get to the point of this meeting and why you're sending me notes."

With a soft laugh, Pierrette waved her hand. "Ah yes, the notes. Just a bit of fun. You didn't enjoy them, I take it?"

"No."

"All right, then. I'll stop." Her response was flippant, more than a bit surprising, and did nothing to counter the sense of foreboding crushing down on Isabelle. Not when that smile affixed to Pierrette's face didn't reflect in her icy eyes. Inarguably, she was an attractive woman, and would undoubtedly be far more appealing if she didn't possess such an off-putting nature. "I've often wondered what happened to you after that night you left," she added.

They both knew that Isabelle didn't simply *leave*.

She'd been forced to wake her sleeping son before they were cast out in the dark of night. But she held her tongue. Kept her features schooled, knowing it was best to pick and choose carefully when to oppose the things Pierrette said.

"You know, I heard all about you long before I arrived in the city," Pierrette continued. "My cousin wrote me, as she often does, and happened to mention the newest courtesan in Paris. A woman who has enraptured most of the male aristocracy. Her description of the woman was so very similar to you."

Pierrette was toying with her, perversely enjoying the tension in the room that at the moment was palpable. Isabelle did not for a moment believe that Pierrette had ventured all the way to Paris from the comfort of her home just because of gossip from her cousin.

"Do get to the point, madame," Isabelle pressed. "Or, I'm afraid, I'll have to take my leave."

"No, you won't, Augustine…rather, Juliette… Oh, and what was the other one? Ah, yes…*Isabelle.*"

At the sound of her real name from Pierrette's lips, her ears began to ring.

Cold fear slid down her spine.

"Good Lord, but you do have many names, don't you? And I hold your whole fabricated world in my hands," Pierrette stated, a smugness to her tone that made Isabelle feel sick.

"I don't know what you're talking about," Isabelle pushed back. It was a pathetic attempt, really. And the only thing she could do when her whole life, and her child's future, was about to implode.

"Let's not play these games, *Isabelle Laurent.* My husband left behind poetry he wrote to you and love letters he'd begun but never finished. What irony, wouldn't you say, that while I pined for him, and he pined for you, you cared nothing about Aubert. I know your father employed actors, and you must have honed your ability to perform back then, but your acting doesn't fool me as it did Aubert and all these men who vie for you. I will say, however, that you're far better suited for the role you play now—a true whore."

Isabelle managed to maintain her neutral expression and her composure, even though her limbs felt numb.

It wasn't shocking to hear Pierrette call her a whore. She'd hurled that name and others at Isabelle the night she'd evicted her and Gabriel from a home that belonged to Roch. The home Pierrette wasted no time claiming for herself as his rightful widow.

The eviction had occurred less than a day after Roch's passing from his accident—a fate that had befallen many a drunkard in Paris. He'd fallen into the Seine and drowned, with an ample amount of his favorite burgundy in him.

And Pierrette had refused to listen to explanation or reason about how they'd both been duped by Roch. It had only angered Pierrette more to suggest Roch was in any way to blame for his double life.

It wasn't likely she'd be more receptive now.

She'd given Isabelle mere minutes to gather a few things. It was fortunate she'd already been prepared in the event of a quick departure, but not from Pierrette.

From Roch.

His imbibing had grown worse over time. His rages lasted longer. Became more volatile. The final straw was the day he'd vaulted into a rage far worse than any other and began slamming his fist repeatedly against the wall, terrifying her to the marrow.

That was the night she'd had enough. She'd decided she'd take Gabriel and leave before that wall became her body. Or worse—Gabriel's. Everything of value she had, she'd painstakingly sewn into the lining of her underthings or packed in a bag she'd hidden, meant for her escape.

She'd planned to leave Roch on the day she'd learned he'd died.

"Madame de Roch, once again I'm going to ask you to get to the point of this meeting."

"I want you to help me obtain a husband for my daughter, Adeline."

Isabelle laughed, stunned by the sheer absurdity of Pierrette's response. "You have just called me a *whore*. How on earth do you think *I* can obtain a husband for your daughter? You have family with influence. Surely you wield more prestige that I do."

"I do. But you have the ability to sway men in a way others don't, and I have a very specific lord in mind. He's wealthy. A perfect match for my dear Adeline. And I hear he's looking for a wife."

"That's wonderful for you and Adeline," she stated blandly.

"Isn't it, though? Aren't you curious who the aristo is?"

"No."

"I'll tell you anyway, since you will be helping to see to Adeline's betrothal and ultimate marriage. I've selected—the Marquis de Fontenay, Luc de Moutier."

Isabelle's heart dropped. Hoping she'd heard incorrectly, she asked, "The...*Marquis de Fontenay*?"

"Correct."

She had to swallow against the knot that formed in her throat before she could speak. "I haven't any influence on him. Or anyone else. If you want him, have members of your family approach him with terms for the marriage contract." God, she wanted to run from the room, away from this horrible woman.

Into Luc's arms.

"I will do just that. But in the meantime, you'll convince him to select Adeline."

"How?"

Pierrette picked up a book that rested on the desk in the duchesse's library. "Use your wantonly ways, of course." Absently, she thumbed through the book. "I know firsthand that men do anything you want in exchange for a tumble with you. And everyone knows you're lovers already. Use your time with him wisely. For Adeline's sake. And yours."

Those last two words sharpened her fear. "What does that mean?"

"It means I know the truth about you. Imagine what would happen if these men were to realize that all this time, they've been grossly deceived. They believed they've spent their time and considerable wealth, from what I've heard, on a woman who is an erotic Venetian courtesan. When, in fact, she's nothing but the daughter of a dead common dramatist, using her acting skills to dupe them in her self-enriching scheme. Whatever would become of poor Isabelle Laurent and her son then? Would she become the lowest of harlots, reduced to lifting her skirts for men of common birth in darkened alleys for a meager sum? Or would she run and hide and create yet another alias? I think the latter. But then, either way, her darling friend Nicole de Grammont would be left to bear the scandal of her duplicity alone."

The knot in Isabelle's throat grew a little bigger. Her son's future was burning down before her eyes. And her beloved friend's reputation possibly along with it. Pierrette was every bit as horrifying as her husband had been. "I'll tell them all that I lied to Nicole. That I deceived her." She couldn't bear the thought that Nicole would be harmed in any way because of her.

Pierrette set the book back down on the desk. "It won't work. She's already told everyone that she knew you and your 'courtesan' mother. She's vouched for you—repeatedly. No one will believe she didn't know who you really are. They'll believe that she helped perpetuate a ruse against those who consider her a friend. It seems a high price to pay to end up friendless and old—just for a no-account like you."

Nicole had risked everything just to help her. "Nicole has done you no harm!" she shot back, outrage getting the better of her.

"True. She's an unfortunate casualty in this scenario. But she needn't be. All you have to do is get Luc de Moutier to marry Adeline."

"Why *him*? Of all the aristos, why Luc de Moutier?"

Pierrette's smile fell. She picked up the book she'd set on the desk and slammed it back down, giving Isabelle a start. "Because I want to take away the man you love just as you took away the man *I LOVED!* she bellowed, her voice ricocheting off the walls.

Snatching the air from Isabelle's lungs.

Before she could respond, Pierrette added, "If you are about to tell me you are not in love with the Marquis de Fontenay, don't! I'll not tolerate any more of your *lies*." She hissed out the last word between clenched teeth. "I was there at the Vicomtesse d'Appel's sojourn, and even with my brief attendance, I could see that you looked at him in a way you looked at no other man. He matters to you. You're highly fond of the handsome, highborn, rich Luc de Moutier. And it will give me great pleasure to see him taken away from you."

Isabelle wanted to scream sense into her and shake her, tell her all this fury and bitterness she harbored toward her was ill-placed. "How are you 'taking him away' when you are asking me to persuade him to marry your daughter by bedding him?" She'd never met Roch's daughter, never heard a thing about her from him. This whole plan was madness.

"That's simply the means to an end. Once they're married, you'll stay away from him, or I will destroy you, that old harlot you live with, and any future you hope to have for that spawn of yours."

"Madame de Roch, I am truly sorry for your broken heart, but I did not take anyone away from you. I didn't know Aubert was married to you. He lied to me, and to yo—"

"Silence!" Pierrette looked her in the eyes. Isabelle saw nothing but cold anger in their depths. Tightly between clenched teeth, she said,

"He loved *me*—until *you* came into his life and poisoned his mind and heart."

Isabelle wanted to shout, *He wasn't capable of love. He was a faithless, conniving, volatile man who doesn't deserve the emotions you carry for him.* But didn't dare. Roch's acting skills were superior to the most seasoned stage performer. He'd convinced Pierrette that his benevolence was authentic. Lord knows he'd convinced her of the same thing for a while too—when, in truth, it was but a ruse to control the women in his life. To bend their wills to his. Pierrette's willful blindness of her husband's true nature was unyielding.

Seemingly incurable.

And part of her pitied Pierrette for clinging to such a hollow, in-authentic man.

"The Marquis de Fontenay is in good standing with the King," Pierrette said. "He is a fine choice for Adeline. Do as you're told and see to it quickly. Don't disappoint me or make me wait long. And don't think to breathe a word of this to anyone—unless you want matters to worsen for you and all those around you. Do consider that the old harlot's children, whom she worked so hard to arrange respect-able marriages for, will be dragged down in her undoing. And her grandchildren are so close to being of marriageable age. You wouldn't want to level all these people's lives, now would you?"

Her skin prickled with fury at herself for being in this vulnerable position when she'd done all she could to avoid this very thing, and at Pierrette for her callousness toward others.

"And if I were to do everything you ask, how will I know you'll not ruin these innocent people's lives afterward?"

"You don't." Again that empty smile cracked across her lips. "You'll just have to trust me. Now, we both know you have plans to meet the marquis. It's best you don't keep him waiting. I'll be watching you."

CHAPTER FOURTEEN

Luc heard the moment his majordomo opened the front door to his *hôtel*, followed by the sound of a voice he recognized immediately. He was on his feet, striding to the double doors of his study in an instant.

Dieu. She was here. *At last...* He'd been waiting two long excruciating hours.

He'd been waiting for this moment forever.

His heart hammered. Every fiber in his entire being roared for her.

Reaching the double doors, he snatched one open, his gaze falling across the vast vestibule onto his dark-haired siren. His one and only Juliette. She was with two larger men he assumed were the servants she'd mentioned. She must have heard the door open as she turned from his majordomo to Luc. Immediately, she approached, leaving the servants behind, the sound of her footsteps echoing lightly.

He stood riveted by the vision she made.

And the luscious little bounce of those sweet breasts with each quickened step she took.

When she reached the halfway point, he noted there was something in her eyes. Something different. Before he could decipher what, she bolted toward him. His back slammed against the door he didn't even remember closing. He grunted. It took a moment before he realized her soft mouth was against his.

Dieu. She was *kissing* him. Urgent presses of her mouth, again and again. Her hands fisting his doublet tightly.

Lust burned through his veins as a particular emotion flooded his chest, fiercer than ever before.

Leveling all the norms of his life.

He *wanted*, for the first time ever, this feeling that welled inside him.

This was so unexpected. He'd never felt such pure joy. He reveled in it, and in every hungry little slash of her mouth against his.

There was a slight awkwardness mixed in with her zeal, and for the briefest moment, the thought that perhaps this too was something that might be new to her flitted through his mind.

Yet another thing he couldn't dwell on.

Not when these perfect lips were finally his. Not when one of his fantasies—kissing *this* woman—had come true. He loved this incredible, uniquely Juliette kiss. He didn't know what to make of it. But it felt akin to a…gift.

And God help him… He didn't want it to end.

He cupped her cheeks and murmured against her lips, "Slow down. Savor it…" Then took command of the kiss, slowing down her frenzy to relish her mouth. Her inebriating taste. He'd imagined what she'd taste like a thousand times.

And she tasted far better than in his wildest fantasy.

He didn't know if they still had an audience of servants. Didn't care a whit if they did.

Slipping an arm around her waist, he hauled her to him tightly, crushing her against his stiff prick, then drove his hand into her silky hair, fisting a handful of her dark locks. Angling her head just the way he wanted. She parted her lips on a breath. He slid his tongue inside her mouth, plying hers with long languid strokes, his own urgency rushing through his blood. She'd seeped into his system long ago. She was like thunder in his veins. The air in his lungs.

There wasn't a single part of him that wasn't starved for her. That hadn't missed her. The very last thing he wanted to do was pull his mouth away from hers—now that her lips were finally his. But there was so much more awaiting them.

And if he didn't stop, he was going to take her right here in the vestibule just to take the edge off their desire. Witnesses be damned.

Reluctantly, he pulled away and gazed down at her. She was up on the balls of her feet. Her eyes were closed. Her sweet mouth was seeking his. She looked so damned adorable. Beyond tempting. And he almost gave in to the allure of those lips again. Instead, he leaned into her and said in her ear, "Follow me."

Taking her hand, he stalked across the vestibule, up the stairs with her in tow, shouting over his shoulder at his majordomo to give her men food, drink, and chairs in the upstairs hallway. And without slowing his stride, he made his way to his private apartments. He didn't stop until he'd thrown open the doors, slammed them shut, crossed his antechamber, and entered his blue-and-gold bedchamber. Closing the door behind him, he then turned his attention to the beautiful woman who now stood in the middle of the room.

He couldn't help but smile. Her eyes were darkened with desire, her breaths rapid and raw. She stood still, waiting for his next move.

Trusting you in a way she's never trusted you before.

And yet again, that filled him with a level of happiness he didn't know he could feel. Hell, he didn't know he was capable of feeling half of what she made him feel.

This woman had changed him. That thought should have been alarming. Should make him walk—no, *run*—away. But instead, he didn't want distance. He wanted more. Of her. With her.

And it had never meant more to him to share in the experience of carnal bondage with a woman as it did with this one.

He pulled off his doublet and threw it carelessly to the floor.

She made his blood course white-hot in a way no other ever had. And he damn well needed that mouth again. The afternoon's sunrays streamed through the windows. He was going to have her naked and bound, every sweet inch of her form illuminated for his viewing pleasure. He was so damned anxious for it, he wanted to tear the clothes right off their bodies.

Isabelle's journal entry about falling from the tree suddenly whispered through his thoughts.

I cut my side and above my right knee...

Perhaps it *was* absurd, as Marc suggested, but he was going to check for any such scars.

Luc opened his vest with a rapid deftness. He loved it that he had her undivided attention. Her hands were at her sides, clutching handfuls of her skirts as she watched him disrobe, engrossed in his every motion. The moment he saw the tip of her pink tongue lick her lips, a dollop of pre-come wept from his cock.

His vest joined the doublet on the floor.

He walked over to her, his approach seemingly breaking the spell. She pulled her gaze from him to her bodice and reached for it, but he clasped her wrist and returned her hand to her side.

"You don't need to do a thing…except relax and enjoy," he told her, plucking loose the ribbon at the décolletage of her gown between the swells of her breasts, purposely brushing his knuckles against her skin as he untied it. He felt her small shiver of excitement. It reverberated through him and down the length of his leaden cock.

"Now then, shall we begin?" He watched for any signs of fear or, worse, panic and saw none.

She nodded, her cheeks pink.

God, how it drove him wild to see a woman's skin flush with desire.

"That's excellent." He worked diligently at the fastenings on her bodice as he spoke. "You are going to follow my instructions. With no hesitation. No inhibition. Just total submission. You are free to ask me to stop at any time you feel you need to. That is how we play our little game. *Understood?*" He chose the word "game" because it was lighter. Innocuous. Rather than to dwell at the moment on how ingrained in his sexuality this was. It wasn't just something he enjoyed in bed.

It was a part of him, part of who he was.

She grabbed him by the shirt and shot up onto the balls of her feet, bringing her lush mouth barely an inch from his. "You talk too much."

He lifted his brows. Not exactly the docile response he typically got from a woman submitting to being bound and fucked.

His lips twitched as he fought to maintain a straight face. "I believe you've missed the submission aspect of this."

She brushed her mouth against his. The light sensation shimmered over the nerve endings in his lips. He felt it ripple down his spine.

"Hmmm? No. I am in compliance with the rules of our game. You said I could stop you at any time… Kiss me. Hard. With your all. Make it go away."

He frowned. "Make what go away?"

"The world. You're the only one who knows how."

Dieu… The things she said…

He slipped an arm around her. "I take all requests under consideration. And I like that one." He yanked her to him and claimed her mouth, driving his tongue past her parted lips. He held nothing back, kissing her hungry and hard. Sucking her tongue into his mouth. Delighting in her sensuous little mews. His hands worked away at her clothing. Her hands tugged at his shirttails. He didn't stop her, despite his earlier words, as they tossed each discarded article onto the floor, breaking contact with her mouth only when necessary.

The faster they dispatched their clothing, the bloody better.

By the time he had her down to her chemise, he wore just his breeches and boots.

He felt the fastenings on his breeches finally give, her hand slip inside and grip his engorged prick, giving it an exquisite stroke from head to base.

His greedy cock jerked in approval in her hand.

His willful beauty.

Luc broke the kiss, pulling her hand away. "I didn't give you leave to touch me. Nor did I give you leave to undress me. You'll *only* do as I ask. No more. No less. No improvisations."

She tilted her head and studied him for a moment, soft pants slipping past her lips. "And if I should happen to improvise again, what then?"

He reached under her chemise and undid her *caleçons*. The drawers fell to her feet. He dipped his head and said in her ear, "There will be consequences." He cupped her sex and massaged her, enjoying her soft moan. Her curls were already delectably damp with her juices. "You'll have to wait to come. I'll make you work harder for it."

He pulled away and looked into her eyes. He wanted to howl with joy. There was still no fear. Just raw passion and keen interest.

He held out a hand to assist. "Get on the bed. On your knees. Face me." His voice was rough with desire. The length of his cock now lightly pulsing in the aftermath of her caress.

Without hesitation, she took his hand and climbed onto his bed and complied with his instructions. Glancing down on the mattress, she noticed for the first time the long scarves on the edge of the bed. He waited for her reaction. She returned his gaze. Still only fire and need in those dark eyes. Once again, she licked her lips. Once again, a hot pulse lanced through his groin.

Grasping the hem of her knee-length chemise, he pulled it off her body and grabbed a scarf. "Give me your hands, Juliette."

Seeing her extend them was a heady rush. He couldn't believe this was finally happening. He bound her wrists together with practiced skill. "I'm going to bind your legs apart as well. Do you have any objections?"

She shook her head. "No," she said, ever so softly. It made him wonder what thoughts were going through that bright mind of hers.

When he was done binding her wrists, he took a step back to devour the sight before him. Naked, except for her stockings reaching above her knees, held in place by red ribbon, and the yellow scarf binding her wrists, she made his mouth water. She'd lowered her arms and clasped her bound hands together. He couldn't see her sides. And her pebbled pink nipples were straining toward him. Begging to be sucked. Driving him to distraction. He touched the scarf around her wrists. "Is it too tight?"

She shook her head again. She'd become very quiet. Too quiet for his liking.

He slipped his fingers under her chin, tilting it up, and gave her another languid kiss. She responded immediately in kind, parting her lips for him. Inviting him into her mouth. An invitation no man could refuse. He stroked her tongue and the soft recesses of her mouth with his tongue before breaking the kiss.

"Are you all right?" he asked.

"I am when you touch me."

He smiled. "So am I." More than he could explain or understand. "There's one more thing I want you to permit me to do."

She crinkled her brow. "Oh?"

He picked up a shorter scarf of red and green from the bed. "I'm going to blindfold you."

For the first time since she'd arrived, uncertainty crossed her features.

"Your men are in the hallway outside my apartments if you need them—though you won't. And I will stop and remove the scarves anytime you choose. Even if it damn well kills me. By covering your eyes, your other senses heighten…"

He cupped her breast, dipped his head, and gave the sensitive tip a soft suck, followed by a little bite. Holding her nipple captive between his teeth for a moment. Making her jerk and whimper, her body instantly arching to him. Wanting more. He released the sweet tip and raised his head. "Pleasure is the goal in our game. It adds to the pleasure. What say you, Juliette? Will you let me blindfold you?"

She glanced past him to the door of his bedchamber, then returned those big fathomless eyes back to him. This time, she gave him a shaky nod. But a nod nonetheless.

Jésus-Christ. His hammering heart practically burst with joy.

Placing the scarf over her eyes, he secured it behind her head. "Raise your arms for me, Juliette, high above your head. Don't lower your arms until I tell you to."

Slowly, her arms rose above her, her nipples lifting higher. Her breathing escalating. Slipping his hand behind her head, he angled it, giving her a deep kiss. Possessing her mouth. Sucking her tongue. Worshiping those lips he'd been denied for so long. *Dieu,* how was he ever going to get enough of her mouth?

Or her?

And what in the world did a man do with these foreign feelings she inspired?

Reaching up, he grabbed hold of the binding on her wrists, to keep her arms from tiring. And keep them in place. Then he lowered his mouth and lightly bit her other nipple. A soft cry erupted from her lips at the spike of sensation. She arched hard toward him. He immediately began suckling her, quieting her down to pants and small mewls. And delicious little squirms she couldn't contain.

He could see her right side now, scanning every inch.

Not a single scar…

Just beautiful satiny skin.

And though the likelihood was small that Juliette and Isabelle were the same woman, he couldn't help but feel a flutter of disappointment. He turned to her other breast and caught sight of something small on her left side. Just above her hip.

He looked closer. A thin white line ran down her side, about the length of his small finger. His pulse began to throb in his throat. He stroked his fingers over it. It was slightly raised.

And definitely a *scar.*

The line from Isabelle's journal ran through his mind again.

I cut my side and above my right knee…

The journal entry had never indicated that the cut was on the right side. *Merde.* It was something he'd just assumed. He lowered her arms, grabbed the end of the red ribbon around her right stocking, and yanked it loose.

The stocking slipped down, puddling around her knee on the bed. Her knees were pressed into the mattress, and he had to shove both the stocking and counterpane down to expose as much of her knee as he could.

And there it was. Another thin white scar he'd never noticed before. About the same size as the other scar.

Stunned, he took a step back. His mind spinning. *Jésus-Christ... Isabelle!*

He scrubbed his hands over his face. Reeling.

Incredulous.

For Juliette to have a scar on her side, that was possibly in keeping with Isabelle's journal, might have raised some suspicions. But to have a scar on her *right* knee, as well—the exact part of her body mentioned in the journal entry—made it undeniable.

This is Isabelle Laurent. Dear Lord, he'd found her.

She *was* alive. In front of him, all along. And it explained the similarities he'd noted about the two women. The way he'd been drawn to Juliette from the start.

The way he'd felt about Juliette from the beginning.

The way Juliette could see the things only Isabelle saw about him— in a way that was different from everyone else.

My God. He'd been Isabelle's lover all this time.

And at this very moment, *Isabelle Laurent* was on his bed. *Isabelle* was constrained in his silk scarves. *Isabelle* was all his for the taking.

"Luc... Please... *I want you.*"

He had to swallow hard. He was so overcome with emotion, he couldn't speak.

Journal passages he'd reread during the many days and nights he'd spent longing for her echoed in his head.

...Down to my very marrow, I feel there is a connection between us. One destined in the stars. If he would simply notice me, touch me, he would feel it too...

He *had* felt it. There *had* been a connection from the very start. This woman was born to be his. There was no one, absolutely no one in the world, who was more in tune with him than this beauty.

And there wasn't a single woman he knew better, understood more, wanted more on every human level than this one woman.

….I want to know the feel of his skin, the taste of his kiss. I want to indulge in all the carnal delights he favors. I want to surrender to his every wicked desire.

He raked a hand through his hair and took in a breath, trying to quell the feelings and questions whirling inside his head and heart.

Bloody hell. His hands were shaking. He'd faced countless battles in the King's navy and while privateering. Fought duels before that. Even sat in prison awaiting his execution.

And never once had his hands shaken. Not ever.

He could have truly lost her, having no idea how she managed to survive as he realized that the man Juliette mentioned, the one who had tried to kill her, *was* none other than that fucking devil Leon de Vittry. He'd never been more grateful of anything as he was that Leon had failed to take her life.

"Luc?" she called out to him again, her tone growing earnest. Her arousal escalating with anticipation. Those gorgeous tits rose and fell a little faster now. Her breaths came a little more raw and rapid. And his eager cock swelled to painful proportions.

…I want to surrender to his every wicked desire…

Dieu, he wanted to fuck her—his *Isabelle*—a dozen different ways.

Stripping off the rest of his clothing, he then sank a knee on the bed beside her, helped her onto her back, then placed her arms above her head once more.

"I'm going to give you everything you've ever wanted. And more." Now wasn't the time to discuss the revelations he'd just uncovered— despite the million questions he had. It was time to relish this moment, this experience—with *Isabelle*.

Seigneur Dieu, this is Isabelle Laurent…

Snagging the remaining scarves from the end of the bed, he looped two through the binding on her wrist and tied each to one of the posts at the head of his bed, rendering her arms motionless.

She tested the bindings, trying to move her captive arms, but they held fast, not allowing her to lower them or move them from side to side. He grazed his fingertips over her taut nipple, wanting to keep her focused on pleasure. The softest, most sensuous little moan escaped from her parted lips.

His cock seeped more spunk.

She squirmed and squeezed her legs together. And he knew that sign. A damned well excellent sign. She was trying to apply pressure between her legs.

A smile tugged at the corners of his mouth. "Are you squeezing your legs together?" he asked the obvious. "Because if you are improvising—"

"No!" She relaxed her legs immediately.

Beautiful Isabelle. So sensual. And an adorable little liar. "I don't believe you," he said, stroking his hand over her silky belly. It quivered under his touch. He stopped just before her sex. "And I haven't decided if there is going to be consequences for your infraction. I do, however, think we should address that sweet clit of yours…"

"Yes, to that last bit! I have no idea what you said before it." She strained a little against her bindings. Trying to reach his hand to rub against it. Desperate for some friction.

"Entirely too willful." He chuckled. *Merde.* How this woman could make his cock pulse in anticipation… "There most definitely is going to be some consequences for your unyielding behavior, *ma belle.*" This was Isabelle—the woman of his dreams. And fantasies. After spending a lifetime fighting and struggling against discord and darkness, what he had with her came easily. And felt right. "I see we're going to have to do something to keep you still." He grasped her ankle. Lifting her leg over him, he situated himself between her spread thighs, then slipped a scarf under her leg and tied it above her left knee. He repeated the same thing with another scarf around the right knee, taking a moment to caress the little scar there with a smile. He'd never adored a scar more. "Now, just relax," he soothed as he bent her parted knees, then pressed them back toward her and again tied the end of each of the scarves to one of the bedposts at the head of his bed, securing her bent knees back.

Her sex was open for his viewing pleasure. Pink and glistening with her juices. This wasn't a dream come true or a double fantasy—having not only Isabelle, but having her bound as well.

It was, in fact, nothing short of a miracle.

And here he thought they didn't exist. At least not for him.

"Do you know you have the prettiest cunt?" He scored his fingers down the soft folds of her slick sex. She didn't squirm this time. Instead, another luscious moan escaped her throat as she sank her teeth into her bottom lip. A hot bolt of fire lanced through his groin.

Jésus, he loved her sensuous responses.

"Are the scarves too tight? Are you comfortable?" he asked, massaging her sex, plying it with soft strokes up, then down, and up once more to her clit, spreading her essence over every gorgeous pink inch. Caressing the swollen little bud between his fingers, giving it just enough sensation on either side of the engorged nub to keep her hungry.

Her head lolled to one side, her short, quick breaths louder now. She was lost to the pleasure flooding her sex and didn't respond to his question.

He slid his fingers into her soft feminine core. Locating that ultra-sensitive spot inside her sheath easily, he curled his fingers and gave it two quick strong strokes. She arched hard with a cry. He leaned down, and, keeping a light pressure on that sweet spot inside her vaginal walls, he sucked her clit into his mouth, enjoying the little whimper she made. Her sheath squeezed around his fingers and released.

More pre-come seeped from his sex.

He pulled his mouth away reluctantly, her delicious taste on his tongue. "I'm going to need an answer. Are the scarves hurting you?"

"No. Hurry. I'm dying…"

He smiled. "No, you're not. You are just terribly impatient." Without removing his hand from inside her, he lay down between her legs, crushing his cock against the mattress, alleviating some of his discomfort. His fingers continued to tantalize that erogenous area inside her sheath. "Learn to savor… You're not going to come until I tell you." He dipped his head and trailed hot kisses along her inner thigh, from her knee, slowly making his way back to her gorgeous cunt.

She squirmed and strained hard against her bindings, arching to him. It was the most sensual sight imaginable. He brought his mouth down on her silky sex, lapping up her juices, swirling his tongue around her clit. Then he lightly bit it.

Making her buck, screaming his name.

He gave the sensitized bud another soft suck and felt it pulsing between his lips, knowing he had it throbbing with need now. The scarves no longer mattered to her. She no longer cared or even thought about them—that much was obvious. She was blindfolded. Bound. Her body so beautiful to behold. She writhed against the binding, arching for him. Wordlessly pleading.

In complete carnal surrender as he drove her to the edge of orgasm and pulled her back again and again.

And yet even as his cock pulsed in time with his wild heart, and his sac was so full of come, one of the most powerful passages from her journal whispered through him.

He is the man I know I will always love...

Ten words that leveled him and melted his hardened heart. Every. Single. Time. These weren't the thoughts he normally had during sex, before or after it. He wanted to burn up the day and night with her. More than that, he wanted to take a risk with her, in a way he'd never risked himself before.

Fuck, he had to claim her, to make her his—the way she'd claimed him.

He eased his fingers out of her and rose to his knees. She instantly balked at the loss of his hand.

"*No!*"

Luc stroked his slick hand down the length of his cock, coating it with her juices, then lowered himself onto her soft form and yanked off her blindfold, suddenly wanting her to see the man who was taking her to ecstasy and back.

Beautiful dark almond-shaped eyes stared back at him. The feral hunger shining in their depths matched his own.

"Easy," he said, resting on his elbows. Then he wedged the crest of his cock against her opening. She gasped. He brushed his mouth against hers and murmured, "Say my name."

"Luc." It rushed out on a pant, warming his lips.

He pressed his prick into her, feeding her an inch of his length. The head of his shaft was engulfed in the wet, warm squeeze of her soft sex. And he was lost to her. Overcome with emotions. Emotions he couldn't deny anymore. Emotions he knew were the very same as those regaled by poets.

He was in love with this woman. Deeply. Madly. Who knew how long?

And he kissed her. A deep short kiss. *Isabelle…* "Say it again. Say my name."

"Luc…"

He claimed her mouth, this time driving his tongue past her lips, as he fed her another inch of his cock. Then another. And another.

"You are mine…" He plunged his whole length in, muffling her cry with his mouth.

Fisting the sheets, he groaned long and hard. He was so large and thick at the moment, making her feel tighter than before. He drove into her snug little sheath again. And again. With each solid thrust, one word repeated in his head.

Isabelle .

Isabelle.

Isabelle.

Spiking his fever. He possessed *Isabelle's* mouth. Possessed *Isabelle's* sex.

Filling all her senses with *him.*

She kissed him, matching his intensity. Her tight grip on his prick was eroding away his sanity. The bliss coursing through his body was blinding. His cock ached for release. His entire body clamored for him to let go. And the tiny flutters and little clenches of her vaginal walls, telling him she was on the edge of orgasm, were melting his bloody mind.

He was practically delirious with desire. Going on sexual instincts alone. Knowing he couldn't hold back much longer in this state.

Not when this was *Isabelle.*

"You're going to come for me. *Right. Now,*" he rasped in her ear, shifting his angle slightly, making perfect contact with her clit with each downward stroke. Knowing the reaction he'd get.

And she gave it to him. Immediately. Screaming in pleasure, she surged up against him, sucking his cock in a fraction farther. Her climax slamming into them both.

He clenched his teeth and buried his face into her neck, her slick walls contracting wildly around his plunging prick, milking his cock. He held on to the final fragments of his control. The stunning sensations were sublime. More than he could bear.

A powerful ecstasy exploded through his senses.

Semen barreled down his cock. He yanked himself out just in the nick of time, then crushed her to him as he poured out everything he had in one hot blast of come after another. The draining sensation was a glorious relief that went on until the final shuddering drop.

It took a moment or two before he could collect his faculties and realize that his languid body was crushing her under his weight. Pressing his palms down on the mattress, he pushed himself up onto his knees. And looked at her. Her eyes shone warmly at him, and there was a small smile on her face.

The smile of a woman who'd been well satisfied.

And he couldn't be happier that *he'd* been the one to put that smile on those lips.

Both their abdomens were coated with the aftermath of his release. Leaning over her, he gave her a quick kiss. "Give me but a moment and I'll untie you." He rose from the bed, forcing his legs to walk across the room to the water basin. He washed himself quickly, returned with a clean, wet cloth, and sat down on the edge of the bed beside her.

Now that the fog of lust, and the shock of who this woman really was, had ebbed, questions began to assail his mind anew.

*****

Isabelle started at the first swipe of the cool cloth. Her entire body felt overly sensitive. Drained. Yet, a sense of joy welled inside her chest.

Niggling thoughts of Pierrette threatened to invade. She pushed them away, desperate to hold on to this moment of deep contentment for as long as she could. Isabelle closed her eyes, allowing herself to enjoy the gentle swipes of the cloth over her belly, not caring a whit about the scarves bound to her limbs. Nor her body's unabashed position. He always knew just how to touch her, in any circumstance. And after what had just happened between them, he clearly knew her body better than she did.

"Are you all right?" he asked, giving her belly another swipe of the cloth.

She was about to respond when suddenly, the cool, wet cloth pressed against her sex. She jumped away, a reflexive reaction, but the bindings didn't allow her to get far. He pressed a hand down on her pelvis, gently pushing her bottom back onto the bed.

"I know you're still sensitive. Try to be still. Allow me to finish." He gently stroked the cloth over her sex again. She squeezed her eyes shut, bit down on her lip, curling her toes, trying to keep from wiggling. She swallowed down the mewls that surged up her throat at each stroke of the cloth over her oversensitized flesh. He gave her a final swipe, then the cloth was gone and his hands were working at the ties on her leg.

She opened her eyes and watched him at his task, her gaze tracing over his handsome profile. The scarf whispered against her skin as he pulled it off and stretched out her leg on the bed. He turned to the scarf around her other thigh and made quick work of that one too, lowering her other leg onto the bed.

He was quiet. And she didn't know what to make of it. Couldn't decipher anything from his features. He rose and untied the scarves around each of the bedposts that secured her arms above her head. Again, without a word. What had happened between them had been so intense and wonderful. Was he somehow displeased?

The edge of the mattress sank once more as he seated himself beside her and lowered her bound wrists from above her head to rest on her belly, then untied the final scarf.

Tossing it to the floor with the others.

He grasped her wrists in his warm, strong hands and began to knead them. "How are your arms and legs? Are they sore?"

She sat up, wanting to get closer to him. Unable to stop herself. "No. They're fine. I'm fine. More than fine." She smiled. "I loved what you did. All of it."

A hint of a smile appeared on his perfect lips. He captured her chin, and she let herself sink into his light green eyes. "Would this be something you're willing to explore further?"

"God, yes…" The words tumbled out of her mouth. She mentally flinched, meaning to be more urbane. But the aftereffects of Lord Seductive were powerful. He'd promised to make her come harder than she ever had. And he'd succeeded. The nerve endings throughout her body still hummed from the sheer impact he'd had on her system. And it was clearly muddling her mind.

His lips twitched with amusement. "I'm pleased to hear that. I loved doing it to you. With you." Then he kissed her. A thrill quivered down her spine. She parted her lips for him, inviting him into her mouth. He seized the invitation, his tongue swirling around hers, slow. Deliberate. Delicious.

Oh, how could she get enough of his mouth? His taste? Him? The feel of his lips melded with hers. She hadn't meant to kiss him when she'd walked through the front door of his *hôtel* today. The carriage ride to Luc's home had been a blur. Haunted by her conversation with Pierrette, she'd been angry and distraught over the leverage Pierrette had over her. And over concerns for Nicole and her family. Of losing any hope of ever seeing Sabine again.

Moreover, of having reality sharply reinforced—that Luc wasn't hers to have and hold—regardless of Pierrette's marriage plans for her daughter.

She hadn't missed the black carriage that had followed her from the duchesse's city mansion to Luc's home.

The moment she'd stepped into his *hôtel* and saw Luc standing in the vestibule, looking as beautiful as always, pulling at her heart, she threw herself into his arms and into a kiss.

Even when she knew better than to do anything that would make herself emotionally vulnerable to him.

Letting Luc be the first man she kissed was wrong. And a dream come true. He had no idea how monumental the kiss was to her. This man's arms were a refuge she shouldn't allow herself. He wasn't his brother who'd married her sister, a commoner. Luc was different. He'd said as much. And everyone knew he was looking for a highborn bride. He was more heaven than she was entitled to by birth and circumstance. But none of that diminished how badly she wanted him— in ways she couldn't have him.

She'd thrown herself into the kiss, then and now.

He lifted his head, breaking their kiss far earlier than she wanted, and simply gazed into her eyes. Once again, she was having trouble reading his expression, deciphering his thoughts. His features were schooled. He was behaving differently.

"Is there something amiss, Luc? You are somewhat…remote. Pensive."

He slipped his fingers beneath her chin once more. "I suppose I am. What transpired just now between us was so good. Better than good. *Incredible.* And I hope I have demonstrated that you can trust me—with more than just your body."

Her chest constricted. Knowing she couldn't tell him what she'd wanted to reveal today, she was forced to stay quiet. And it hurt so much.

It was obvious by his expression that he expected her to respond. When she didn't, he said, "I read *The Princesses' Adventures* volumes. Both of them."

Her heart leaped to her throat and immediately began to pound. Slow, hard thuds. She didn't like the unexpected turn in their conversation. "Oh? Did you enjoy them?" She managed to keep her tone light.

"I did. Very much. I found them fascinating, and I learned something by reading them."

Her every instinct spiked with alarm, yet she managed to keep her tone cool. "And what was that?"

"That my sister-in-law Sabine's twin, Isabelle Laurent, wrote them."

Her stomach dropped.

He cupped her cheek and gently stroked his thumb across her lips. "I know this because, as I've mentioned to you before, I've read Isabelle's journals. I know her writing style. Her voice. I know her desire to write princess adventure stories. I know she's alive. Would you like to know what else I learned?"

No! she screamed in her head.

Because now things were complicated.

Now telling him the truth of who she was put people's lives in the balance. Including her son's quality of life and future.

Now there was possibly a carriage waiting for her outside to make sure she was complying with the wishes of a madwoman.

It took a moment for her to summon her voice. She forced a smile, when she'd never had to fabricate one for him before. "Didn't you say she is dead and buried on your property? Forgive me, but this sounds a little far-fetched."

A half smile pulled at the corner of his mouth. But it never reached his eyes. And that unnerved her further still. "I would agree. It definitely sounds far-fetched. Ludicrous. And even unlikely too. Except…"

"Except what?"

He released her cheek, his gaze dropping down her body. Reaching out, he brushed his fingers against her left side, then her right knee. "These little scars confirm that *you* are Isabelle Laurent."

CHAPTER FIFTEEN

Isabelle leapt off the bed. "You're mad!"

Luc watched as she scanned the floor. The instant she spotted her chemise among the clothing strewn about the room, she raced to it, scooped it up, and threw it on.

Covering her beautiful form from his sight.

She was visibly shaken, and it was clear her intent was to bolt from the room. She dropped her gorgeous derriere onto the end of his bed and began yanking on her stocking.

Luc rose from his spot on the side of the bed and approached, then lowered himself onto his haunches before her. He brushed her hands away and helped pull the stocking up above her knee. Grasping the red ribbon off the floor that had held it in place, he then secured it around her thigh, in the very spot he had affixed his scarf earlier. Wishing that that was what he was doing once more rather than helping her dress so she could flee.

"Isabelle—"

"Don't call me that!" She tried to stand, but he managed to stop her with some gentle pressure on her shoulders. He hated that her breaths had escalated due to distress—instead of sexual excitement.

"If you wish to leave, so be it. I won't force you to stay." He placed her bare foot on his thigh and picked up the other stocking from the floor. There was a hint of tears in her eyes. And it gutted him. "But let us at least be truthful with each other." He slipped the stocking over her foot and up her leg.

"You don't know what you are talking about. You don't," she insisted.

"I know what Leon tried to do to you. I know that it must have been terrifying to be locked in a burning building, facing such a horrifying death. Flames closing in on you. Perhaps you were even with Gabriel at the time. That I do not know." She averted her face. Wouldn't look at him. Wouldn't say anything. She was gripping the edge of his bed so fiercely, her knuckles were white.

"I understand that your late husband was abhorrent. And I understand why, having survived all that you have, you wouldn't trust easily. Or at all. I do understand what it's like to be betrayed so deeply by those who should be trustworthy, you don't wish to bother. Or try. Or risk trusting again... Or even feeling." He wanted to use her real name once more but didn't want to upset her again.

At least she was still there. And listening.

"I've come to know Isabelle intimately well. She isn't the sort of woman one easily forgets. You are fiercely loyal and protective—and you've sacrificed much to protect those you love—your son, your sister, and the rest of your family. Haven't you? Vittry was the reason for this whole ruse of pretending to be dead. Wasn't he?"

She bit her lip but said nothing.

He continued. "I know you. I know all your likes and dislikes. I know you are witty—the journals are full of charming stories. I know what an enormously talented storyteller and writer you are. How sensual you are. How responsive you are to my touch. You are a loving mother—the sort envied by all sons. And I believe, especially after today, that part of you trusts me and that whatever the reason you are unable to tell me the whole truth has something to do with the son you love so much."

That caused a tear to slip down her cheek. She quickly swiped it away.

"Sabine and my brother looked for you. I helped them look for you too, *chérie*. And since I read those journals, I have wanted you." He stopped short of mentioning her emotions for him in her journals. He'd no clue how to discuss such feelings.

Another tear slipped down her cheek and again she swiped it away. Only this time, she shot him a look with pain and anger in her dark eyes.

"What did you want? Sex from some ingénue scribbling fanciful notions in a journal? That woman from those journals is dead. You need to understand that."

He picked up the other red ribbon from the floor and tied it around her stocking. "No," he countered. "Her circumstances are different. But the heart and soul of that woman is still alive—as are all her passions and wants."

She leapt off the edge of the bed and onto her feet, moving away from him. "I have to go. Please send a maid in to help me dress." Her voice was charged with emotions, and she moved about the room, snatching up the rest of her clothing from the floor.

To avoid looking at him.

He rose, reached out, and grasped her arm. She jumped on contact and shot him a look that tore his heart. So much pain was in those eyes. And he understood that level of anguish.

"Easy. I'm not going to force you to stay. I can help you with your clothing—"

"No." It was firmly dealt.

"Very well. I'll summon a maid. But I want to tell you something first. I think it's only fair that if I'm asking you to reveal all your secrets, I should reveal all of mine." That captured her attention. He was able to pull her clothing bunched in her arms away from her now that he'd piqued her curiosity, and the focus was no longer on her. Luc tossed the items on the bed.

He led her to the settee and motioned to it in silent invitation for her to sit, waiting patiently until she finally did and looked up at him. His heart had begun to race and his stomach roiled, knowing the darkness he'd kept at bay was about to come to light—when he'd fought so hard and successfully against that—the greatest battle of his life.

He thought he'd go to his grave with the information he was about to reveal. But this was Isabelle, and it was important to him for her to know. To hear *everything*. To have just one human being know the complete truth. And perhaps—by some miracle—purge the shame from it all.

He'd never craved acceptance from anyone. Except his father—until it was beaten out of him. But, *Dieu*, how he wanted *this* woman's understanding.

And so much more.

You already had one miracle occur today. You found Isabelle. Maybe, you might get a second. Or maybe she'll run from the room.

In disgust.

She waited quietly. Watched him closely. He scrubbed a hand over his face and took a deep breath, grappling with his words. Foul memories were surging to the surface. He could feel a bead of sweat form on his brow. Old anxieties and fears echoed in his body and oozed into his stomach. *Jésus-Christ.* It was all happening again. Like an encore performance from a hideous play, all the emotions he'd felt as a boy were crawling through him. Pervading every fiber of his being. He leaned forward, resting his elbows on his thighs, and clasped his hands. He instantly felt a pull on the muscles of his scarred back.

An ugly reminder he got from time to time of his ugly past.

"Fucking is the only time I allowed myself to feel anything." That took her by surprise. From the corner of his eye, he saw her lovely brows rise. "I suppose I should add reading novels and poetry. And your father's plays. Perhaps it's the reason I enjoy sex and the arts so much." He gave her a small smile, then looked down at his clasped hands before he continued. "I don't give a damn what anyone thinks. But I care what you think. You've asked me certain questions. I want to answer them—completely. Truthfully." He didn't want his past to be the reason she couldn't trust him. His past had done him enough harm. He didn't—wouldn't—let it harm anything he had with Isabelle. "You've asked about my temper. About my duels. Why would I fight in so many duels? Why was I so angry? I've been purposely evasive. I'd never respond to those questions from anyone who dared to ask— and there aren't many who would have dared. But I want to answer them for you. *Just you.*" He took in a fortifying breath, trying to quell the agonizing emotions rising inside his gut. "Most of my boyhood, I was beaten for sport by Charles and the cousin I've mentioned named Bellac—that is until I was big enough and strong enough to fight back." He wasn't going to offer the horrific details. Those words would never make it out his mouth. Not ever. He had to stop and swallow twice before he could force more words out. "The older I got, the more fury I felt inside. I couldn't vanquish it. Nor the emotional torment that came with it—even after they'd stopped. I turned to dueling, challenging my peers, purposely leaving no slight uncontested. Dueling was supposed to release the anguish I was choking on."

Her warm hand was suddenly on his arm. He turned his head to look at her. Her eyes were large, shimmering with tears. And understanding.

"You...you wanted to...*die*." It wasn't even a question.

Fuck. There was that intuition she had. He'd left it unsaid. Hadn't even explained fully. She could have interpreted his words differently. Yet she'd simply known.

He had to look back down at his clasped hands once more. Emotions were knifing him in the chest. Everything inside him was screaming *STOP!* And he couldn't speak and battle back the agony slicing his insides while seeing pain in her eyes.

He forced a small smile. "I believe the only duel I partially wanted to win was the one that sent Bellac to hell. I was volatile, brash, with reckless wishes. And it's what led me to the King's navy, thinking war would put an end to it all. That I wouldn't likely return. But instead, it changed me as a man. I am grateful to have served my King and country, and to have fought with the men whom I commanded. And as horrible as it was to be arrested and imprisoned as a traitor, it solidified my desire to rise above everything that had happened and triumph over it." To put his boyhood behind him at last.

He took a moment to shore up his defenses before looking at her. *Merde.* He'd laid himself completely bare. Would she be repelled by what he'd told her? Would she see him as having been weak for wanting his anguish to end on a dueling field before his twenty-second birthday? Or as a casualty of war?

He dragged his gaze to her.

Tears were slipping down her face. She looked at him with compassion and... Was that *awe?* A knot formed in his throat.

She cupped his face tenderly and pressed a kiss to his lips. He could taste her tears. "He was a monster. Your father and cousin were both monsters. No one should do that to a boy. *No one.* And I'm so sorry for the suffering they put you through. I understand how torment can continue long after your tormenter is no longer there. I marvel at the inner strength you had to overcome what would have been insurmountable to many. And I am so very glad you didn't lose your life on a dueling field, in a ship battle, or on a gibbet."

And then her warm lips were on his again.

Dieu... Her words were like a balm over every wound he had inside. He shut his eyes and pulled her onto his lap, returning her kiss tenderly. Lovingly. Worshiping her perfect mouth. And her. He'd held on to his secrets for so long. Too long. Having had no one to tell. Never wanting anyone to know.

Or to sit in judgment of the lowest moments of his life.

He could still taste tears on his lips, and, *merde*, he wasn't entirely sure they were just hers.

And he wanted, needed more from her today. Wanted to share more with her. And to have her to share more with him.

He pulled back, noting that her breathing had begun to quicken slightly. It wouldn't take much to turn this into another carnal encounter. But he had more to say. "No one but Isabelle noticed that anything was amiss about me. Just you." He caressed the side of her cheek with the backs of his knuckles. "I want to thank you for that."

Her eyes were soft and full of emotion, but she held her tongue.

At least she wasn't trying to run from his home anymore.

He smiled. "I have something I want to show you. But, unfortunately, we are going to have to put our clothes on."

*****

Isabelle descended the grand staircase of Luc's *hôtel*, holding his hand.

She'd been afraid to trust him for so long, in constant conflict over wanting to believe everything he said. Wanting to distrust him. And just plain wanting him, more than anything.

Yet the truth was he was every bit the man she'd imagined him to be. And so much more. The wounds he'd suffered from his childhood, both inside and out, didn't diminish him in her eyes one bit.

It only made him perfectly imperfect.

Human. And real. So brave and strong.

A courage that went far deeper than the battles he'd fought and won as an officer in the King's navy. Or as a privateer. His bravery and strength reached back all the way to his boyhood and rose to the level of hero in her eyes.

Regardless of whatever happened between them, she knew two things: She was determined to fight back against Pierrette's demands and not allow Nicole, Luc, or herself to be pawns in that woman's little game. Secondly, she would enjoy whatever moments of bliss she could with this man and cherish them for a lifetime.

No more hidden truths between them.

If he could bare all, if he, knowing who she was, understood why she'd held her tongue for so long—with no volatile outburst as Roch would have done—then there was no reason to keep anything else from him.

She was doing what didn't come easy to her—she was placing her complete trust in someone.

"Gilbert," Luc called out. His rich voice broke into her thoughts.

The dark-haired young servant stopped dead in his tracks in the vestibule and bowed. "Yes, my lord."

"Madame Carre has agreed to grace us with her presence and dine here this evening. Tell the cook we wish to impress her and that supper will be served one hour earlier than normal." Luc smiled at the younger man.

"Yes, my lord." Another quick bow and he was gone.

She gazed up at Luc. That knee-weakening smile was now directed at her. A fresh wave of joy crested over her. It felt as though she'd slipped inside the pages of her very own *Princesses' Adventures* novels.

"Does that meet your approval, *chérie*? I trust that will give you sufficient time to return home to Gabriel and see to him before he retires for the night?"

His consideration of her son moved her deeply.

You meet with my approval. You always have…

She returned his smile. "Yes. Thank you." It didn't escape her notice that he had begun to call her "darling." She had to fight the urge to read anything into the endearment, lest she embarrass herself by flinging her arms around him and never letting go.

He led her across the vestibule to a set of double doors, still holding her hand. Grasping the door latch with his free hand, he gave her a wink. "After you."

Then threw open the door.

She stepped inside. Her heart lost a beat. The room was massive, with a wall of windows and three sets of double glass doors that stretched across the opposite wall, facing the courtyard. But it wasn't the vista that took her breath away, nor the grandeur of the room. It was the three other walls lined with shelves and filled with books, from the floor to the high ceilings.

More books than she'd ever seen in her life.

A single book was a small fortune. A costly treasure in and of itself. Her family had once owned a moderate number of novels.

This immense collection surrounding her was more than a king's ransom. Slowly, she turned around and drank it all in.

"This is one of my libraries," he said with pride. "There is one at each of my châteaus. I've lost some books after the Crown confiscated our properties and title, but I am working to replace them. What is here is being duly recorded by my secretary."

She shook her head, her smile returning. "No small task."

He chuckled. "No, it isn't, but it is mostly done."

She walked toward the nearest shelves. "This is an incredible library, Luc." She ran her fingertips along the leather spines of the volumes before her, loving how much they meant to him. Luc walked over to a shelf feet from where she stood and pulled out a book.

He held it out. "I think you might like this one."

She approached and took the book from his hands. The author's name grabbed her attention. A large grin she couldn't contain formed on her face. "*Isabella di Morra.*"

"Yes. I think we both like her works. I would like to gift it to you."

She shot her gaze up from the book to his face. "I couldn't..."

"Yes, you can. I insist."

"But, this poetess is one of your favorites."

"I have many favorites." He turned and walked toward the large ebony-and-gold desk at the end of the room. Wearing a white shirt, black breeches, and boots, his tall strong form was mesmerizing to behold. She allowed herself to appreciate the sight. It set her insides aflutter. "I've recently discovered a new author I favor. The characters are captivating," he said over his shoulder. Reaching the desk, he turned back to face her, then gestured toward some volumes beside him.

Curious, she approached to see who his new favorite was, still holding the book of poetry by Morra in her hands, and immediately recognized her books. Her cheeks heated.

He sat on the edge of the desk, studying her closely. Those engrossing green eyes, scrutinizing her face. And, perhaps, her thoughts.

What in the world did one say when the man you'd dreamed of for years has learned of your girlhood affinity for him?

"I will say it again, as it bears repeating. You're an extraordinary writer," he said. "Your writing is engaging. And I don't say it because I am one of your main subjects and characters."

She murmured her thanks, mortified that her blush only deepened. It was a great compliment coming from a man who was so well-read.

Coming from Luc de Moutier.

"I don't suppose the purpose for bringing me here is to have me to talk about books—a comfortable, innocuous subject—and well...lull me into divulging more?" she gently teased.

He laughed. "I will confess, there is that. But I also wanted to share this library with someone who'd appreciate it." He brushed an errant curl off her cheek. "Allow me just once to hear from those gorgeous lips your real name."

She owed him as much. He'd spoken his truth with courage. She needed to do the same.

"Before I do, I wish you to know I am placing great faith in you. Something I do not normally do."

"I know. And I will not betray your confidence. Not ever. I would never hurt you."

She'd heard those words from other men. From Leon. From Roch. She swallowed, placed Morra's book on the desk next her novels, lifted her chin a notch. And took a leap of faith.

"I'm Isabelle Laurent."

He softly swore, snaked an arm around her waist, and yanked her to him. Then swooped in with a kiss as though he wanted to seal the name on her lips. Her body sparked to life. She immediately fisted his shirt against his strong chest and returned the kiss, hungry for more, wanting to make up for all the missed kisses she could have had with him.

And foolishly denied herself.

He broke the kiss sooner than she would have liked. He was about to speak when she blurted out, "You are the first man I've ever kissed."

His brows shot up, clearly surprised by the unexpected confession.

"I've never kissed a man before you," she continued. "Roch despised the mere thought— for which I was eternally grateful. And I've never given any man leave to kiss me—except you."

"*Dieu*... I don't know what to say... I'm flattered and honored—" was all he could say before she leaped into more confessions.

"I hadn't ever done some of the things we've done in the boudoir. Or the library. Then there was that time in the gardens...and, well, if you haven't already guessed, I haven't the sexual experience others think I have." Words were spilling from her lips unrestrained. As though a dam had just broken. Everything she'd been forced to hold back flooded out of her. "Besides submitting to Roch, I've only been with the Marquis de Cambry. Do you know him?"

"I—"

She began to pace. "He was gentle, kind." *Unlike Roch.* "But he didn't have your sexual repertoire. I didn't realize men even knew the things you know of the carnal arts."

He caught her arm, arresting her in her tracks. "Isabelle—"

Dear God, hearing her real name from his lips sounded heavenly. "Could you tell?"

His brow furrowed. "Could I tell what, *chérie?*"

"That I was a novice at some of the things we did?"

A smile formed on his handsome face, and he pulled her by the arm back between his parted legs and wrapped his arms around her waist. She wanted to return the embrace, but rested her palms against his chest instead.

Mindful not to touch his back.

He leaned in and pressed a kiss to that sensitive spot below her ear. A tiny tingle quivered down her spine. "I noted some sexual curiosity that suggested certain things were new. But that didn't lessen the experience. The carnal connection between us is exquisite. I love fucking you. I love making you come for me. And I love the way you come." His voice was a low, sensual murmur.

Her blood heated with every quickening beat of her heart. "What a coincidence. I love making you come for me and the way you come too," she whispered in his ear. Then lightly bit his earlobe. She delighted in the sound of his groan.

"Oh, no, you don't." He pulled back, his hands on her shoulders, but a smile was on his lips. And oh, how she loved that smile. It made her feel joy just seeing it. It always had. "We are going to continue our talk. Without any of those delicious distractions—for now."

She nodded in agreement. "There is much to talk about."

Pierrette. And Sabine. Her sister was the topic she wanted to discuss most. And was most afraid to mention. Until now, there had been a glimmer of hope she'd see Sabine again.

The time had come to see if that hope would be utterly dashed.

"Why don't we begin at the beginning?" he said. "What happened that day of the fire in the servants' outbuildings? If you are not the person buried in the grave at my château as everyone believes, then who is?"

"Gabriel's mother."

He frowned. "What do you mean? What are you talking about?"

"I did not give birth to Gabriel. His mother was a woman from the village. She would come for food while she was pregnant with her son and continued after her babe was born. I always managed to sneak her something to eat. She came every day, and so I became concerned your father would learn of what I was doing. He'd have been furious to know his food was being given away—and especially to one of the peasants on your lands. And I did not wish to suffer his wrath as many of the other servants had. I asked Virginie to meet me that day at the servants' outbuildings. That is where she, Gabriel, and I were when Leon's men started the fire. Gabriel was only an infant. He and I survived. But Virginie perished. I became his mother that day." She felt the usual sting of tears in her eyes and a knot in her throat over Virginie's death. The mental images of the inferno, always lurking on the fringes of her mind, invaded her thoughts. The terrifying flames. The eerie sounds of crackling wood followed by the crashing timbers all around them.

It was the stuff of nightmares. Nightmares that had torn her from sleep many times and sent her racing to Gabriel's bedside to make certain he was all right.

She tamped down the memory.

Luc pulled her tightly against him. She allowed herself to lean on him—something she normally wouldn't do—and rested her cheek against his shoulder. Feelings of being safe engulfed her heart.

And she liked that. So much.

"I can only imagine how terrifying that must have been," he murmured. "I wish I'd been the one who'd ended Vittry's worthless life. I'll see to it that a proper stone is placed over Virginie's grave. Something discreet yet fitting for her."

She shot her head up, surprised and moved by his promise, her eyes filling with fresh tears, blurring his face. She forced them back. "Thank you. That would be lovely."

"What about Gabriel's father?"

"I know little about him. I'd never met him. Virginie was recently widowed and all alone. There wasn't any family to care for Gabriel—on either side. Gabriel and I had no one that day of the fire, except each other. I have raised him, and I couldn't love him more had he come from my own womb. He is my son."

"How on earth did you make it off our lands without Vittry and his men seeing you?"

"I simply ran with Gabriel in my arms. Didn't stop until we reached the main roads. I was in desperate need of any transportation at all to get as far away as I could. Then I thought a miracle happened. Roch was in his carriage and stopped to help. An aristo with wealth. He didn't ask questions in the beginning. He was kind then and offered to take me to a wet nurse for Gabriel. After Roch's death, I came to Paris to begin anew. With a new name. A new persona. Determined to make certain Gabriel would have a good life and a future free from poverty."

He gave a nod. "You are indeed his mother. Only a mother would go to such lengths for her child. I don't often say this to people, but I admire you. Your strength. Resilience. And courage." A warmth glowed in his beautiful eyes. And she cautioned herself not to presume more than what was there. He reached out and brushed another of her errant curls from her cheek. "So, now I fully understand why you wouldn't allow a man to kiss you. And I comprehend why you would not accept any married lovers—to keep your affairs uncomplicated."

She stepped away from him, breaking the embrace, needing some distance to be able to speak without the deluge of romantic emotions that was presently swamping her heart. He was beyond potent—both to her heart and body.

The longer she remained in his arms, the more strongly he affected her.

"Yes, that had a lot to do with Roch's wife, and since we are on the subject of her, there is something important I must tell you about Pierrette de Roch."

*****

Luc cocked a brow, awaiting her next comment. He couldn't imagine what could be relevant or important to him about a woman he'd never met.

"She's a recluse. She never leaves her country estate, but now she's here in the city."

An uneasy feeling slid into his gut. "Does she know who you really are?"

"She didn't before, but she does now. I never expected to see her in Paris. I never expected Roch to leave letters with my real name. Letters she discovered after his death."

"When did you see her? How do you know she's here?"

"She was there at the Duc and Duchesse d'Allain's salon today. I just spoke with her in private. She'd been sending me anonymous notes for a while. Ugly little missives with nothing more in them than insults. It is all rather bizarre and twisted. Pierrette harbors a great deal of animosity toward me. Accuses me of stealing Roch from her. I've tried to explain to her that I did no such thing, but she is now threatening to reveal my identity—and threatening to ruin Nicole's reputation for aiding me in my, as she called it, 'self-enriching scheme' if I don't help her daughter marry a certain aristo."

Bloody hell. "That is madness. Which aristo?"

"You."

"*Me?* You jest?"

"No, I don't. Please give me your word that you will not further complicate this by attempting to see Pierrette or reason with her. To intervene in any way is likely to only make her angrier, and that would make matters worse. I've yet to speak to Nicole about this. I believe we should defer to her wishes on managing the matter, whatever they are. She has much to lose."

"By Roch's widow's threats, so do you and Gabriel."

"We will be all right. All of us. I'll make certain," she managed to say with conviction. Yet, he sensed she was worried. Again, he marveled at her fortitude. "Do I have your word?"

"You have my word and my pledge to help, as much or as little as you wish—without marrying Roch's daughter." He wasn't going to add to her distress. Nor was he about to marry this madwoman's offspring.

"Thank you. I would never ask you to. And I am unwilling to allow any of us to be a pawn for Pierrette."

"But why does she want me?"

He saw her stiffen ever so slightly. Then she shrugged. "Who knows the workings of that woman's mind."

Again, he sensed there was more she wasn't saying.

She looked down as though in thought, then met his gaze. "Luc, there is another matter I wish to discuss with you… It is about Sabine. I wish to see my sister again. I want Gabriel to meet her. To meet his cousin Isabelle. I want to hold both of them. I want her to know that I am alive. That I did everything I could to keep Leon away from her and the rest of our family—and I wish to see them too. I know it is much to ask, but perhaps you can take me to her?"

His stomach fisted, a reflexive reaction to a subject that struck a raw wound.

What she was asking of him was no easy task either logistically or emotionally, for it would mean he'd see Jules again. In their final conversation, when his brother had attempted to break down barriers— barriers Luc had erected between himself and Charles's favorite son for Luc's own sanity's sake—he'd slammed the door permanently shut on any relationship with his brother.

The thought of seeing him again was gut-wrenching.

"Isabelle, that isn't easy. You need a fully armed sea vessel to safely navigate the waters in the West Indies. It is far too dangerous otherwise. I don't own a warship."

"But the King does. France is at peace. The warships aren't needed. Perhaps you can speak to him? You were an officer in the King's navy and a privateer for the Crown. Didn't the King allow privateers to rent the ships they used? I have funds—"

"The King was not aware that I was renting his warship at that time, as I was under the command of his favorite privateer then, Simon Boulenger. Simon was once the commander of a fleet of privateer ships. He has his own warships and had rented some from the Crown as well when we were still at war with Spain. That is how your sister, family, and Jules reached the West Indies and Simon's island, Marguerite—on one of his warships. And yes, for the King's *gain*, he did permit the use of his ships to attack Spanish vessels and relieve them of their silver cargo. Not to simply voyage across the sea."

"Do you mean to say there is *no* way to see Sabine again?"

Jésus-Christ. He felt as though someone just punched him in the stomach. Seeing the devastation in her eyes winded him. "I did not say that. Perhaps they will return someday for a visit…"

"Why would they? My family and Sabine are there. And you have made it plain to your brother that you don't wish to see him. Even you don't believe that they'll return. You have said as much."

Fuck. He raked a hand through his hair. "This is complicated and more than just an issue between my brother and me."

She went silent and simply stared at him. A direct, unwavering, penetrating gaze, as though she could read his every thought. Then looked away and shook her head.

When she returned his regard, she simply said, "I must leave. Please have someone summon my men."

Merde. "What about dining with me?"

"I fear I've lost my appetite. I'm going home."

"I wish you'd reconsider."

"Oddly, I was going to say the same thing to you." She walked toward the doors of his library.

"What should I reconsider, *chérie?*" he called out.

She stopped and turned around. "I wish you'd reconsider your lying to me after purporting to be honest."

"I am not lying."

"You are. Perhaps you are even lying in part to yourself. I have asked for a great deal, I know. I should not have made such a request and put you in this position. And for that, I apologize. I can understand why one wouldn't wish to make such a great journey. So be it." He didn't miss her voice cracking with emotion. "But the obstacle here is not obtaining the warship—though I will concede that there is significant difficulty there. And it isn't the long voyage. The true obstacle *is* your brother. I know your father treated you horribly. Unspeakably cruel. But it isn't your brother's fault, any more than it is yours. I'd wager he isn't even aware of what happened to you. You haven't ever told him, have you? He deserves the truth from your lips. And he doesn't deserve to be punished for your father's sins."

Her words slammed into him. Anger surged inside him and scorched through his very entrails. "Jules is *not* a victim!" he shot back.

"Nor is he a villain. I remember him with you at the theater. I saw him once intervene in an altercation between you and another gentleman one night. He loves you. He'd tried to protect you. He may have even kept you from a duel that might have killed you. You suggest that everything you've been through is over. Behind you. But, and I say this to utter the truth with no ulterior motive, you will never be completely done with what your father and cousin did until you've made peace with Jules."

What she said robbed him of his physical breath, knifing deep into his wound. The last thing he wanted to hear was that he wasn't done with Bellac and Charles.

The last fucking thing he ever wanted to hear.

He steeled himself against the pain and the ire it incited, battling back the excruciating memories that suddenly threatened to materialize in his mind. He didn't want to see his father's face or any part of that room where his nightmares originated. Or his perfect, unmarred brother. Not now.

Fuck, not ever.

Luc placed his hands on his hips and shut his eyes a moment before opening them again. He managed one sole word past his clenched teeth.

"Go!"

CHAPTER SIXTEEN

Isabelle was numb.

Her carriage approached home. She stared blankly out the window.

She'd lost her sister—for the second time. This time for good.

And Luc as well.

She'd pushed him too far today—though what she'd said about his brother was true. It was only a matter of time before what they'd had would come to an end. They had lived in the present with no future.

The entire day had been incredible. And horrible. And though she was exhausted down to her marrow, she wanted to see her precious boy and their beloved oversized dog, curl up together with them on her bed, and read a story.

Tomorrow, she would address the problem with Pierrette. Speak with Nicole.

Tomorrow, she would let herself feel. Mourn her losses. Find a way to heal, and forge a path forward.

But the rest of this day belonged to Gabriel and Montague.

The moment her carriage pulled up to the front of Nicole's *hôtel*, she noted the toppled stone planter at the bottom of the steps. Purple flowers rested on the ground, surrounded by dirt, and two large pieces that had broken off the planter.

It was odd. Not something easily toppled. Definitely not something Nicole's staff would have left on the ground.

An instant uneasy feeling formed in the pit of her stomach.

As soon as the carriage stopped and the door opened, she practically leaped out, and raced up the stone steps. She'd just reached the front door when it was flung open.

Delphine greeted her, sobbing hysterically.

Isabelle grabbed her hands. "What is it? What has happened?"

Delphine pulled her inside, crying uncontrollably. Sounds that were meant to be words emitted from her mouth, but Isabelle couldn't make any sense of them.

"Oh, good God. She is trying to tell you your son is gone." Pierrette's voice pierced the air.

Isabelle shot her gaze up to Roch's wife standing in the vestibule, four sizable men with her. It took three rapid heartbeats before the words sank in.

"...*your son is gone.*"

Her heart thudded in her throat. And for a moment, she thought she couldn't possibly have heard correctly.

"What do you mean, *gone?*"

It was then she noticed two male servants on the floor, with facial scrapes and cuts. The majordomo, Joseph, sat on the bottom stair, holding his head, blood streaks on his hand.

And Annette, dear God, Annette, Gabriel's nurse, was in the far corner, weeping into her hands much the same way Delphine was. Both women looked disheveled as though they too had been in a physical altercation.

"They...they took him," Delphine sobbed.

Isabelle's limbs went cold. She screamed out Gabriel's name. And again.

She was met with wild barking from Montague—in the distance. Sounding as though he were locked in Gabriel's room.

But no Gabriel.

She raced toward the stairs. But someone caught her by the waist, lifting her feet off the floor and dragging her back to the center of the vestibule.

"Where is *MY SON?*" she demanded, trying to break free from the crushing grip of Pierrette's man, digging her nails into his arm to no avail, kicking her captor in the shin. She heard him grunt, but his grip never slackened.

Oh God! She'd walked in without Yves and Serge. The men had driven away—gone to attend to the carriage and horses. She'd left herself vulnerable.

She'd left her *son* vulnerable having taken them with her in the first place.

"*Where is he?*" she shrilled, frantic. The other servants leaped to her aid despite their injuries, only to be grabbed by the other men and easily tossed aside.

Pierrette stood silently, looking bored.

"What have you done with him? Where is Gabriel? Let go of me!" She was screaming and fighting, beyond panicked. Managing to twist around, she curled her fist and landed a blow to the side of the brute's face.

"What on earth is happening?" Through her hysteria, Isabelle clearly heard Nicole's voice.

"Wonderful, the other harlot is here," Pierrette stated blandly to herself.

Ignoring Pierrette, Nicole addressed the brute. "Unhand her!" But he didn't comply. Nicole spun around to face Pierrette. "Who the bloody hell are you? How dare you intrude into my home, harm my staff, manhandle my friend."

"She has done something to Gabriel!" The anguished words tore up Isabelle's throat. She landed another swift kick to the man holding her in an iron grip around the waist.

Nicole visibly blanched. *"What—?"*

Miffed, Pierrette waved a hand. "Oh, no one has done anything to your brat. Do calm down… *Everyone!*"

Isabelle stopped fighting for a moment. The more she exerted herself, the tighter the goon squeezed. She was having problems catching her breath, and she needed to focus. Be strong.

To help Gabriel.

She shook down to her very entrails. "What have you done with my son? Where is he?"

"He is safe," was all that Roch's wife offered.

"*Where is he?*" she said through clenched teeth.

"He is in my possession until the trial—should there be one."

"Trial? What trial? For what? And what do you mean, *should there be one?*"

"A trial for custody of my husband's son."

None of this was real. This couldn't be real. Her mind was spinning. "What are you talking about? Roch was *not* Gabriel's father."

Pierrette smiled. "That is to be determined."

"The only matter that need be determined is your madness. And that should be easy," Nicole shot back. "Return that boy at once!"

Pierrette cocked a brow at Nicole. "You have played everyone for a fool with this daughter of a dead playwright. I would be careful if I were you. Now then, the King has decided that the boy should be with me, a woman of good standing and elevated bloodlines, instead of a common prostitute. I have in my possession a *Lettre de Cachet*. If you are unaware of what that is, it is an Order of Confinement, signed by the King under royal seal." Pierrette looked over at Isabelle, her next words directed solely at her. "These men are here to remove you from this home, just as they removed the child, and will escort you to the prison that awaits you."

"*Lettre de Cachet* is often for an indefinite confinement. *Without* trial!" Nicole exclaimed.

"You are having me *arrested?*" Isabelle laughed without mirth. "What for?"

"You can't be trusted not to interfere with this matter and would try to kidnap the boy."

Tears blurred Isabelle's eyes. "You can't do that to him. I'm certain he's terrified. If you wish to hurt me—"

"I have. I have the most precious person to you."

"What about Luc? I thought you wanted him for your daughter," she all but spit out.

"I couldn't care less about him. And I don't have a child, you fool. I was never able to give Aubert one. Mind you, he was rather busy with you. It's your son I want. I only used the Marquis de Fontenay as a way to ensure that you and your two brutes wouldn't be here. It's the reason I had you followed. I told you you were nothing but a worthless whore. The promise of promiscuity sent you running and allowed me to easily gain access to the boy. I hope you enjoyed yourself."

Tears spilled down Isabelle's cheeks without restraint and her measured tone dissolved as she raised her voice and shouted, "How evil must you be to hurt an innocent child just for your twisted sense of revenge!"

"You will *finally* truly know, as you sit in your confinement and rot, what it is like to be kept from someone you love. Day after day. Night after night. I have done society a favor—every woman married or about to marry—in having you removed from our midst."

"You will not do this!" Isabelle screamed, her voice reverberating in the vestibule. "You will give me back my son!" She lunged at Pierrette.

Then everything went black.

*****

Footsteps approached Isabelle's room.

They had placed her in a convent in the country. Yet it was still a prison. She'd been there one week, two days, and at least nine hours. Longer than that since she'd seen Gabriel.

A small bed in the corner. Simple linens. A small window that let in some light. A washbasin. And she had access to a small *sale de bain*.

Small and narrow was what her life had become. She existed with a singular purpose.

Escape.

She'd find a way to get out of here. Because they were not keeping her from Gabriel. Fear and worry for him and his well-being battered her heart. She didn't sleep. Barely ate—just to keep her strength. And paced.

Back and forth.

Back and forth.

Back and forth.

Surreptitiously observing everything, looking for any weakness in her captivity to gain her freedom. Once out, she would retrieve Gabriel.

Then they'd leave France. Forever.

Footsteps stopped outside her door. She heard the key in the lock. Then the thick wooden door creaked open. One of the older sisters from the Convent of Mont-Dieu entered, followed as usual by a large man with a weapon in hand. It was so Isabelle wouldn't attempt to overpower the nun and obtain the keys to her freedom.

The male guard was not allowed to be alone with her.

Given her "corrupted soul," according to Mother Superior, Isabelle was likely to trade sexual favors for freedom.

And she'd be correct on that score.

It was the reason, she'd been told, that they hadn't put her in a regular prison—with all male guards—choosing to confine her to a convent instead.

If given the chance, she'd surrender her body. Endure it. Then scrub it from her mind and never think of it again. There was *nothing* she wouldn't do to get Gabriel out of Pierrette's hands.

Not once since her confinement had she allowed herself to cry. She refused to weaken and give in to despair, no matter how dire the circumstances were.

While there was breath in her body, she'd save her son.

The nun's expression was stern. Her disdain toward Isabelle was the same as that of the other women at the convent. The nun stepped aside, and then the man lumbered to the corner of her room. He was least ten years her senior. His skin and hair were dirty from physical labor. She didn't miss the way he ogled her breasts repeatedly.

She suppressed a shudder of revulsion.

"That will be all. Thank you." The familiar voice made Isabelle's heart jump with joy.

Nicole... Thank God!

Instantly, a knot welled in her throat. She raced across the room and threw her arms around her dear friend and squeezed her tightly.

"I'd like to be alone with her," Nicole said, returning her embrace.

"No, Mother Superior specifically stated that you may have a brief visit in our presence only," the nun replied.

Isabelle pulled away. "Have you seen Gabriel? How is he? Where is he? Have they harmed him? Is he all right?"

Nicole gripped her shoulders and squeezed affectionately. "I have not seen him, though I have been working to that end. However, I have been assured that he is fine. He has been visited by my lawyers. That witch will not allow me to see him personally."

Isabelle squeezed her in an embrace again, all too aware of the nun and guard watching them. In her ear, she earnestly whispered, "Get Gabriel out of France. Anywhere away from Pierrette. I *will* escape this place and join him."

Once again, Nicole pulled away and looked her in the eye. "We are going to get him back to you. I am doing all that I can."

God, what did she ever do to deserve this woman in her life?

"How do I thank you enough for all you have done for me and Gabriel? I would need several lifetimes. You have done so much, and I have done nothing in return but bring you grief."

"Nonsense."

"Pierrette has threatened to harm your reputation—if she hasn't already."

"Yes, by revealing your name, which she has done. And yes, she has attempted to harm me as well."

"I am so very sorry…"

"For what? You are not responsible for the vindictive actions of another. There are people who are simply riddled with contempt. They live their lives in self-imposed misery and wish to inflict that on others. You needn't worry about me. I have encountered my share of Pierrettes in my life. This is not the first person who has attempted to diminish me in society. I doubt she'll be the last."

"Have you lost any friends or acquaintances because of this?"

"No one that matters. She will not succeed in shaming me for the way I wish to live my life and for the alliances I choose to keep. Do not let her shame you for the life you've led."

"I will *not* allow her to take Gabriel away from me."

"That's it, my darling. That is the very attitude we must maintain. Now then, they can hold you here indefinitely, without trial—which is what Roch's widow wants. But I have been to see a number of judges at the *Palais de Justice*—Paul de Brilhac and Nicolas de la Toison, to be exact—and have pushed for a resolution to this matter. They will not simply return Gabriel to you. There will have to be a trial for custody. Since Pierrette is claiming that Roch is Gabriel's father, you will have to convince the judges that she is lying. You will have to tell the truth about his mother and father. I have campaigned for this trial so that Pierrette can no longer have claim over you and your son. Give me your word that you will not do anything to anger the judges I have spoken to in the meantime."

Isabelle understood what Nicole was talking about. She didn't want her to risk everything on an escape plan.

"You have my word."

"Good. A trial will get you out of here—for good. Is there anyone who knows the truth? Anyone who knew Gabriel's mother?"

"Delphine. She worked with me at the Moutier château where Virginie would come begging for food. She knew her."

"That's good." Nicole offered her an encouraging smile.

"No, it is not. Pierrette is of noble blood. Delphine and I are not. Her words have more weight."

"Allow me to keep working on this matter. I am not without influence. I have been able to gain entry here, and that was virtually impossible." Nicole smiled. "Together, we will get Gabriel back—using the law."

"Please push to visit Gabriel. To see with your own eyes that he is well. Tell him that I love him. That I have not abandoned him. Tell him to look at the stars each night and that I will do the same and we will gaze upon them together."

Nicole clasped Isabelle's hands and squeezed. "I shall."

"What of Luc?" she couldn't help but ask. She deeply regretted her parting words. He'd already had his share of anguish without her stirring more. Even if he never wanted anything to do with her again, she wished she could apologize to him. Know he was all right.

Nicole shook her head. "He is gone, to one of his châteaus, I think. He is not in the city. He's unaware of what has happened."

"He isn't coming back." At least not to her. "I am not permitted to send any letters. Would you write to him and tell him how sorry I am about how we parted last and to have caused him distress? I simply want to know he is well. And you are correct. We must focus on Gabriel. We must win this trial."

No matter how impossible it was.

Because losing was not an option.

CHAPTER SEVENTEEN

Isabelle was placed in yet another locked room, with a simple table and chair.

She was mere feet away from the *Chambre de Justice*—where three judges would assemble. Where she would fight for Gabriel's return.

The trial date had arrived—three weeks from the day she'd last seen Nicole. They hadn't allowed her dear friend to visit again.

Yet Nicole had managed to cause this trial to occur—in a world dictated by men. And Isabelle remained indebted to and in awe of the most incredible woman she had ever known.

Thankfully, she was no longer in the convent garb she'd been given there. Thanks to Nicole, one of Isabelle's finer gowns had been sent. Her hair was neat but adorned with no embellishments. She knew, as well as did Nicole, that her appearance had to be on par with Pierrette's.

Even if her bloodlines were not.

Elegant but demure.

For Gabriel's sake.

Again, Nicole had managed to perform miracles. Lord knows, Isabelle was in need of a significant one today.

She smoothed her skirts for the tenth time, struggling to keep her fidgeting fingers still. She prayed they'd come take her from this room soon and get on with the matter.

The anxiety was suffocating.

The sound of a key turning the lock grabbed her attention. *Finally!*

Pierrette swept into the room with a swish of her green gown. She was smart enough to keep a male guard with her.

Isabelle balled her hands into fists. An almost blinding rage shot through her. She'd never had a physical altercation with anyone in her life. But at the moment, that guard and her promise to Nicole were the only things that were keeping her from pummeling the woman before her.

"Get her out of here," Isabelle demanded, addressing the guard.

"That's a lovely gown, my dear." Pierrette responded as though they were at a soiree, ignoring the order Isabelle had given the guardsman. He didn't seem inclined to follow it. "You do know it doesn't change the fact that a whore wears it. That harlot friend of yours may have forced this trial, but you will not win against me."

Isabelle took three sharp, quick steps toward her, deriving only a small measure of satisfaction in seeing the woman's smug expression change. And her quick steps back.

Isabelle stopped inches from her face.

"Your lies and sheer heartlessness will not win against *me*. You have allowed yourself to become hardened and hateful because you pine for the love of a cruel man who willfully withheld it from you. Wasting years of your life. And for that, you have already lost. If you have done *any harm* to my son, I promise you—*no, I swear it*—you will rue this day and every single one thereafter until you finally take your last breath on this earth and go to hell."

She had to turn away to keep from strangling the life out of her.

"You little bitch. You have no idea what you put me through. You bewitched him. Denied me his love, and now that he is dead, I shall never know it again, for he wasted it on the likes of you," she hissed out at her as Isabelle continued to walk away, putting distance between them. "I have always wanted a son. And you have raised a whiny, insolent little creature who cries and screams ceaselessly. I will show them I am the better choice for him—a parent who will curb his discourteous humor."

Isabelle saw blood red.

She whipped around and lunged at Pierrette. The guard caught her by the waist, but not before she managed to crack her palm across Pierrette's face.

The stunned look on Pierrette's face wasn't enough to dim her ire or diminish her anguish.

"You will pay for what you have done to that innocent boy!" Isabelle said.

Pierrette left the room in a rush, holding her cheek.

*****

The courtroom was warm and filled with spectators.

A hush fell over the room as Isabelle paused at the threshold and steeled her courage. She would not fail. She would not fail Gabriel.

She entered, poised, with elegance. Her chin up. Her steps strong.

And she looked at no one. Though, from her peripheral vision, the bright colors told her that most observers were from the noble class. The wave of whispers upon her entering the room was instant. It rippled through the mass.

She ignored it. Didn't even attempt to decipher what they were saying. Focused simply on reaching the opposite side of the large courtroom without her knees giving way under the crushing weight of her fears.

Grasping her skirts, she climbed the two wooden steps into the defendant's box, then turned to face the crowd. It was Vannod's face she happened to notice first. He looked her in the eye, then looked away. The same thing occurred with a number of men who'd openly vied for her at every social event.

Clearly, word of who she really was had spread. They were all here for entertainment.

Not support.

Quickly, she scanned the crowd until she found Nicole, needing one friendly face in this horde. In a deep purple gown, she looked regal and beautiful as always. She smiled at Isabelle.

She mustered a sliver of a smile in return and a nod. Schooling her features, she relied on the acting skills she'd attained since childhood to give the outward appearance of calm. Assuredness. While doubts gnawed at her confidence.

Isabelle squeezed the wooden railing before her and took in a fortifying breath.

You can do this. You can.

"Mademoiselle Laurent?"

She looked down at the elderly gentleman before her dressed in black robes. "Yes?"

"I am Félix Tabart. I will be representing you today at the request of Madame de Grammont."

"Yes, of course."

"We are only permitted a few moments to confer. I am told Delphine is prepared to attest to your story of Gabriel's mother, Virginie. But Delphine isn't here. At least not yet."

Isabelle's gaze shot up and scanned the crowd again, searching for Delphine's face.

"Where is my son?" she asked.

"He is in Madame de Roch's care." She wanted to object that instant, because Pierrette was not giving Gabriel the care he needed. "I have seen him myself. He has no signs of physical harm and he bears a proper weight."

Isabelle could offer just two words. "Thank you." Knowing he wasn't being beaten and was being fed gave her some comfort.

He continued, "You will have to give your testimony first if Delphine is not here by the time we begin. I should warn you that I have it on good authority Madame de Roch will have servants claim you had no child when you came to live in Château Mayenne."

She wasn't surprised Pierrette had managed to coerce the servants to lie where she'd once lived with Roch. "I have had much time to think on this matter, Monsieur Tabart, and I believe that proving the existence of Gabriel's birth mother is difficult." She scanned the mass once more, looking for one particular man. Even if he too came for the entertainment of this matter and not to support her, at least she'd know he was well. "Especially without the Marquis de Fontenay to verify that she is buried on his lands. Also, I fear if I admit that I did not give birth to Gabriel, he will be taken from me nonetheless."

"That is a possibility."

"Then I am going to tell them of my wanton ways. Of my untamable desires. If I muddy the waters enough, there can be no finding that Roch fathered Gabriel."

"I'm afraid I cannot encourage you to lie."

"I won't. I will take care to choose my words carefully."

Tabart gave her a nod as the three judges entered. A spike of excitement fluttered through the crowd.

Pierrette's lawyer, a pot-bellied older man of similar age to Monsieur Tabart, addressed the three judges. "Most honorable lords," he began, and told them the tall tale of a boy, born out of wedlock, whose best interest it was to be with the widow of his highborn father rather than his common mother of ill repute.

Isabelle swallowed down her screams of denial as he went on to describe the widow's "loving nature." Her willingness to "open her heart and home to the boy."

She glanced at Pierrette, expecting to see her smug look. Instead, she sat near her lawyer, looking sullen. Seemingly lost in thought. One of her cheeks slightly more pink than the other.

"I tell you," Pierrette's lawyer continued, "the boy's behavior and manners are at present those of an untamed little beast."

Isabelle blinked back the sting of tears. For her sweet son to be behaving in any hysterical fashion at all was only because he was confused and terrified.

"We are urging that custody be granted to Madame de Roch, a woman of standing. Of nobility in her pedigree that can be traced back in all four bloodlines for many generations. Whereby the boy would benefit in having private tutors and proper lessons in etiquette..."

Gabriel had an excellent tutor and proper lessons in etiquette. She'd seen to it. Each lie he told about Gabriel battered her soul.

"...We will show, through a number of witnesses, that the male child in question, the Vicomte de Roch's only male issue—"

The doors slammed open, making Isabelle jump.

Luc stood on the threshold, a scowl on his face. Without hesitation, he stalked toward the front, his tall, powerful body dressed in black boots and breeches and a costly light green doublet. A perfect match to his eyes. He moved with masculine grace, carrying himself with his usual inherent authority gained from being a former naval officer, seasoned in battle and a man of superior birth.

At least a score of people filed in behind him, some carrying books, others journals. And Isabelle recognized each person, one by one. Marc, then Delphine, who flashed her a large smile, as though she knew some wonderful secret. And others she hadn't seen in years who'd been servants, like her, to Luc's father.

Her heart began to fill with hope.

She tried to quash it, afraid of any devastating disappointment.

"What is this intrusion about?" one of the judges asked over the rush of whispers around the room.

"I have a matter before this court relevant to this proceeding," Luc stated.

Pierrette's lawyer exchanged whispers with his client, then interjected, "The Marquis de Fontenay can wait to be called as a witness for the defense if that is his wish."

"No, I cannot wait. Sit down," Luc's order was sharp, as was the look he gave the man.

The lawyer complied, his face reddening.

Isabelle saw Nicole nod to Tabart. He spoke up. "My honored lords, I have no objection to allowing the Marquis de Fontenay to speak. If he feels what he has to say is relevant, he should be permitted to relay his information."

The judges conferred a moment before one said, "Very well, what have you to say, sir?"

Luc tossed a look over his shoulder and gave a nod to a man holding two volumes. The servant approached. Isabelle instantly recognized her old journals in his hands.

Her cheeks warmed. *Good God. What is he going to do with those?*

"There once was a young woman who had an affinity for me. Years ago, she keenly watched my every move, every expression from the darkened corners of her father's theater. And she noted it all down, her every romantic sentiment, every passionate yearning—for me alone—recorded in those volumes." Luc gestured toward them as the servant held them up. "You may review them, two hundred pages in all."

"What does this have to do with this matter of the legal custody of Gabriel Laurent?" the judge asked.

"The woman I speak of is Isabelle Laurent." He cast her a glance.

A murmur erupted from the spectators.

"Silence!" the middle judge commanded the crowd.

"Several years ago, she left her family and came to my château to work, just to be near *me*. There are twenty servants behind me, ten more outside—if that is not enough—all of whom worked with Isabelle at Château Serein and can attest not only of her employment but of her affections for me."

Once again, more murmurs arose.

Before any of the judges could object to the noise, Luc continued, his voice raised above the din. "Gabriel was sired and born on Moutier lands. He belongs to *me*."

Isabelle's soft gasp was eclipsed by the eruption of the throng.

Again, Luc didn't wait for the calming of the crowd. "Any suggestion that Gabriel was sired by the late Vicomte de Roch is a *lie*." He looked pointedly at Pierrette.

Pierrette looked away.

"Quiet! That will be quite enough chatter," the judge demanded.

"Everyone has heard of what happened to my family, thanks to Leon de Vittry and his accomplices," Luc continued. "Isabelle Laurent tried to save my life and those of my family at the time—writing letters to warn them. She tried to warn me too, though I did not get her note—all of which put her own life in peril. Vittry purposely burned down the servants' outbuildings at Serein while both Isabelle and Gabriel were in it. She escaped with the babe, keeping herself, Gabriel, and her family safe from Vittry until she learned of his death only recently. She was in hiding on one of Roch's properties, having come to him with the babe already born. Once again, Roch could *never* have fathered the boy." Again, he looked at Pierrette. She stared at her folded hands clenched tightly on her lap. Never lifting her gaze.

"I was not about to allow Gabriel to be held captive by a delusional woman bent on some misguided revenge. This morning, my men and I entered Madame de Roch's *hôtel* after she left and reclaimed my child, who is now safe in *my* custody."

That knocked the breath from Isabelle's lungs. She placed a hand over her lips to muffle her sob of relief.

And elation.

A roar from the spectators reverberated around the room.

This time, Luc waited patiently for the judges to quiet the throng before he continued.

"Now, you have been made aware that Isabelle's and my lives have been intertwined for many years. And everyone knows Isabelle and I are lovers. We have been since the moment we were reunited at the Comtesse de Grandville's masque."

Marc nodded. "Yes, that is my sister, and this is true," he interjected with a smile and then patted Luc on the back.

Isabelle mentally flinched for Luc over Marc's touch. She saw Luc stiffen, then nod to his well-meaning friend. "Yes," he said. "Our affair has kept the gossipmongers' tongues wagging. But here is something you don't know." Luc took a book from one of the men near him and held it up. Then he turned to her. "You wrote *The Princesses' Adventures* novels, didn't you?"

She moved her gaze to the book in his hand, then returned her attention to him. "Yes."

A chorus of gasps ricocheted around the room.

"And I am one of the princes in these books, am I not?"

"Yes."

"Why?"

She gazed into his eyes. The room and all its occupants fell away. *Tell him the truth. There is no point fighting it any longer.*

"Since the moment I first saw you at my father's theater, I have wanted you. Longed for you. You have been in every beat of my heart. In every breath of my body. I would not have survived all that has happened had I not known you. I see you every time I close my eyes. You are in all of my most cherished dreams. You are my Fair Prince. I love you. I always have. I always will."

A small smile tugged at the corner of his mouth. He turned to the judges. "I've spoken to the King. I have a letter from His Majesty." Luc reached into his doublet and pulled out a small scroll with the royal seal on it. "His Majesty has rescinded his original *Lettre de Cachet.* Isabelle Laurent is free to leave. And I demand the court's official ruling—an official incontestable recognition—as to Gabriel's sire—me."

The judge looked at Pierrette and her lawyer. "Have you anything to say?"

The lawyer shook his head and glanced at his client. By his expression, he prompted her for a response.

From Pierrette came only five words: "I don't want the brat."

The judge nodded. "It is hereby officially recognized that Luc de Moutier, Marquis de Fontenay, is the sire of Gabriel Laurent. That is all. In the name of his Majesty, King Louis XIV of France, this matter is closed."

The three judges stood and left as the crowd erupted. Cheers and some applause echoed through the room. Isabelle leaped out of the defendant's box and raced to Luc, dodging through the crowd, frustrated by the obstacles that were in her way. At last, she broke through and threw herself against his hard, muscled form. Jumping up onto the balls of her feet, she fisted his doublet and crushed her mouth to his.

He tasted like heaven. And happiness. And that delicious, sumptuous heat that was uniquely Luc. Her body ignited for him. His fingers laced through her hair. Tilting her head, he slid his tongue inside her mouth, kissing her deeply. She felt his emotions travel through her, telling her of his affections for her in the best way he knew how. She drank it in, thirsty for more.

He'd leveled the walls she'd built to the ground.

And she was overjoyed that he had.

"Isabelle, we must stop. We have a significant number of spectators, and this is about to become rather carnal," he murmured against her mouth. But she could hear the smile in his voice. "Once we get home, that sweet little sex of yours is all mine."

Home. Where her son awaited her. Where Luc lived.

Out of her multitude of mistakes, she'd managed to do some things very right. She had her son and Luc.

Nicole came up to her. Isabelle threw her arms around her and showered her with thanks and love. She could hear Marc clearing the room of the spectators, encouraging them out onto the street. With a final kiss to her cheek, Nicole and Marc were the last to leave.

She was alone with Luc. "Is Gabriel all right? Did Pierrette harm him? Can we go see him now?"

"He's fine. We found him locked in one of the bedchambers. He was frightened and upset, but he was not harmed."

Tears blurred his beloved face. "Thank you for everything you've done."

He sat on the edge of the wooden railing that divided the room for the spectators. "That's odd. I was going to say the same thing to you."

"I haven't done anything."

"That isn't true. You've affected me in more ways than I could have ever imagined."

She looked down briefly. "Not all positive, I fear. I should not have caused you distress the last time we spoke. I should not have expected you to do the impossible by obtaining a ship. Sometimes the desires of my heart have been too grand. I certainly should not have mentioned your brother. I've been worried about you."

He cocked a brow and stretched out his long legs. "Why?"

"Because of how upset you became…"

He reached out and grasped her hand. Turning her palm up, he pressed a kiss to the sensitive spot on her inner wrist. The light sensation sent a thrill through her. "I survived Charles, Bellac, war, and imprisonment. I can easily manage any comment you wish to make. And your comment about my telling Jules the truth was, as much as I hate to admit it, correct. I've thought about your words a great deal since we parted. Jules deserves the whole truth about what Charles and Bellac did to me. My brother doesn't deserve my disdain because he was treated…well, differently than I. I want to speak to him. I don't want Charles to cause any more ill effects in my life. I wish to heal the rift between Jules and me. As to doing the impossible and obtaining a ship, I have done just that."

Isabelle's heart lost a beat. She couldn't have heard him properly. "You…you are going to take me to see Sabine?"

He grinned. "I am.

Stunned, shocked, she managed one single word. "How?"

"After some negotiations with His Majesty, I will be renting one of his warships. I had already begun to assemble a crew. Mostly men who have served with me. Some are at my *hôtel* preparing for departure. They helped me retrieve Gabriel."

Emotions tightened in her throat. She grabbed his doublet and rained kisses all over his face, tears of pure joy slipping down her cheeks. He laughed and captured her face between his palms.

"Wait. There is more I wish to say before I take you to Gabriel."

"I can't imagine what you have to say that could make this day any better. First your tale about being Gabriel's father, then saving him from Pierrette, then the added assurance you'd brought—the letter from the King. And now the voyage…"

"I told our story because I wanted people to know that it was special. That it spanned many years. And as to the tale of being Gabriel's father—that isn't necessarily a mere tale, unless you wish it to be."

Then he released her face and lowered himself down on one knee. A squeak rushed up her throat. Her hands flew to her heart. She began to tremble.

She dropped to her knees, cupped his face again, and kissed his lips. "*Yes!*"

He chuckled. "*Chérie,* I haven't asked you anything."

"Oh yes, of course. Please proceed."

He shook his head, amused. "Isabelle Laurent, will you—"

"YES!"

"—marry me?" he finished, chuckling again.

"Well, I suppose I should think about it—yes! Yes, I will marry you! I love you." Then she kissed him, reeling with joy. And love.

CHAPTER EIGHTEEN

Luc had been in his study a few hours, giving Isabelle some time to be alone with Gabriel. They were upstairs in his private apartments, and squeals of delight could be heard from the vestibule. He'd finalized further plans with his second-in-command for their departure in a month before dismissing the man and heading upstairs to the woman he could not wait to marry in three weeks.

But there was something bothering him.

He'd rehearsed his marriage proposal the entire night before and during the carriage ride to the court proceeding.

Yet it hadn't been complete.

He'd left something out.

And it needed to be rectified. Though it wasn't an easy task he'd set himself. They were words he'd never uttered in his life. Never thought he would.

Reaching the doors of his private rooms, he opened the door and strode across the antechamber to the bedchamber's double doors. He could hear Isabelle and Gabriel talking and laughing, the joyful noise making him smile as he approached.

One of the bedchamber doors was ajar. He pushed it open.

Gabriel and Montague noticed him first. The boy let out a whoop and jumped from the bed at Luc. He caught the boy in his arms. Montague offered several booming barks.

"Gabriel!" Isabelle admonished. "You mustn't do that. Montague, that's quite enough."

Luc laughed. "It's all right."

"*Maman* says you're going to be my father." He gave Luc an impish grin, then a quick tight hug, his arms circling Luc's neck.

"That's correct. And did your mother tell you that we are going on a great ship and sailing across an ocean?"

"She did! I have an aunt and an uncle and a cousin too!"

He smiled. "You do."

"I will do my best to be a good son," Gabriel promised. Those words tugged at Luc's heart. It was something he'd tried to be as well. An impossible achievement with the man who'd sired him.

"You already are," he told the boy who'd easily won his heart. "I promise that I will do my best to be a good father."

Gabriel hugged him again. In his ear, he heard, "You already are."

Smiling, he set the boy down. Unquestionably, he had his mother's magic. Gabriel inspired the same tender emotions. "I need a private word with your mother."

Isabelle stepped forward. "It's getting late. Why don't you lie down, and I will be back shortly."

Gabriel nodded. "All right." He ran and jumped onto the bed. "Come on, Montague." He patted the spot beside him. And just like that, the giant dog plopped himself on Luc's bed.

He was too preoccupied to say anything. He simply took Isabelle's hand and led her to the antechamber, then closed the door.

"There is something I need to say." He rubbed the back of his neck. "I had meant to say it earlier. But I didn't and I don't want you to think I don't wish to. Because I do."

What the bloody hell? He sounded like a babbling idiot.

Her brow creased. "What is it?"

The most difficult thing I've ever tried to say.

"I know how to bed a woman. I know how to seduce her. Yet I don't know how to love a woman—or anyone. I've never loved anyone in my life. But I wish to learn how to with you. And Gabriel. And even the horse-dog, Montague."

She smiled at him. More of a beaming, take-his-breath-away sort of smile. Love shone in her eyes. And *Jésus*, how that melted him—each time. It was a feeling he'd grown to adore.

"I can assure you that you have done mightily fine thus far."

"Not yet. Not until I declare my affections." *Dieu*, why was this so damned difficult? Lord knows he'd read enough love sonnets to know what words to say, but they needed to be his words. Not another's. Luc raked a hand through his hair. *Damn it. Just say it.*

"The author of those captivating journals made me laugh. She made me want her. She made me fall in love with her. Then I met a woman who was just as engaging. Alluring. Witty. And I fell in love with her too. It matters not what name you use, Juliette Carre, Isabelle Laurent—or Isabelle de Moutier, I love them all. I...love *you*."

He never thought he'd use those words in his life. They were foreign in his mouth.

Yet he'd never made an utterance that felt so good. And was so right.

A single tear slipped down her cheek, but her smile never lessened. She stepped closer and cupped his face tenderly. "As I've stated, I can assure you that you have done mightily fine thus far, Lord Seductive, my Fair Prince, Luc de Moutier, my soon-to-be husband. I love them all because they're you." Then she kissed him, her soft, warm mouth melding with his. Her tongue slipping past his lips. He gave it a suck. She gave him a sensuous little moan. It reverberated down his spine to his cock. He was stiff as a spike in an instant.

Her hand reached down and stroked along the contour of his erection through his breeches, all the way to the sensitive tip. And squeezed. It was his turn to moan.

"I need you," she whispered in his ear.

"What about Gabriel?" *Merde*, he'd never had sex with a child under the same roof, much less in the other room.

She reached back and locked the door, then untied his cravat. It dangled from her hand as she held it out to him. Her breathing had already quickened, inciting his own. "You'll have to be quick about it. Something hard and fast."

The saucy little tilt to her head and the fire that burned in her dark eyes made the request impossible to refuse.

He took the cravat from her, a smile tugging at the corners of his mouth. Leaning in, he said in her ear, "Take your clothes off before I tear them from your sweet form." He bit her earlobe, enjoying her little shiver of excitement.

God, how he enjoyed playing with her in the boudoir.

Her hands flew to her clothing, pulling and unlacing, casting it off as fast as her eager fingers would allow. Luc watched as he removed his doublet, his shirt, breeches, and boots. *Jésus-Christ*, just watching her adorably frenzied method of undressing made his cock swell to painful proportions. His prick already felt as hard as iron.

Impatient, he stopped her, lifted her, and placed her bottom on the round table at the center of the room. He pulled off the balance of her clothing, shoes, stockings, caleçons, and the final veil covering her body, her knee-length chemise. He allowed himself to take in the vision before him. "You are so beautiful. Your nipples are so puckered and taut. They need to be sucked, don't they?"

She bit down on her lip and nodded. The quick, awkward little jerks of her head that made him smile, even when he was so fucking aroused, his sac ached.

"Good. Now, on your back, arms above your head. Wrists together."

Seeing her comply made his cock jerk with anticipation. He walked around, stopping beside her, and bound her wrists together. Not having any scarves in his personal antechamber, he improvised. Snagging one of the ribbons he'd tossed to the floor from around her stockings, he looped it into the cravat around her wrists, then secured it to the leg of his table.

A sudden pull and moist warmth closed around the crest of his cock, taking him by surprise. He darted his gaze downward. Her head was turned toward him, and she'd drawn the head of his prick into that incredible mouth.

Then she sucked.

He tossed his head back with a groan. He moved his hand to the back of her head, pulled her to him. And gave her slow, shallow pumps of his cock—despite the urgency bubbling in his blood. He took a brief moment to bask in the glory of her mouth before he withdrew.

Every nerve ending in his prick railed against his action.

He bent down and brushed an errant curl from her cheek. "Did you just improvise?"

"No, it wasn't me," was her cheeky response.

It drew a laugh from him. "I'm going to let this go for now as we are under some time restraints. So, unless you have any objections, I'm going to fuck you now, and I'm not going to pull out." He walked around the table, stopping between her parted thighs, and gripped her hips. He rolled his hips, allowing his shaft to glide through the dewy folds of her sex, coating his cock with her warm, slick juices.

"No objections!" she said as he stroked his prick over her clit.

"Excellent, because I'm going to fill you with come," he said, wedging his cock at her entrance. And drove his whole length into her with one solid thrust.

She bit down on her lip, muffling her cry of pleasure, and arched up off the table. His cock buried to the hilt, her exquisite sex squeezed around it, he waited for her body to relax. When she lowered her back onto the table, he reached between their bodies and captured her swollen little clit.

And lightly pinched it between his finger and thumb.

She gasped and lurched, but he held on, keeping the pressure on the bud strong enough for her to feel it. To allow the sensation to build. She wiggled and jerked her hips, her breathing turning into pants. His name rushed past her lips.

"I need to…" She squirmed. "I have to…"

"Come? No, you don't. Not yet. Hold it back for me," he told her, then leaned forward and sucked one of those delicious little nipples into his mouth, plying it with slow steady suckles, still holding her little clit captive. She mewled and writhed beneath him, trying to get some friction from his cock buried deep inside her.

"I can't, Luc… *Now!*"

He released her nipple, then turned to the other one. "Fight it back," he said, then sucked the pebbled tip of her other breast, giving it the same carnal care. He could feel a light pulsing beginning in her clit. He didn't relent on the pressure of his pinch, waiting for those magnificent little spasms to move inside her sex, along the length of his buried cock.

She arched and squirmed as much as she could under his weight. Her desperation and sexual fever mounting. Releasing her nipple, he soothed her, coaxing her into fighting back her climax a little longer, telling her how good it was going to be. Then it began, the light flutters of her vaginal walls. Then stronger contractions rippling along his cock. The occasional clench and squeeze of her snug cunt driving him half out of his mind. She'd reached the edge, unable to pull back from it any longer.

He released her bud. Gripping the edge of the table near her head, he dragged his length back out. Then drove back in.

"You're mine… *Isabelle*. You're going to come with me." He kissed her, his tongue possessing her mouth. His rhythm was hard and fast. His every downstroke came in contact with her sensitized bud.

She surged up against him, his mouth muzzling her cry as her orgasm exploded through her senses. He let go with her. Pouring his prick into her, her sex clutching and releasing him, milking semen from his cock in one glorious rush after another until he'd completely purged his prick.

It took a moment before he heard it clearly. A small knock at the door from his bedchamber. A little voice said, "*Maman?*"

And the distinct whine of a dog.

Dieu, Gabriel.

Luc shoved himself off Isabelle's warm form and cleaned himself and her with the first thing he saw—his shirt. He untied her just as quickly and pulled her up to a sitting position. She looked at him, confused, her cheeks pink, her body relaxed and sated. Then she heard it too.

"*Maman?*" Followed by a little jiggle of the locked door handle.

"It's Gabriel," she exclaimed in a whisper.

"Yes, I know. Dress." Luc scooped up the chemise and tossed it to her.

"Just a moment, my darling," Isabelle called out to the boy as Luc yanked on his breeches. She tossed on her chemise and *caleçons*.

"*Maman,* the door is locked." Another whine came from the dog.

"I know, darling. I'm coming to unlock it." She frantically tied the *caleçons* in place, then shoved her chemise down and smoothed her hair.

Luc reached the door to his bedchamber with two quick steps and placed his hand on its latch. "All right?" he asked her, making certain she was ready for him to open it.

She nodded and rushed forward.

The moment the door opened, she crouched down, and Gabriel was in his mother's arms. "I had a frightening dream, *Maman.*"

"Not to worry. I'm here. Montague is here," she said, smiling at the dog. "And Luc is here."

"You mean *Papa.*"

She smiled at Luc. "Yes, that is exactly what I mean." She rose and then entered Luc's bedchamber with Gabriel holding her hand.

The giant white dog followed contentedly behind, tail wagging.

Luc rested his hands on his hips and smiled. *Papa.* It took some getting used to. And yet he loved it as much as the boy who'd made him a father.

He walked into his room to find Gabriel lying on Luc's bed, Isabelle holding the boy, lying beside him on her side. She patted the center of the bed, where there was plenty of room for him. His smile grew, and he climbed into bed, mimicking her position. She snuggled her bottom into his groin. He wrapped his arms around her and whispered in her ear, "I love you." It was easier to say this time. And he damn well intended to say it to her every day of their lives.

There was a sudden pounce on the bed followed by the brush of fur against his side. Luc glanced down his body and found Montague lying on the bed behind him, watching him, his chin resting on Luc's side.

"Isabelle," he whispered in her ear.

"Hmmm?" By her response, she'd begun to drift into sleep.

"Where does the dog sleep?"

Gabriel yawned. "He's part of the family. He sleeps with us."

"Montague is partial to human beds and obstinate about leaving them," Isabelle sleepily concurred.

Luc glanced back at Montague. His ears were perked. His chin still resting on Luc. Luc reached down and playfully scratched between Montague's ears. The giant dog relaxed them in appreciation of the petting.

Luc had his own family now. And a ridiculously large white dog.

Each had managed to awaken his heart when he thought it was long since dead.

As he closed his eyes, he had one final thought before slipping into sleep.

He was definitely going to need a much larger bed.

EPILOGUE

The island of Marguerite lay in the distance.

Their tender bobbed on the blue-green waters that surrounded the lush island. Two men from the crew rowed, carrying Luc, Isabelle, Gabriel, and Montague closer and closer to the shore.

A large throng had gathered on its beaches. Isabelle's heart pounded as she scanned the crowd, looking for the one beloved face she hadn't seen in too many years.

"*Papa*, does this island belong to France?"

"No. Caribs, pirates, and civil wars became too much trouble. They wanted no part of it, selling the French islands to their governors. This is a private island owned by Simon Boulenger, the commodore of the fleet of privateer ships that once sailed for France, before the war with Spain ended. I sailed under his command."

"Pirates and Caribs? Are we in danger on the island, *Papa*?"

"You needn't worry, Gabriel. This island is heavily fortified. The only reason we have not been attacked is because they've recognized our ship is French."

"But they don't know it's us," Isabelle said, still searching the faces in the distance for her sister.

"Not yet." Isabelle heard the smile in her husband's tone but didn't turn around.

Where's Sabine? The babe in her womb gave a light kick. Isabelle absently moved her hand to her belly and gave it a soothing rub.

"She's right there," Luc said in her ear, as if he'd read her thoughts.

She darted her gaze in the direction of his extended finger.

Dear God. Sabine!

Her sister stood beside a man she instantly recognized as Luc's brother, Jules de Moutier. Sabine's hand was over her brow, shielding the sun from her eyes. But she recognized her sister's form, her blonde hair—instantly.

Isabelle leaped to her feet and waved both arms.

"*Dieu.*" Luc caught her around the waist to steady her. "*Chérie*, sit down. You're going to fall in the water."

Isabelle yelled her sister's name, emotions she hadn't allowed herself to feel since leaving home surging inside her.

Sabine's hand dropped for a moment, then returned to her brow as she slowly moved away from the crowd and closer to the shoreline.

Looking unsure.

The tender was ever so close now. The land so temptingly near. Isabelle yelled out her sister's name again.

This time, Sabine screamed, "*ISABELLE!*" and again, "*'Sabelle! 'Sabelle!*" Grabbing her skirts, Sabine ran into the water, pressing against the lapping waves, fighting to get to her.

Isabelle hadn't heard that affectionate name her sister used to call her by in so long. She jumped into the water.

"Isabelle!" Luc exclaimed. Montague began to bark. But she didn't turn around. The waves pushed her toward the shore, aiding her along. Sabine's arms were outstretched to her. Tears streamed down both their faces. Sabine still fought against the current. Isabelle couldn't get to her fast enough. A strong wave shoved her forward, and she caught hold of Sabine's hands. The next wave shoved her into her sister's arms.

A cry came from both of them as they held each other tightly, not wanting to let go. Isabelle closed her eyes and buried her face in her twin's wet hair. Then she pulled back, needing to see her face.

She cupped Sabine's cheeks. Her sister did the same. Their tears mingled with the seawater splashing against them.

"I don't know… I don't understand…how you are alive…" Sabine sobbed with joy. "And, oh!" She felt a kick from Isabelle's swollen belly that was pressed against hers. Sabine's gray eyes widened. She placed her hands on Isabelle's swollen stomach. "You're…?"

"I am. And I am alive and well, with a son, Gabriel, and married to someone you may know. Luc de Moutier."

Sabine let out a shriek of joy just as Luc caught up to Isabelle, grasping her elbow. "Perhaps we should go to the shore?" was all that left Luc's lips before Sabine threw her arms around him and squeezed him tightly. Waves splashing against the three of them. Isabelle saw Luc flinch only slightly. Her sister looked up at him and said, "Thank you! How did you find her?"

Luc smiled down at her. "My very wise sister-in-law gave me some journals that helped."

Jules reached them just then, a giant grin on his face.

"This is Isabelle!" Sabine told him and hugged her again, as more waves splash against them.

Jules placed a hand on his brother's shoulder. "I don't know how to thank you enough for finding Isabelle and for bringing her here."

Luc shrugged, smiling good-naturedly. "No need to thank me. My wife and I wanted to pay you a visit. There is much to catch up on and discuss."

"Wife?" The older Moutier brother turned to her, still sporting his big grin, kissed her hand, and said, "Welcome to the family. I am thrilled you are both here."

"Thank you," she said.

"Pardon me. Is there a reason the four of you are having a conversation in the sea?" a handsome man called out from shore, his arm around a beautiful dark-haired woman whose eyes were filled with tears watching their emotional exchange. Sabine was back to hugging Isabelle. She laughed and said, "That is Simon Boulenger and his wife, Angelica. We are all delighted he found someone to steal his heart. Now, come. I can't wait to let our family know you're here." Sabine held her hand as they made their way to the beach.

The tender reached the shore just then, and Gabriel jumped out, racing to her. He was instantly showered with affection from his very wet aunt and uncle, who told him about his cousins awaiting them at home—Isabelle and two-month-old Luc.

They walked out of the water toward the crowd that was eager to greet them. Isabelle couldn't wait to see the rest of her family.

"Good Lord. Is that some sort of small horse?" Jules asked.

"No. He's a dog," Luc assured his brother. "He's part of the family and he likes human beds."

"And chicken," Gabriel supplied.

Simon slapped Luc's brother on the back with a laugh. "Glad he will be staying with you, Jules."

Isabelle walked hand in hand with her sister and Luc toward the waiting carriages as Gabriel gleefully raced back and forth along the beach with Montague.

Her heart was full.

Her world now complete.

A HISTORICAL TIDBIT

I have a confession to make.

I didn't make up the character of Nicole de Grammont.

You see, several years ago, when I first read about an extraordinary woman named Ninon (Anne) de Lenclos (1620-1705), a French courtesan, a writer, later in life a teacher (teaching the art of lovemaking to men), I *knew* she had to be a character in one of my books. She was educated, witty, smart, and loved sex unabashedly. Rising from modest beginnings, she amassed wealth and respectability in a world that was ruled by men and strict moral authority from the Church. She made no apologies for her life or her beliefs. She purposely refused to marry to remain independent.

She knew how to draw men of consequence to her and knew how to keep their interest. She put her wealthy lovers into categories: those she had sex with for a price. And those she favored and had sex with for free. Men were always trying to get into the latter group (naturally) and stay there—by using charm and funds. She was sought after by men well into her sixties. It was reported that one of the most powerful men in France, Cardinal Richelieu, once offered her a small fortune to spend the night with her. She kept the money and sent a friend to spurn his offer, because she wasn't attracted to him. It's been said that she told him, *"If you are a great lover, this is too much money. But if you aren't, this isn't nearly enough."* When she had children, a number of noblemen came forward to claim the babes as their own and provided for them. She died at eighty-four, having lived life by her own rules.

The poetess Isabella di Morra really existed too. Her tragic life and the poetry she left behind, as mentioned in this book, were all true. Paul de Brilhac and Nicolas de la Toison were the names of real judges in France during this time.

As to the court proceedings in this novel, court battles for custody of minors—especially children with significant inheritances—were not uncommon in France during the 17th century. Many family members would attempt to gain custody of the child, and control of their fortune, sadly, not always for the benefit of the child in question. Greed was not invented in modern times.

If this is your first Fiery Tale and are wondering why I set it during the reign of the Sun King, Louis XIV of France? Louis was a lusty king. His glittering court was as salacious as it was elegant. It was during this very time period that the father of fairy tales, Charles Perrault, author of *The Tales of Mother Goose*, wrote stories that have delighted generations: *Cinderella*, *Sleeping Beauty*, and *Little Red Riding Hood*, to name a few. *Three Reckless Wishes* is based on his famous fairy tale *Three Foolish Wishes*. Many believe it's where the saying, *"Careful what you wish for,"* may have originated. I hope you enjoyed your time with Luc and Isabelle in the opulent time when fairy tales were born!

Much love,

GLOSSARY

Antechamber	The sitting room in a lord's or lady's private apartments (chambers) within their hôtel or château.
Caleçons	Drawers/underwear.
Cabinet	Office. A room often found in a lord's or lady's private chambers/apartments. Some *cabinets* were so large, they were used for private meetings.
Chambers	Another word for private apartments. A lord's or lady's chambers consisted of a bedroom, a sitting room, a bathroom, and a *cabinet* (office). Some chambers were bigger and more elaborate than others.
Chambre de Justice	Chamber of Justice.
Chère	Dear one. (French endearment for a woman, *cher* for a man).
Chérie	Darling or cherished one. (French endearment for a woman, *chéri* for a man).
Comte/Comtesse	Count/Countess.
Dieu	God.
Duc/Duchesse	Duke/Duchess.

Hôtel/Château	The upper class and the wealthy bourgeois (middle class) often had a city mansion in Paris (*hôtel*) in addition to their palatial country estate(s) (*château*).
Lettre de Cachet	Orders/letters of confinement without trial signed by the King with the royal seal (*cachet*).
Merde	Shit.
Ma belle	My beauty. (French endearment for a woman).
Palais de Justice	Palace of Justice/courthouse.
Salle de Bain	*Bathroom.* A small room located in one's private apartments/chambers in either a château or hôtel. The room usually had a fireplace, a tub, and a toilet (that looked like a chair with a chamber pot). The room was small on purpose so that the fire from the fireplace would keep the space warm while one bathed.
Seigneur Dieu	*Lord God.*
Vicomte/Vicomtesse	Viscount/Viscountess

READ AN EXCERPT OF UNDONE

*A *USA TODAY* Bestseller!*

Inspired by the tale of Rapunzel, Lila DiPasqua offers a steamy, emotionally charged historical romance in the acclaimed Fiery Tales Series...Rescuing this beauty from the 'tower' is only the beginning...

Maintaining her ruse as a commoner, and trusting no one has kept Angelica safe. But a chance encounter with a handsome stranger lands her right where danger lies. Now, this sinfully handsome man with arresting blue eyes and a polished manner thinks he's saved her life, when in fact he's placed her in great peril. She's intent on keeping him and everyone else at arm's length. Yet, the smoldering attraction between them is difficult to deny. And impossible to ignore...

As commander of a number of privateer ships, Simon Boulenger dresses and speaks like an aristocrat, and has obtained wealth. But he is still not a noble. Or an officer in the King's Navy. His lifelong dream to elevate himself from his station of birth and attain a respectable place in society is dead. Worse, he's ensnared in a deadly scheme, and must get out.

But how is he to stay focused on his dangerous mission when the mysterious beauty has him utterly intrigued? He can't afford the distraction any more than he can resist the carnal hunger she stirs. Simon soon discovers that she's not only a passionate soul mate, but a woman born into privilege. A woman he can never have. But they're in too deep. Their hearts are at risk…as well as their lives.

*****

Simon approached her slowly, his brow slightly furrowed.

Unable to stop herself, Angelica took in his male beauty. He, not the books, now dominated the room. How was it possible that he looked even better than before?

A few wayward strands of his dark hair played against his lashes, but it was his mouth that captured her attention.

Such an appealing mouth…

She looked away, horrified by the workings of her mind. It had to be her headache that was distorting her thinking.

He stopped before her, towering over her.

The bookshelves against her back kept her fixed in place. She was keenly aware of the limited space between their bodies, his proximity causing her body to warm.

"I asked you a question." His voice was quiet but firm.

Gazing up at him, she tried to clear her head by taking in a deep breath, but it only served to draw in his wonderful scent. She couldn't quite describe it, but it was tantalizing in the extreme.

What was the matter with her? She shouldn't be reacting to him this way. She'd chosen a cloistered existence, or rather, it had chosen her. Nonetheless, she'd accepted her future long ago.

"You should not be wandering about alone." He spoke softly, his voice deep and rich in her ears. It reverberated through her belly with wicked appeal. Lightly, he stroked his knuckles along her bruised cheek. "You should be in bed. You are still injured."

She closed her eyes briefly. Get hold of yourself. This was the second time he'd touched her. Instead of drawing back, as she would have expected, she found herself wanting to draw near. It was a stunning reaction. As stunning as the tiny tingles that sped up her spine at his caress.

"My malady has much improved," she said, hoping she didn't sound as discomposed as she felt.

He lowered his arm and his gaze.

It took two wild heartbeats before she realized he was staring at something on the floor. She forced her gaze down, her insides still quivering with the residual pleasure of his small caress. The book she had dropped lay on the woven rug.

He was staring at her again, one dark eyebrow slightly cocked, before he retrieved the fallen item.

"You–I'm afraid that you startled me, and the book–I dropped it…" Definitely not your most eloquent response, Angelica. She turned her gaze away to a safer sight than the far too attractive Simon de Villette.

"You can read this?" he asked.

Her eyes darted back to his. The book was in French. She wasn't about to divulge that she could indeed read every word in the book of love sonnets. In fact, she was gripped with the most powerful urge to devour each and every beautifully romantic line.

She quashed the silly yearning.

"No. It's written in French, is it not? I couldn't possibly…" His penetrating gaze made her uneasy. She wished she could read his thoughts behind those disarming light-colored eyes.

"But you can read, Angelica." Yet again he managed to unbalance her by the way he spoke her name. It was astonishing what it did to her insides every time he said it.

He'd done nothing but show kindness toward her. His manner was gentle, attentive. His words spoke of concern for her welfare. Yet she was forced to stoop to deceit. She simply couldn't lower her guard. Not for a moment. Not with a single soul. Keeping her secrets had kept her safe. And she wasn't about to break with precedent.

Besides, this man *was* dangerous. No one had ever inspired these physical responses from her before. The sooner she left France, the better.

"I learned to read at the convent," she lied. Again. "I teach there…the children in the orphanage…" At least that was the truth, albeit clumsily told.

He placed the book back on the shelf. "Why?"

"Why?" She knitted her brow in confusion.

"Yes. Of what use is it to teach the children of commoners?" Despite his words, she had the distinct feeling he was not expressing his personal view of literacy and the lower class. He was trying to draw information from her.

She chose her next words carefully. "At the convent, we believe everyone should have the opportunity of an education, noble or peasant. Male or female."

"Your pardon, Captain." The French phrase came from the doorway.

Relief washed over her when she saw the old male servant standing at the threshold of the library.

"Your meal awaits you in the dining hall, sir."

Simon gave a nod. "Merci, Henri." He turned to her. "Have you eaten?"

"No…"

He smiled. "Good. Then you will join me this evening for supper." He tossed out phrases to Henri in French, ordering him to set another place in the dining hall.

Though she'd wanted to speak to him, the thought of dining alone with him was daunting. She seemed to be completely out of sorts in his presence at the moment, struggling to get her mind and mouth to work together.

"Perhaps Gabriella would like to join us?" she said with a polite smile. If he would summon her friend, she was certain she could get through the meal and convince him to return them to the convent.

"She has already eaten. We are the last to dine this evening." Amusement flickered in his eyes. "Are you nervous to be alone with me, Angelica?"

"No." Her smile remained frozen on her face. "Of course not." He didn't frighten her. Though her reactions to his physical appeal were another matter altogether.

"Do you find my company unpleasant? Would you rather dine alone?"

"Unpleasant? No, absolutely not," she quickly assured, wishing at the moment he were old, potbellied, and missing some teeth. "I would be pleased to dine with you, if you consider this suitable attire." She touched her garb.

A slow, gorgeous, knee-weakening smile formed on his appealing face. He leaned in, and in her ear softly he said, "You are beautiful just as you are."

His unexpected words astounded her. As did the look in his eyes when he pulled back. He actually looked…sincere. No one had offered her a compliment, not for a very long time. And certainly not about how she looked. She touched her plain garment once more, so different from his costly attire. He was being far too kind.

He placed her hand in the crook of his arm. "Let us proceed. This will be an excellent opportunity to learn more about each other."

Oh God…

THANK YOU for reading THREE RECKLESS WISHES!

Want my next release for just **99¢?** Sign up for my **99¢ New Release Alert** newsletter at www.LilaDiPasqua.com. Each new release will be **99¢** for a SHORT time only. Get notified. Don't miss out!

FIERY TALES SERIES

Novellas
Sleeping Beau
Little Red Writing
Bewitching in Boots
The Marquis's New Clothes
The Lovely Duckling
The Princess and the Diamonds

Holiday Novella
The Duke's Match Girl

Anthologies
Awakened by a Kiss
The Princess in His Bed

Full-length novels
A Midnight Dance
Undone
Three Reckless Wishes

Lila DiPasqua is a USA TODAY bestselling author of historical romance with heat. She lives with her husband, three children and two rescued dogs and is a firm believer in the happily-ever-after. You can find her on BookBub, Facebook, Twitter, Instagram, and Goodreads!

Made in the
USA
Middletown, DE